TALES FROM THE PAVILIONS

TALES FROM FAR PAVILIONS

Compiled by

Allen Synge and Leo Cooper

ARROW BOOKS

Arrow Books Limited
17–21 Conway Street, London W1P 6JD

An imprint of the Hutchinson Publishing Group

London Melbourne Sydney Auckland
Johannesburg and agencies throughout
the world

First published in Great Britain by Pavilion Books Limited
in association with Michael Joseph Limited 1984
Arrow edition 1985

Set in Linotron Ehrhardt by
Rowland Phototypesetting Limited
Bury St Edmunds, Suffolk
Printed in Great Britain by
Cox and Wyman Limited, Reading

ISBN 0 09 940050 2

Contents

Acknowledgements

The following friends, sleuths, and authorities have been instrumental in leading us to some richly rewarding wickets.

These include Mary Lomas – the Irish cricket historian F. A. Reid, Stephen Green – Curator of the MCC, Colin Webb, A. R. Lewis, Alan Duff, Robin Marlar, Michael Parkinson, Godfrey Smith, Henry Porter, Patrick Moore OBE, Michael Hoyle, Professor Kenneth Bourne at the LSE, D. J. Foskett OBE, Bob Kingdom, John Pitt, John Minch, K. J. Cole, Derek Anns and that excellent all rounder Terence Prittie. Benny Green's anthology *The Cricket Addict's Archive* led us to a number of contributions as did the Office of the Hong Kong Government, the Northern Ireland Office, Lloyd's of London Press, The Admiralty and the Danish Cricket Association.

Our special thanks must also go to *The Cricketer* whose pages proved a mine of both information and material, and to whom we are indebted for many contributions. Similarly *The Journal of the Cricket Society* and its editor James D. Coldham have been of considerable help to us. Nor could we have produced this anthology without the, as always, invaluable guidance of *Wisden*.

Some of our contributors first appeared in a number of newspapers which include *The Times, The Sunday Times, The Daily Mail, The Irish Times, Irish Independent, Ce Matin, The Birmingham Post, The South China Morning Post,* and the *Helsinki Cricketer*.

A number of our team have already appeared in print and we would like to thank their publishers for letting them come out to bat. They include Dudley Owen Edwards *The Quest for Sherlock Holmes* (Mainstream Press), James D. Coldham *A History of German Cricket* (The Journal of the Cricket Society), Peter S. Hargreaves, P. C. G.

Labouchere, and T. A. J. Provis *The Story of Continental Cricket*. We would also like to take this opportunity to wish them and their publisher Hutchinson, every success with the sequel *More Continental Cricket*. Other members of our team to appear in print are Edward Rae *White Sea Peninsula* (John Murray), Olave Baden-Powell and William Hillcourt *Two Lives of a Hero* (Heinemann), W. E. Bowes *Express Delivery* (Stanley Paul & Co.), Sam Kydd *For You the War is Over* (Bachman and Turner), P. G. Wodehouse *Piccadilly Jim* (Barrie and Jenkins), Jack Fingleton *Cricket Crisis* (Pavilion Books), Fred Lillywhite *Tour of America 1859*, A. A. Thompson *Odd Men In* (Pitman Publishing Ltd, London), Sir Pelham Warner *Cricket Between Two Wars* (Chatto and Windus), George Mell *This Curious Game of Cricket* (George Allen and Unwin), Arthur Grimble *A Pattern of Islands* (John Murray), Michael Green and his publishers Hutchinson, Philip Snow *Cricket in the Fiji Islands* (Whitcombe and Tombs, Dunedin, New Zealand), *Ceylon Cricket Annual, 1899* (A. M. & J. Ferguson), Frank Tyson *The Cricketer Who Laughed* (Stanley Paul and Co.), F. S. Ashley Cooper *Cricket Highways and Byways* (George Allen and Unwin). The pieces by William Rushton on cricket in Corfu first appeared in *Cricket '78* (Test and County Cricket Board). It is good to see that cricket has already featured in a number of foreign publications, and we have been delighted to borrow from *English and American Studies in German*, Editor Werner Habicht (Max Niemeter Verlag) and *Atta Spel Sih Liv* by Merete Mazzarella.

Just as important as the above are our foreign correspondents. Without their batting and bowling skills our side would have been severely weakened. A number of their despatches appeared in the newspapers detailed above. Some pieces however appear here for the first time. We would like to thank them for turning out to play for us. Our foreign correspondents include in Ireland Tony Coleman, Tony Gill, H. Morgan Dockrill, Ces Cassidy, Roley Jenkins and Sir Arthur Conan Doyle. Our Scottish tales came from J. F. Carnegie and Jeremy Madden Simpson, whilst J. F. N. Hodgkinson, J. Peckover, Ernest Sandford, and George Walker brought us news of the French variety. Our Dutch

colleagues number amongst their team Peter Beecheno and
Kess Bakker. In connection with Germany we would like to
thank Professor James Trainer, Graham Lees, Secretary of
the Munich Cricket Club, Major M. Oliver, Jonathan
Ignarski and Ernest Burgschmidt. James D. Coldham, Igor
Olenski, and Denis Foley helped to lift the Iron Curtain and
bring us news of Russian cricket.

Our youngest contributor Piers Pugh-Morgan supplied
some much needed information on the Mediterranean and
takes his place amongst the other members of the 'Med'
team, Mrs E. M. Slatter, Christopher Matthew, William
Rushton and Michael Green. Our section on Israel was
greatly strengthened by the inclusion of Mrs Yehudit Lipman. We are also indebted to Major E. W. Stanton, Commander B. H. C. Nation, G. R. Hovington, Gavin Ewart and
Fred Stead who all supplied us with tales from Military
Pavilions.

Out in the wider world our contributions have been
secured from David Niven, C. P. Snow, H. G. Robinson, H.
Brearley, John Laffin, Bill Feeder, Miriam Young, Ian
Keys, R. W. Butler, Tony Sharp, F. M. Saunders, Gaston
Berlemont, E. A. Cordell, Brian Johnston, R. J. Hayter, H.
Sharp, Fleming Baird and Gerald Howat. Last but by no
means least we would like to acknowledge the contributions
of Charles Burton, and Marvin Cohen.

Many pieces have reluctantly had to be discarded simply
because they failed to meet our definition of a foreign cricket
experience. Derek Anns's extraordinary account of The
Orleans Club's encounter with Rickling Green CC on
August 4th and 5th, 1882 appeared to qualify first because
the name 'Orleans' suggested a French origin and secondly
because among the contributions to the Club's long unsur-
passed total, was a certain Mr P. J. de Paravicini who, alas,
proved, on closer enquiry, to be a very English Old Etonian.
This epic encounter is perhaps the most lamented of our
omissions, particularly since we are still uncertain about the
nationality of Mr B. Posno who in contrast to Mr G. F.
Vernon's 259 and Mr A. H. Trevor's 338, was accorded the
following entry in an historic scorebook, 'C. Silcock b R. S.
Spencer . . . 0'.

For the record the result was Rickling Green CC 94, Orleans Club 920.

Every side has its behind the scenes workers and our team is no different. Our thanks go to Simon Holt for collecting the permissions for this anthology, to Beryl Hill for her work on the manuscript, and to Marsh Dunbar for her administrative help.

Every effort has been made to trace the copyright holders of the materials used in this volume. Should there be any omissions in this respect, we apologise and shall be pleased to make the appropriate acknowledgements in future editions.

Preface

The idea for this book stemmed from *Strangers' Gallery –
Some foreign views of English cricket* published in 1974 by
Lemon Tree Press. It was really this book that introduced us
to each other. Both of us felt after several discussions and
exchanges of anecdote that we could take the idea a step
further. At about the same time as we were talking about the
project Peter Tinniswood flashed outside our off stump
with the publication of his hilarious books *Tales From the
Long Room* and *More Tales From the Long Room*. These
concentrated our minds wonderfully. While we recognised
that we would be foolish to attempt to emulate Tinniswood's
highly original approach to the wicket, it occurred to us that
there might be even taller stories from more distant long
rooms which would have the additional merit of being true.
Out came that heavy-roller cliché, 'Truth is Stranger than
Fiction'. And behold, we had an ideal batting strip for
people, famous and hitherto unknown, living and long dead,
with unusual experiences to recount of cricket in foreign
lands (by our arbitrary ruling, 'foreign' means those countries, islands and polar regions which do not as yet enjoy
Test status).

For the record, neither of us are particularly good cricketers. Both of us nevertheless take a keen interest in the
game. In our time we have played (unnoticed, perhaps)
alongside the great and famous, and in our time too we have
talked to them or gazed at them in awe, if only in pubs after
the game. Middle-aged groupies we are. Both of us have
also played cricket in faraway places. We have, too, experienced that great comfort drawn from the experience, when
you are thousands of miles from home, of feeling secure on
a cricket field; taking part in an unending ritual that is
part of our heritage whilst around the game's boundaries

Australians, Dervishes, Fijians, Nazis and Scotsmen look on with puzzlement or amazement.

Many contributions to this anthology are very funny, almost by accident. It is certainly not meant to be just a funny book. Unusual matches have been played, no doubt, all over the world for years about which none of the participants remember anything. However, it is the endless possibility of happenings on the cricket field that seems to be reflected here. It is difficult or wrong perhaps to single out any particular contribution, but surely James Coldham's account of the Worcester Gents tour of Nazi Germany must leave even Peter Tinniswood typewriterless and the story of the railway passenger marooned on a remote station in Scotland and forced to play cricket with the station-master and the porter takes some beating although we hesitate to swear to the absolute authenticity of this one.

Here it all is, anyway. We hope that the publication of this book may serve to produce even more unusual reminiscences. What we all tend to forget is that the first-class game as we know it is but the tip of the iceberg. Someone somewhere in the world is playing cricket at any time and in so many cases returning, at the end of a sun-blessed day, to some Far Pavilion bar to relive that day's play again. This book is offered merely as a reflection of so many happy hours, not perhaps spent playing the game, but talking about it or watching it. It is also, we hope, a tribute to the game itself and the way that, having insinuated itself into our lives, it remains there, dormant perhaps, but ready to be transmitted in unusual anecdotes to unsuspecting victims at a moment's notice. There is no cure.

Finally, some words of thanks. Behind these pages are dozens of good friends and pub and club acquaintances who just happened to know a man who could lead us to a man who played cricket in Patagonia. They are acknowledged above. We would particularly like to thank Godfrey Smith of the *Sunday Times* for giving our idea so much exposure and thereby releasing a flood of helpful letters and telephone calls. Without his contribution this book would have been a rather slimmer volume.

AS & LC, London 1984

The Celtic Fringe

Stumped and Bowled in Tipperary

It was all Cromwell's fault. If that bloodthirsty killjoy hadn't taken it into his head to order his Major Generals to confiscate every cricket bat in Ireland for burning by the public hangman we might now be enjoying Anglo-Irish encounters at least as keenly fought as the yearly battles at Twickenham and Lansdowne Road (it's not recorded what Cromwell did about balls). As it is, Tipperary is a long way from the Kennington Oval in a cricketing sense. '"Dev" maintained that rugger was well suited to the Irish temperament. Cricket definitely less so,' writes Terence Prittie who then describes a game in North Tipperary which is as rich in affectionate humour as any thing to be found in England Their England

The quality of the Nenagh side had improved beyond measure, and old Paddy Flannery had been forced to retire for the second time, but travelled with the team to watch them play and to chuckle and chirp like a grasshopper from the tall grasses beyond the outfield. A formidable batsman had been enlisted in the shape of Dr Tony Courtney, a legendary figure in the neighbourhood. A mountain of a man, he had been capped for Ireland several times at rugger and there were many tales of his feats on the field of battle, usually concerned with French or Welsh who were unwise enough to 'play dirty' with him and his friends. He had more than once driven over a 295-yard hole of the local golf course. Later in life he was to become a recruiting agent for the IRA, picking likely lads from a street corner which gave him a clear view of the doors of four public houses.

Dr Tony, on this occasion, was well-set when my father put himself on to bowl. Thirty years earlier he had bowled well for his regiment. Now, his arm was a trifle stiff, but he still had plenty of ideas. His first three balls were models of the defensive slow-medium off-break bowler's art, pitching just short of a length eighteen inches outside the off stump. Dr Tony watched them go by with an impassive face.

The fourth ball was a dream for the hitter off the front foot, a half-volley just clear of the off stump. Dr Tony's left leg went out, down came his bat like a flail, and there was the clean smack of the really full-blooded drive. Left to its own, it would have been a six, but it was hit with the flat trajectory of the perfect golf-drive, and rose slowly. Reaching my father in a split second, it must have been eight feet up.

For a man of nearly sixty, my father did well to pick out the line of the ball when off-balance. He leapt acrobatically and slightly to one side, and took the ball full on the palm of his left hand. It dropped like a cleanly-shot jack snipe, stone dead, at his feet. He stood, rubbing the injured hand, with a meditative but most unpleasant look in his eye. Dr Tony, with a solicitous look on his face – after all, my father was host, ground-owner, organiser, the lot – took several tentative steps down the wicket. He could have had no possible idea of going for a run. My own thought was that he was going to apologise.

Suddenly my father stooped, picked up the ball and threw it at him. I say 'at' without any doubt, for I could follow the line of the ball, and could see the look in my father's eye change to a glint of triumph as he saw that he had aimed straight and true. The ball hit Dr Tony above a flapping pad on the right knee-cap, the one with which he had been having trouble ever since a Welsh wing three-quarter had come half-way across the field to put his boot into it. He staggered, and fell. From his knee, the ball rolled slowly on towards the stumps, tapped on one like a tentative beggar at the door, and a bail dropped almost unwillingly to the ground.

We won the match by ten runs. The *Nenagh Guardian*, reverting to earlier, erratic habit, entered the incident into the score-sheet as 'Dr A. Courtney, stumped *and* bowled by Lord Dunalley, 28'.

TERENCE PRITTIE

The Wanderers' Irish Tour
(*to the tune of 'The Cork Leg'*)

If Irish cricket has yet to produce a Hobbs or a Bradman, the hospitality it extends to visitors is certainly legendary. Was it those welcoming 'jars' that inspired Sir Arthur Conan Doyle, touring Ireland with the Stonyhurst Wanderers, to pen perhaps the worst set of verses ever produced by a best-selling novelist?

My Stonyhurst lads, just listen awhile,
And I'll sing you a song in right musical style,
A song that will raise on your faces a smile,
Concerning our trip to the Emerald Isle.
              Ri-tooral-rooral, etc.

A finer team than ever went o'er
Was never seen in the world before,
For we had eleven men and more
Who unless they got out might be reckoned to score.

Oh, how can I tell of what fell to their lot,
Of the balls that they hit, and the balls they did not,
How the batsmen were cool and the bowlers were hot,
And the fielders were – well, goodness only knows what.

The Phoenix came out with their heads in the air,
The Phoenix went back in a state of despair,
For Henry's performance it made them all stare,
And we won by an innings and fifty to spare.

And Trinity, oh, but we walloped them well,
To George and the Doctor* the honours there fell,
And Hatt's fast expresses dismissed them pell-mell,
And the heat was as great as in – Coromandel.

In conclusion the Leinster their colours have struck,
Where the present composer compiled a round 'duck'.
There we fought against audience and players and luck,
And pulled off the match by sheer coolness and pluck.

So fill up a bumper to one and to all,
Who handled the willow, the gloves and the ball,
May cricketers ever their prowess recall,
And may Stonyhurst flourish whatever befall.

*Sir Arthur had recently been awarded an MD by Edinburgh University.

SIR ARTHUR CONAN DOYLE

Waterford's 'Second XI'

Keeping match fit in the face of Ireland's legendary hospitality was clearly a problem for Tony Gill and his international tourists of the Jack Frost XI. But in the preliminaries to a fixture at Waterford he was afforded a glimpse of the steely competitiveness which Irish smiles sometimes disguise.

Groggy from Cork, we arrived at Waterford more or less prepared, if not in the best of shape, to face the pick of the local cricketing talent. The opposing captain welcomed us with extensive quotations from W. B. Yeats and his own work, for he was himself a poet. Finally he let drop the information that we would be playing the Second XI in the afternoon's encounter. As tactfully as possible, we pointed out that our fatigued appearances could be deceptive. We reminded him that Jack Frost's XI contained a number of very able players; not to mention the odd international star.

'That's why we're calling ourselves "the Second XI"', the poet-captain answered with a cunning smile. 'Just in case you beat us.'

TONY GILL

In Dublin with Hutton

One of the editors is not entirely amused by Alan Duff's impressions of cricket at Trinity College, Dublin, having been educated there and retaining memories of many hard chases in what seemed an extremely fast outfield.

But no anthology on distant pavilions could keep it out, not least because of the glimpse it offers of a great English batsman in the twilight of a career forged on infinitely sterner wickets

My very first outing with the MCC was in 1960 to play Ireland in Dublin. We played at Trinity College and in the best Irish tradition of hospitality the mower had broken down three weeks before so that the outfield was like a meadow. Len Hutton had retired the previous summer but was playing to make it his last first-class match – he wanted to go out on a century. I have two abiding memories of the game. First, it was too wet to start and both teams retired to the pub to drink Guinness. When we started after lunch, at the fall of the first wicket I rushed up to the captain for permission to 'leave the field' – but before I could reach him he had also turned tail along with four other members of the side. At the fall of the second wicket four other members disappeared which just left Sir Len himself who serenely walked off while play was in progress! On the second day we were batting. I got in to join Sir Len at about 12.45. He was the only one capable of coping with a mud pitch and fast off cutters. Every now and again he stroked one serenely past the close in-field and said 'That must be four', but time after time it pulled up in the meadow grass and we only got one. At 1.20 I finally got a full toss which I put away into the meadow and got off the mark with one. The great man himself walked down the wicket to me – I thought for a little pat on the back that I could tell my grandchildren about – but all I got was 'Watch it, son – only ten minutes to lunch, you know!' He finally made 80 something – worth at least 150 in other conditions – and quietly returned to England with a 'bad back' so he could not come up to Ulster where we played North of Ireland CC in their centenary match.

ALAN DUFF

Ireland Humble the Mighty West Indies

*It can be risky for an Englishman – and certainly for a
West Indian – to be patronising about Irish cricket. They
will immediately be referred to the score of a match
which will live for all time in the country's annals:
Ireland v. West Indies played at Sion Mills, Londonderry, 2 July 1969. Result: a spectacular win for
Ireland. There is some evidence suggesting that the West
Indian team had been entertained at a brewery on their
way to their Waterloo on the playing fields of Sion Mills.
However, witnesses are reluctant to come forward. And
who in any case would wish to diminish this fantastic
result? The Irish Times of 3 July 1969 was justifiably
lyrical*

It wasn't cricket – it was a massacre. And wonderful to
behold, it was Ireland who handed it out and the West
Indies, the most flamboyant of all cricketing nations, who
were on the receiving end of a nine-wicket beating. Sion
Mills, unfamiliar venue for international cricket, has never
seen anything like the happenings that took place there
yesterday.

Unbelievable, unthinkable, impossible, yet incredibly
true, the West Indies were shot out for 25. And they were
lucky to reach that figure, for at one stage they had nine men
back in the pavilion with 12 runs on the board, blitzed to
destruction by the Irish pace attack of Douglas Goodwin
and Alec O'Riordan, who bowled with great fire and
accuracy on the damp wicket.

To aid them, the Irish bowlers had veritable 'vultures' of
fielders who were ever ready to swoop on the mis-hit or
edged ball.

Against an unchanged pace attack, the West Indies batsmen floundered and finally capitulated after 100 minutes at
the crease. There will be no calypsos written about this
one.

The fall of the West Indies wickets came like this: 1/1,
2/1, 3/3, 4/6, 5/6, 6/8, 7/12, 8/12, 9/12, 10/25. And the
figures of the men who wrought the destruction will be

etched indelibly into the minds of the people lucky enough to be present – Goodwin five for 6 and O'Riordan four for 13. And to think that Ireland had lost the toss.

It took Goodwin just one ball to start the rout. Camacho, who had scored a single off O'Riordan's first over, faced Goodwin and the Irish captain, dropping one just short of a length, tempted Camacho into an injudicious stroke and Dineen, fielding at mid-wicket, gratefully accepted the chance. Ireland were on their way.

Joey Carew was the next to go – a victim of O'Riordan, who had the tourists' opener snapped up at square leg by Hughes. Surely, it was all too good to last. Yet better things were to follow as the tourists groped about on the slow wicket.

Basil Butcher, whose cricketing talents have been appreciated from Sydney Hill to Lord's, left no lasting impression on the spectators who stood on a railway embankment in a town in Co. Tyrone. He called for a sharp single in O'Riordan's fourth over and his partner, Foster, could not make the necessary ground before Ireland's Colhoun broke the wicket. Three for three.

Butcher was next to go, brilliantly caught by Duffy in the gully off a lifting ball from O'Riordan. Butcher had made two and his side six, off just 12 overs.

Goodwin was not going to be left out of the picture, however, and he had Clive Lloyd caught at midwicket by Waters and then claimed the scalp of John Shepherd, thanks to Duffy's vigilance in the gully. Fifty minutes had gone and the West Indies were tottering. The masters of stroke play had managed to get eight runs and had lost six wickets in doing it.

They were to get no respite. With 12 runs on the board they lost their seventh wicket. Findlay skied one from Goodwin and Waters held on to the catch, after first causing a slight flutter with a bit of juggling.

Clyde Walcott, who is manager of the team, and who in his time has been at the wicket in many a crisis, could not stop the rampant Irish and he was next to go back to the pavilion, caught in the covers by Anderson off O'Riordan.

Without addition, Colhoun caught Roberts off O'Riordan, and nine of the tourists were out and just the round dozen on the board.

The last pair, Shillingford and Blair, were at the wicket and they did their best to hurl defiance at the Irish. They managed to add 13 runs to bring the total to 25 before Goodwin stepped in to bowl Blair for three and bring the innings to an end.

Shillingford was not out nine, and was the West Indies highest scorer. Not one of them had managed to get into double figures.

Waters and Pigot opened for Ireland and no opening pair can ever have walked to the wicket in a happier position. Pigot left no doubt about his intentions and in Shillingford's first over, he took five which included a four which was hooked down the leg side.

Ireland reached 19 before they lost Robin Waters, caught by Findlay off Blair, but Michael Reith and Pigot saw the tourists' total passed safely and Ireland were home, by nine wickets, unless, under the one-day rule, both sides could complete two innings and that did not happen.

So Sion Mills, an unlikely venue, had seen a sensational result, and the West Indies who on Tuesday had held England to a draw on the hallowed square at Lord's are unlikely ever to forget a little village in Northern Ireland and the day that Ireland took her place among the cricketing nations of the earth. It was enough to make W.G. stir in his grave, but then he never did like the foreigners!

Irish Times

THE SCORE

West Indies	*First Innings*	
G. S. Camacho	c. Dineen, b. Goodwin	1
M. C. Carew	c. Hughes, b. O'Riordan	0
M. L. C. Foster	run out	2
B. F. Butcher	c. Duffy, b. O'Riordan	2
C. H. Lloyd	c. Waters, b. Goodwin	1
C. L. Walcott	c. Anderson, b. O'Riordan	6
J. N. Shepherd	c. Duffy, b. Goodwin	0

T. M. Findlay	c. Waters, b. Goodwin	0
G. C. Shillingford	not out	9
P. Roberts	c. Colhoun, b. O'Riordan	0
P. D. Blair	b. Goodwin	3
byes		1
		25

Second Innings

G. S. Camacho	c. Dineen, b. Goodwin	1
M. C. Carew	c. Pigot, b. Duffy	25
M. L. C. Foster	c. Pigot, b. Goodwin	0
B. F. Butcher	c. Waters, b. Duffy	50
C. H. Lloyd	not out	0
C. L. Walcott	not out	0
leg-byes		2
		78

	First Innings				*Second Innings*			
	O	M	R	W	O	M	R	W
O'Riordan	13	8	18	4	6	1	21	0
Goodwin	3	8	6	5	2	1	1	2
Hughes					7	4	10	0
Duffy					12	8	2	12
Anderson					7	1	32	0

Fall of Wickets

1–1, 2–1, 3–3, 4–6, 5–6, 6–8, 7–12, 8–12, 9–12, 10–12.
1–1, 2–2, 3–73, 4–78.

Ireland	*First Innings*	
R. H. C. Waters	c. Findlay, b. Blair	2
D. M. Pigot	c. Camacho, b. Shillingford	37
M. Reith	l.b.w. b. Shepherd	10
J. Harrison	l.b.w. b. Shepherd	0
J. Anderson	c. Shepherd, b. Roberts	7
P. J. Dineen	b. Shepherd	0
		56

Ireland   *Second Innings*

A. J. O'Riordan	c. and b. Carew	35
G. A. Duffy	not out	15
L. F. Hughes	c. sub b. Carew	13
leg-byes 2, no balls 4		6
		69

*D. E. Goodwin and O. D. Colhoun did not bat in either innings.

Umpires: M. Stott and A. Trickett

	O	M	R	W	O	M	R	W
Blair	8	4	14	1				
Shillingford	7	2	19	1				
Shepherd	13	4	20	3				
Roberts	16	3	43	1				
Carew					2	0	23	2

Fall of Wickets
1–19, 2–30, 3–34, 4–51, 5–55, 6–69, 7–103, 8–125

A Famous Victory

Ireland's victory by 9 wickets over the West Indies, all out 25, at the Sion Mills ground, Londonderry, 2 July 1969

Some Contests acted out on humble Swards
Are no less Epic-filled than those at Lord's.
Come Muse! provide my pen with rhyming skills,
That I may sing the Field of Sion Mills,
(Whose fame may lie forgotten and unsung
Unless some Aid Divine inspire some Tongue,)
Where Ireland's Chosen, facing fearful odds,
Achieved a stature little short of Gods.

Oh to convey that memorable scene!
The Pitch (see *Wisden*'s note) was 'em'rald green',
That claim for Girls and Diamonds I'll amend:

'An Em'rald Pitch is NOT a Carib's friend,'
For Ireland's heroes strove like men inspired,
While one by one the Visitors 'retired';
Their faces long, their crease-duration short,
For Hospitality goes ill with Sport.

No Shepherd now appeared to lead the Flock;
No Butcher to attack or slay or block;
No rising Star to Foster hope's illusion,
Since nothing reigned but horror and confusion.

At 3 for 3, then 8 for 6, (no byes)
To Sion's hills in vain they raised their eyes.
At 12 for 9 the fact was plain to all
Their eyes had served them best by watching ball,
For such the ill success with which they played,
'Twas clear those hills withheld th'expected Aid.
The tail wagged doggedly through snick and drive,
And (with one bye) progressed to 25.
Those dark bare Mills and hills had sown such panic,
They held the genius loci for Satanic.

The Irish now cut loose with pull and sweep,
And found the troubled Waters far less deep.
Unrivalled Day! Good Win! Immortal Score!
Peace has its Victories more renowned than War.

H. MORGAN DOCKRELL

---

*An Irish friend draws our attention to yet another
feather in Ireland's cricket cap*

Though cricket was invented by the English it has travelled
the planet, indeed the only Nobel Prize-winner ever to
appear in *Wisden* is not an Englishman at all, but an
Irishman, an author, poet and playwright. His name is
Samuel Beckett, but then with a name like Beckett, how
could he not play cricket?

JEREMY MADDEN SIMPSON

The Thinking Woman's Game

If it is true that Irishmen take their lead from their women there must be a bright future for cricket in The Emerald Isle. A roving reporter from Irish Independent *recently came upon a group of fanatical league cricketers. Significantly they were all wearing skirts*

In early evening sunlight, a team of cricketers are crouching in a semi-circle, fielding a series of shots, from their leading batsmen, in a brisk practice-coaching session. Behind them, in the shade of Merrion Clubhouse, the opposing side are donning their shin-pads, grip-gloves and headbands in preparation for pitched battle. Their captain moves onto the pitch to toss a coin with the home captain for choice of first innings. The silver disc spins in the sunlight – and comes down on the home side.

The opening batsmen pad up, smoothing down their short white skirts. The Ladies League match between Merrion and Leinster is under way.

'Some of the girls are hockey players who want to play a team game during the summer,' says a burly male cricketer. 'But most of them simply want to play cricket. They practise very hard. It's not a game to them. It's *the* game.'

To the uninitiated like me, the game is highly complicated. You don't have to be Einstein to spot a bowler or batsman, the evidence is ricocheting in front of your eyes. But unravelling the rules that govern the actual method of playing is altogether more complex. And the Cricket Club handbook is hardly enlightening.

Take Law 23. It deals with the complications of a 'dead ball'. (A ball dies, apparently, if caught by bowler or wicket-keeper.) The rule states: 'A ball is not dead when it strikes an umpire, unless it lodges in his dress.' This immediately raises questions like – what happens if the umpire is dead as a result of being struck by the ball? And where could the ball lodge in his dress?

Then there's the stunning Law 39. Appropriately headed 'Stumped', it ordains that 'the striker shall be out Stumped if, in receiving a ball, not being a no-ball, he is out of his ground otherwise than in attempting a run and the wicket is put down by the wicket-keeper without the intervention of another fieldsman'.

Attempts by Merrion players to translate this piece of cricketese caused deep creases in foreheads, but no easy explanations. The only interesting and decipherable rule, Law 16, number six – 'If both captains agree, intervals for drinks may be taken' – doesn't seem to come into play much. In fact, the watching cricketers were quick to dispel the notion that strawberries and cream and the odd bottle of champagne should enter the proceedings at some point or several.

'There's very little time for social breaks during a game,' said a male player, severely. 'They take their cricket very seriously.' And he nods towards the pitch, where the two teams have commenced play.

After a match that would do credit to 22 Irishmen, the Merrion supporters 'invade' the pitch and start running around the returning players, embracing them soccer-style, and the Leinster team look as indisposed as a brace of parrots. But over pots of tea, and towering stacks of sand-wiches and fruit cake – washed down with cooling pints of Smithwicks and Harp – the losing team's agony recedes into the middle distance. There would be future opportunities for revengeful victory.

With white cricket jumpers wound around shoulders, and the minor cuts and bruises incurred in battle starting to glow on foreheads and arms, the talk turns to fielding and batting technique and the all-round appeal of the game.

The players – all secretaries, bank officials, or insurance agents by day and budding Ian Bothams by night – say that cricket appeals mostly because it provides as much mental exercise as it does physical exertion.

Secretary Aisling White (19) who is playing her fourth season for Merrion Club, says: 'Cricket is like a drug. We practise every Monday and Wednesday from 5.30 to 9 o'clock, and most of my weekends are tied up with Club activities. I did play hockey and some tennis, but cricket training starts as early as February, so it does demand dedication.'

And a demure fielder adds: 'Of course, there's the additional kick of playing a traditional male sport. Of all male-orientated games, cricket is the most logical one to choose. It is more subtle than soccer and more dangerous than rugby. It's really the new Thinking Woman's game.'

CES CASSIDY, The Irish Independent

Some could argue that Scotland really has no business in this anthology. After all, our northern neighbour has provided us with two England captains and an outstanding spin bowler in Ian Peebles. However, Roley Jenkins, the great Worcestershire and England bowler, was to discover to his cost that, in cricket as in law, Scotland has its own legal system

We were playing Scotland. Their team included that prolific scorer of runs, Rev. J. A. Aitchison who, I recall, scored hundreds against the Australians and South Africans, among others.

On this occasion, I bowled three beautiful overs to him, beating the bat about ten times. Twice he shouldered arms to the 'wrong-un' and l.b.w. appeals were turned down. I said 'sorry' to the umpire for appealing – I forgot we were playing under Scottish Law.

When I had bowled the last ball of those three overs, I ambled up the wicket and addressed the batsman:

'I am told you are a parson.'

'Yes, that's right, I am.'

The moment was too good to lose. I looked hard at him and said: 'If I had your b . . . . . dy luck, I would be the Archbishop of Canterbury.'

ROLEY JENKINS, The Cricketer

Platform Cricket

This strange tale is all the more remarkable in that the action takes place at a railway station far from the beaten tracks of cricket

Before the days of the common use of motor cars, a commercial traveller found himself at a lonely railway station in the north of Scotland which was manned by the station-master and a porter.

When he was told that he would have to wait four hours for the next train he asked the porter if there were any places of interest nearby, perhaps a castle, stately home or garden, or even a cinema or sporting event. The porter said that there was nothing, but if the traveller cared he could join him and the station-master in a game of cricket, which was their usual way of passing the time.

The station-master took the bat and the traveller was put on to bowl, with the porter as fielder. The first ball removed the station-master's middle stump and the porter went into ecstasies of joy which to the traveller seemed excessive.

He asked the porter why he was so pleased and received the following reply: 'Well, you see, he has been in for four years.'

J. F. CARNEGIE

French Cricket

Rien à Déclarer?

France is little more than an hour away as the Channel ferry ploughs; but as far as cricket goes it can seem light years distant. Here is one striking example of the different customs to be encountered on the other side of the English Channel

In 1979 a cricketer tried to take his bat through the French Customs at Calais. He explained what it was used for, but the official was completely baffled by it. He then handed him a list of a thousand items, inviting him to select a suitable category. Eventually the bat was admitted into France as an 'engine sportif sans movement mécanique' and a duty of 1.25 francs had to be paid.

GEORGE MELL, *This Curious Game of Cricket*

Cricket's Belle Epoque

Anglo-French cricketing contacts were not always so unsatisfactory. The cordial 'Entente' established during the Second Empire saw genuine attempts on the part of the French authorities and media to come to terms with the English game, as a doyen of cricket historians recounts

When the MCC were in Paris in 1867, a Frenchman remarked to 'Bob' Fitzgerald: 'It is a truly magnificent game, but I cannot understand why you do not engage a servant to field for you instead of having so much running about to do yourself.' And in a report of the play it was recorded: 'The bowler, grasping the ball in the right hand, watches for the favourable moment when the attention of the batsman is distracted, and then launches it with incredible force; the batsman, however, is on the alert; he strikes it to an enormous height, and immediately runs.'

This quaint view of things recalls the fact that, whilst the Emperor (Napoleon III), Empress Eugénie and Prince Impérial were watching a match between Bickley Park and Beckenham, long-on brought off a difficult and spectacular catch. A minute or so later a gentleman-in-waiting, hat in hand, approached the successful fieldsman with a message from the Emperor, thanking him very much for his performance, and asking him to do it again. On another occasion the Emperor asked whether a certain West Kent match was being played for money, and Frederick Edlmann answered in his most dignified manner, 'No, sire; for honour.'

At least once, however, the same Napoleon proved a good friend to cricketers. He had visited the Paris Cricket Club and had the game explained to him, and this circumstance saved the club, for a few days afterwards an old Oxford man, while making a run, tripped, fell and broke his arm. The matter was at once reported to the police, and the club was about to be suppressed as dangerous, when an appeal to the Emperor prevented so dire a calamity.

Reference to the Paris Cricket Club recalls that, in 1865, there was published a handbook of twenty-four pages entitled, *La Clef Du Cricket; ou Courte Explication De La Marche et Des Principales Règles De Ce Jeu. Par An Old Stump*, MPCC. It dealt with cricket generally and gave the twenty rules of the Paris Cricket Club.

The club was formed in July 1863, and among its early presidents were the Duke of Edinburgh and the Duc d'Aumale. In 1865 it presented to the Prince Imperial an outfit consisting of two bats, two sets of stumps (silver mounted, with ebony bails), two balls, pads, gloves and spiked boots; also a treatise on the game. The articles were enclosed in a handsome and massive mahogany case lined with green velvet, on the lid of which was an engraved silver plate bearing the inscription, 'A son Altesse Impérial, Monseigneur le Prince Impérial'. The gift called forth the following acknowledgement to M. Drouyn de l'Huys, the club's President:

Sir – The foundation of a cricket club cannot fail to promote the development of the public health, if the practice of the game should become as general as I desire, and as your efforts give reason to hope. I heartily applaud this institution, and accept with pleasure the implements of the game which you have had the kindness to offer to the Prince Impérial. You are well aware, Sir, of my sentiments of high esteem and goodwill for yourself.

Eugéne

At the same time the Prince forwarded two thousand francs to the club as a mark of the interest he took in its welfare, and in the following year, when he became a member, promised to subscribe one hundred francs annually.

The Emperor, when he visited the ground in 1866, confessed 'Je n'y comprends rien du tout.' The Empress rejoined in English: 'I understand a great deal, and I hope that next year the little Prince will have learnt this interesting game.' Despite his ignorance of the finer points of cricket, His Majesty proved a good friend to the club, and before the commencement of the season of 1867 granted it an important concession by giving it permission, through the Prefect of the Seine, to enclose and level its ground in the Bois de Boulogne.

The unconscious humour of which the French mind has proved so prolific was never more in evidence than in a 'Guide', in which, by means of a conversation, an attempt was made to explain the intricacies of the game:

'Let us, then, observe the cricket game, my dear Gaston.'
'But, my dear Henri, the cricket game I do not understand.'
'Eh, bien, here is the tram; let us seat ourselves, and as we go I explain. There are eleven men on each side, two umpires, two wickets, a ball, and some guards, since the ball is so very hard. A player sits at the wickets, and, behold, one hurls down at him the ball, the no-ball, the wide ball, the leg-break, the googly, the head-break, the rapid, the very slow. C'est terrible! Mon Dieu, you will admire! The batter, who has a flat club, makes the strokes – the on-drive, the off-drive, the back-cut, the upper-cut, the leg-pull and the left hook, strokes of a skill incroyable. The crowd cries, "Brava!" like M. le Professeur Hall at the Opera. But alas! The batter misses the ball; the wicket is knocked down. One cries

"How out?" and the umpire nods his head. Thereupon the batter retires, and they place upon the board his score and the letters l.b.w. Sometimes the umpire cries "Over!" and all walk over to the far side for the sake of exercise. The game, Gaston, is of great simplicity. And – I almost forgot – wearied by the continual striking of the ball, the batters, too, for the purpose of recuperation, run swiftly up and down between the wickets.'

'It seems very dangerous, Henri.'

'True! For me, I would rather exercise myself with diabolo or dominoes.'

The description was written in all seriousness, and to this day the author of it probably considers that he produced a valuable treatise on the game. Many years ago, I can recall, a *maire* of a seaside resort much favoured by English families decided to promote a fête for the benefit of the younger visitors in which 'Juvenile Sports', with cricket as the chief attraction, were to be held. The good man, wishing his plans to obtain as much publicity as possible, decided to make an English translation of the French posters and handbills. The idea was sound, but unfortunately the announcements in English were headed 'Childish Games', much to the righteous indignation of the visiting youth old enough to take part in a properly organised match. It was amusing, too, when a fast bowler, after delivering two or three overs, was approached by a gendarme, who warned him, 'Not so fast, sir, if you please – not so fast!'

F. S. ASHLEY-COOPER, *Cricket Highways & Byways*

Other Frenchmen have been overawed by the destructive capabilities of the cricket ball

Le bal s'elance avec un velocité terrible.

HIPPOLYTE TAINE

Only Bullfighting can Compare With It!

The newspaper Ce Matin, *reporting a match between Nottingham and the Athletic Club of Paris in 1951, went so far as to compare our gentle game with bullfighting, according to the* Birmingham Post *translation*

'On the lawn there were two teams of eleven men, all dressed in white as for tennis, some wearing small caps. A resemblance is also seen to football or hockey because of men whom one saw crouched ready to defend the goals.

'These goals, if you please, are formed of three sticks stuck in the ground, supporting two small wooden carved objects. This forms a wicket. When the ball attains the wicket the goalkeeper is eliminated.

'These goalkeepers – each holds with two hands a wooden racquet with which he defends his wicket. Their legs are protected by white armour. In short, the principle is that of football.

'A man runs ten metres in the direction of a batsman and throws the ball straight at him. The batsman brandishes his racquet and redirects the ball towards the outside. Men run, one of them seizes the ball and the score changes. Finished for the moment, says the referee, 21 points to Nottingham.

'Should a batsman send the ball out of the ground it is ten points for him. The stroke is rare. On striking the ball the batsman dashes towards his vis-à-vis, and if no one has caught the ball it is a point for his team. In the second half this will be the job of the other team.

'The rain fell as between the Orcades and the Shetlands; but they, with that indifference formerly shown during the blitz, remained stoic.

'Then occurred an incredible thing. Mr Blackburn of Nottingham, correctly received the heavy ball (wood and rubber surrounded by leather) on his wooden racquet. But with terrible force the projectile deviated and struck him in the face. He stepped back, staggered and fell upon the grass. Blood flowed in a stream from his wound. "Nottingham 37 points", the referee announced, while they removed the unfortunate batsman on a stretcher. The rain increased and the match was stopped.'

Summing up, the French critic wrote: 'For a national and esoteric sport only Spanish bullfighting can compare with it.'

Note: Blackburn, whose facial injury was superficial, was treated at the Paris hospital and discharged.

Translation by ERNEST SANDFORD

It's not entirely a history of misunderstandings. Cricket was to score a notable convert among the French Impressionist movement

I believe I am finally going to take the house in L'Isle-Adam. Unhappily it is right next to the cemetery, but the garden is six or seven times bigger than ours, we shall be able to play cricket. . . .

CAMILLE PISSARRO, *A letter to his son*

'Steady, Oudard, Steady!'

Again, two dedicated French batsmen find an affection-ate place in J. E. Peckover's memories of his Edwardian schooldays

In the ordinary way one does not associate cricket with the French and yet, oddly enough, two of the most enthusiastic cricketers I ever knew were Frenchmen.

For several years (1905–9) I and one of my two younger brothers were incarcerated in a small and gruesome pre-paratory boarding school at Upper Walmer, Kent – a school I have long since preferred to call Hades House School.

Cricket was one of the very few school activities that offered temporary surcease from a quasi-martial routine involving canings, impositions, threats and invective. Even the headmaster became human when playing cricket.

The lot of an assistant master was not much better than that of his pupils. Rarely did a master remain at the school for more than two terms at the most; some there were who remained with us but one term.

There were, however, two Frenchmen, who, if my memory does not deceive me, remained at Hades House for two successive summer terms – Monsieur Peruchot and Monsieur Oudard.

M. Peruchot was a swashbuckling extrovert, animated, voluble and tense. He was of medium height and powerfully built. M. Oudard, on the other hand, was by nature reserved.

Their contrasting temperaments were highlighted on the cricket field.

In the course of time the two Frenchmen became almost fanatical in their devotion to cricket. At first they were drawn to the game in the spirit of curiosity; cricket to them was seen as a novelty, but, as they began to learn more and more about the game, they became completely cast in its spell; ultimately they even began to discuss cricket, employing in the process the proper cricket terminology. Neither master displayed any great talent for the game, true, but what they lacked in skill they made up for in keenness.

M. Peruchot would come out to bat, hatless, *sans* batting gloves, his shirt sleeves rolled up level with his brawny biceps, a pad on his left leg.

He wore a stiff white boiled shirt, a white starched collar, a flowing black cravat, black riding breeches and yellow leather boots with long pointed tips. Having taken guard M. Peruchot would spit on his hands; twist the handle of the bat and cast a stern glance on the schoolboy fielders surrounding him.

He had but one scoring stroke – a wild golf drive. If it ever connected with the business portion of the bat, the ball would almost certainly soar to the boundary; even a mis-hit would quite likely net him a single.

M. Peruchot very quickly learned that his best chance of scoring was to leap from the crease and endeavour to meet the ball on the half volley. He was agile on his feet but, alas, more than once the slippery soles of his walking boots betrayed him. On missing the ball he would swivel his torso sharply and in scrambling back to the crease he might fall flat on his face only to be stumped. If, however, he stayed at the wicket long enough to get his eye in he would give us, the fielders, a merry chase.

When M. Peruchot bowled he gripped the ball tightly in the palm of his right hand and after a short run let loose with everything he had. He might bowl a wide, or send the ball clean over a batsman's head; again he might, every once in a rare while, hit the stumps. Like his batting, his bowling was cyclonic and totally unpredictable.

M. Oudard, on the other hand, did not bowl, preferring instead to concentrate on batting. He wore on the cricket field black trousers and black walking boots. When batting he also took the precaution of wearing a left pad but, unlike his compatriot, he wore batting gloves, kept the sleeves of his white shirt unrolled and eschewed a cravat.

He was for the most part a stonewaller; indeed when blocking he never raised his bat more than a few inches at the very most and at the moment of stopping the ball he would give a little jump that made it appear as if the impact of ball on bat had all but knocked him over.

Every so often M. Oudard would seemingly become bored with blocking whereupon, imitating M. Peruchot, he would let go with a wild drive, only to miss. At such times, rising from a bench set down in the small cricket tent and running forward, hands cupped, M. Peruchot, of all people, would roar 'Steady, Oudard, steady!' In answer M. Oudard would raise a hand and addressing his confrère in French call back, 'Don't worry Peruchot, old chap. From now on I shall play very, very carefully. Watch.'

M. Oudard would thereupon resume his stonewalling, only in a very short while to execute yet another wild and futile drive, whereupon the oral exchanges would be repeated all over again.

For myself I shall never forget the animation the two masters brought to the game; indeed they bolstered our spirits both on and off the field. In conclusion, may we fervently hope the two obscure French cricketers of yore survived the 1914–1918 war to live out rewarding lives.

J. E. PECKOVER, *The Cricketer*

Papa Joue Au Cricket

It's not quite French, nor even French cricket; yet as Mr
D. J. Foskett OBE points out the following verse will be
poignantly meaningful to any 'papa' summoned by the
Headmaster to play in the annual Fathers' Match

Papa joue au Cricket
C'est une grande allumette – une deux-jour allumette.
Papa est dans le pré tout le premier jour.
Il laisse tomber deux attrapes.
    et manque trois balles dans le profond, qui vont à la borne
    pour quatre. Beurre-doigts!
Son capitaine le met sur à bouler. Il boule deux larges, et
    trois pas-balles. Il est frappé pour six. Il boule des
    plein-jets et des long-sauts et des demi-volées. Il est ôté.
    Il a l'analyse: – Pardessus, 3; Pucelles, o; Courses, 38;
    Guichets, o.
L'autre côté accourt une vingtaine de haute taille.
Papa s'assied dans le pavillon.
Il est dernier homme dedans.
Il regarde son capitaine, qui fait un siècle.
Aprés un premier-guichet debout, les guichets to imbent.
Le filateur en prend quatre: un attrapé à court troisième
    homme, un dans le ravin, un autre à niais moyen-dessés,
    et le dernier vaincu par un qui va avec le bras.
Le marchand de vitesse fait le truc de chapeau parmi les
    lapins: un joliment pris à jambe-carrée, un dans les
    glissades, et l'autre battu et boulé tout au dessus de la
    boutique.
Les joueurs courent. Le guichet-teneur casse le guichet.
    Celui qui court n'est pas dans son pli. It est couru dehors.
Papa est dedans.
Il saisit sa chauve-souris.
Il marche à la poix.
Il prend milieu-et-jambe.
On boule. C'est un casse-jambe.
Papa ferme ses yeux. Il coupe en retard. Il manque.
On boule. C'est un Chinois.
Papa ferme ses yeux. Il accroche. C'est un coup de vache.

La balle lui frappe le genou. Le pre hurle, 'Comment ça?'
   L'arbitre lève son doigt.
Cloches d'enfer!
Papa est dehors, jambe-devant-guichet.
Il n'a pas cassé son canard.
Hélas!

Discovered by D. J. FOSKETT
Translation by GEORGE WALKER

From The Windmill End

A Fight For Survival

Once, when one of us was at the Frankfurt Book Fair, we sold a book on Mountaineering for Beginners to a Dutch publisher. This was considered by many to be a triumph of British salesmanship and by the time the Fair had ended had become a legend attended, as always, by colossal exaggeration. Neither of us were therefore surprised to find that cricket flourishes in Holland. This first extract from Wisden *magazine shows that such was the enthusiasm that very soon after the end of the Second World War efforts were being made to start up the game again*

During the Second World War cricket became increasingly difficult and the league (of which there were several) competition was abandoned entirely in 1944. Many grounds had been confiscated by the occupying forces and the people in Holland suffered badly from five years' oppression and terror. German troops inspecting the HCC (Hague Cricket Club) ground at The Hague one day were intrigued by the equipment, so the groundsman Harry lined them up around the slip-catcher as if for fielding practice. Having shown this bunch of invading non-cricketers the general idea with a tennis ball he then handed the Hauptmann some cricket balls. When the first teeth started flying amidst bloody yells of agony, Harry beat a hasty retreat and disappeared for some weeks. Despite this incident the ground was saved!

Immediately after the war concerted efforts were made to revive the game and a chronic shortage of equipment was alleviated to a large extent by the creation in England of a 'Save Dutch Cricket Fund' under the presidency of Sir Pelham Warner. Their generous donations of bats and balls gradually put cricket back on its feet again. Soon after the liberation exciting contests were also fixed with British regiments still serving in Germany and little by little international contacts were established once more.

Amongst post-war stars prominent players were Wally van Weelde, ebullient and forceful thumper of the ball, whose scorching drives will be remembered with mixed feelings by many opponents; Manus Stolk, unobtrusive and meticulous opening bat; and Robbie Colthoff, an exciting right-handed striker and brilliantly agile wicket-keeper, whose fine technique avoided any serious damage and enabled him to start his professional career as a surgeon with perfectly straight fingers. In the opinion of many experts Peter van Arkel, regarded as one of Holland's best-ever batsmen – like Colthoff a doctor now – and Ernst Vriens, prolific wicket-taker with his sharply turning off-breaks, could both have gone a long way in English county cricket. Tony Bakker, although not always in favour with the establishment, served the All Holland team extremely well with many a flamboyant and memorable innings. The current national XI contains the veteran Rene Schoonheim, neat wicket-keeper/batsman, Steven Lubbers, who turned professional and had a few seasons with Derbyshire seconds, and the promising batsman Ron Elferink, who in last year's ICC tournament made 154 not out off the Fijians.

KEES BAKKER, *The Cricketer*

Holland v. Australia

Wisden *records the bare facts of a day, and indeed an incident which must have set the whole of the Low Countries buzzing – or at least some of them (and, of course, Mr Potter's head)*

At The Hague on August 29, 1964, Holland won by 3 wickets. An unfortunate accident marked this carefree match. Ian Potter received a fractured skull while batting and took no further part in the tour.

Wisden

Dames At The Wicket

A friend of ours, asked if he could remember the name of one Dutch cricketer, thought for a while and then said with a quizzical smile, Tulip Sinji? It was he who introduced us to the contributor who here gives us a charming account, among other things, of Ladies or 'Dames' cricket as played under his tutelage

Mention of 'Ladies cricket in Holland' to the average player or spectator in England, raises quizzical eyebrows. After the initial shock, a spreading smile heralds the inevitable follow-up: 'Do they play in clogs and wear Dutch caps ha ha!!' One becomes resigned to this reception of a slightly bizarre topic, and the mental vision it produces, e.g. blonde pigtailed Amazons hurling Edam cheeses at equally formidable batswomen wielding brass bedwarmers, on a field of tulips under the baleful gaze of spectral windmills. This, I must confess, would have been my reaction if the subject had been broached to me years ago, but such is the enchantment of this most glorious of games, one is always being surprised by something never before experienced.

My introduction to Dames (pronounced dá-musz) cricket in Holland was a physical confrontation, not a giggle in the pavilion bar; it therefore came as more of a shock! Let me set the scene, so you may appreciate my involvement and enthusiasm from that moment on.

Some ten years ago I left England because the climate 'bowled me over' so often that the medical profession suggested my retirement from the home pitch, rather than become a fertiliser for it. So I travelled Europe, happily finding sunshine in Spain and the invigorating clean air of Scandinavia an effective boiler clean for my rusting system, but subconsciously missing my flannelled friends and the sound of leather on willow.

During a visit to London in 1978, I chanced to meet an old friend and Sussex player, Leslie Lenham, who is one of the founder members of the National Coaching Association, and he suggested that I help the furtherance of the game by coaching abroad in the lesser known cricketing countries. Seduced by his ale, honeyed conversation, and thoughts of Dr Livingstone, I agreed. A month later a telephone call from Holland turned my cricketing beliefs and considerable cricketing experience upside down.

Accepting the offer to be player coach I set off to Holland, knowing that the game had been played there for a hundred years, several touring sides coming regularly to England. My only worry was communication, Dutch being a difficult language (and still to me, at times, double Dutch). Arriving over a weekend, I proceeded to the cricket ground on Monday evening to start the coaching activities, and on being instructed that on Monday I would have the Veterans (the 40 club of Holland) and 'Ladies' to look after, I naturally assumed that the term 'Ladies' applied to the more portly and social members of the Veterans. Imagine rounding the pavilion to the nets and being faced by twelve very attractive and athletic girls clad in white, throwing cricket balls about! My first reaction was that they were the tennis section having a skylark, but when they marched up, solemnly introduced themselves in the most perfect English, shook my hand and kissed me on both cheeks I was stunned. Recovering my poise, stiff English upper lip and all that is expected of an Englishman abroad, I tottered over to the nets thinking 'even James Bond never faced these odds'.

The first thing that struck me was their approach to the game, the serious attention and efforts to do the 'right thing', no chatter or playing about; whatever one demonstrated or instructed was followed with dedication. It was indeed the dream that film directors, orchestra conductors and sports coaches have, but which seldom materialises. To complete this seeming fantasy of the mind I was welcomed back in the bar by these nubile creatures, bearing trays of ice-cold lager for my refreshment, and requesting further information on the game.

Several calming glasses later, trying to unscramble my mind and assume a Bond-like nonchalance, I ventured enquiries as to the whys and wherefores of Dames Cricket in Holland. Having heard of women's cricket in England but never witnessing a performance on the field, I was intrigued as to how the gospel had spread to these parts and when it originated.

It transpired that it all began in 1930 in a town called Haarlem through the motivations of the local hockey club, the hockey since being a breeding ground for many players. Expansion gradually took place in the pre-war years, a ruling body, the NDCB and a league formed in 1934. Encouragement was given by the English WCA and several sides came over to provide more experience. During the war years cricket obviously stopped because of difficulties in obtaining equipment and other more serious restrictions. Revived again in 1947 and encouraged by some farsighted men, the clubs began to flourish, with tours to England and South Africa taking place. Interest waned in the early 70s, but the efforts of some younger committee members and players began a revival, which has in the past few years escalated from 200 to over 600 players. These players are split into 40 clubs, more being formed each year, and split into four divisions, promotion, relegation and national championships being fiercely contested, with the standard of play improving each year.

Those readers who have yet to see women playing cricket should not give condescending smirks and mutter 'but it's not real cricket', but go and see a top-level game. They will be pleasantly surprised. To emphasise this point, all the higher-order batsmen wear thigh pads, such is the pace some 'quickies' are achieving now, and bruises of battle are displayed with pride.

Cricket is a minor sport in Holland, the major proportion of the people have no idea what the game is about. Many times people have wandered into a ground and politely enquired, 'Are the two gentlemen in white coats doctors or butchers?' 'Neither actually,' is the solemn reply, 'they're neutral umpires to stop us killing each other!' This statement emphasises the Dutch approach to all their sports: they 'go at it' with everything they have, and training sessions are treated with as much effort and concentration as the actual game. But one peculiar fact has emerged and has surprised other cricket coaches over here, many being ex-county, or current test players from overseas: that is the mental approach of the Dames, whether naturally talented or not.

I well remember one girl working at her bowling action and control for nearly four hours one evening until I pleaded with her to stop. On my inquiry the following week as to her performance over the weekend, she shyly replied: 'Six wickets, four with outers and two with inners.' What more can one ask for as a coach? – except how to explain to a father why his two daughters require half his garden for a practice net!

Hard as their approach to the game is, the 'third innings' in the club house is just as important to the Dames. Sometimes the evening develops into many of them having dinner together then on to a disco, 'to keep the body moving and improve the footwork', a good way to combine practice and pleasure.

Taking them on tour to England is a great experience, good cricket, combined with excellent team and social spirit making it all worthwhile. A system of fines has been introduced for misfielding, dropped catches, swearing and general misbehaviour. Several umpires have been startled to hear the captain say to a miscreant: 'That will cost you 10p for the misfield and 10p for swearing.' It acts as a better deterrent than the formal admonishment in many cases. Perhaps some of the Test captains should introduce this system to reduce the hysterical outbursts one unfortunately witnesses these days, and which are copied by the youngsters. For once the ladies keep their mouths shut!

The Dames have in the past few years gained the respect of the men and boys, because of their attitude, playing ability and social assistance within the clubs. Pretty barmaids, scorers and secretaries are always an asset, whatever anyone says. This respect has led to the regular provision of good pitches, equipment, and willing umpires, all of which are essential to the improvement and furtherance of their game. This is unfortunately not the case in England, where their 'sisters' have to struggle for recognition, especially for good pitches. English cricket clubs please take note. You can be missing out in more ways than one, better a cricketing girlfriend or wife than the 'reluctant dragon' grumbling in a deck chair.

Sitting in deckchairs brings me to another point of the Dames game – 'attire'. When I first arrived and became involved, all the girls wore skirts and long socks, all very nice and feminine but hardly practical on a freezing spring day, blue-kneed, waiting to bat and batting with a confusion of skirts, thigh pads and pads to contend with. My suggestion that trousers were more in keeping with the game, besides providing a modest 'rear view' was accepted. During the next tour to England a startled sports shop proprietor and his goggle-eyed assistants were entertained by a sporting 'Folies Bergères' fitting out fashion show. Since then trousers have been the standard form of Dames dress on the Dutch cricket fields.

All cricket grounds, as one should expect in Holland, are flat, but many are extremely attractive, surrounded by trees with first-class pavilions and facilities, providing real cricket atmosphere. All the pitches are artificial, either matting or simulated grass, which provide a fairly true but slightly higher-bounce wicket. The girls, however, like to play on the 'green green grass of home' and love the tours to England with the sloping grounds and changing wickets. Many of them go to the cricket weeks organised by the WCA and there meet other girls from Australia, New Zealand, West Indies and India. This helps to establish contacts between the countries and give the Dames more playing experience, as the season in Holland is limited to three months because of the demands of hockey on most of the grounds.

When you ask them what the lure of the game is, why they become fanatics, their answer is always. 'A team and individual sport, fascinatingly involved, and unpredictable'. Where have we not heard this before? So their approach to the game is not dissimilar to the men's. Most of their games are played on Saturdays, and they avidly follow the fortunes of the men on Sundays. Such is the standard some of them have achieved, that several men's team secretaries, bedevilled by last-minute 'drop-outs', unhesitatingly reach for the telephone, knowing that a competent and willing 'fill-in' is readily available; therefore no quarter is asked or given in these situations from the opposition, as 'points' are at stake.

As a final tribute to their efforts to 'do it right' I must recount an incident in a match between the national Dames team, and a men's club who invited them for a 'practice' game before we went on tour to England. Having dismissed the men for 160, the Dames were on 130 for 4, when a tall, attractive girl, having reached 70, essayed another hook at the fast bowler she had twice deposited into the woods, and edged it into her mouth. Lying in a pool of blood, surrounded by the players and a crestfallen bowler, her first comment was. 'Sorry, it was my own fault, my head was in the wrong place, it should have gone in the car park.'

Many people ask me why I give so much of my time to Dames cricket. The above is part of the answer, their devotion to the game, and the spirit with which they play, the remainder. Cricket is cricket, whether played by schoolboys, Test players or women, and it should be supported and encouraged to ensure its continuity. After all, looking to the future, who is the best coach of children? A cricketing mother can impart encouragement, basic technique and knowledge at an early age, thereby paving yet another way to the wicket.

My association with the Nederlands Dames, their friendship and humour, have made the past years some of the happiest of my life and led to meeting my 'soul mate', who is their captain. Her cherished dream is to lead the Dames down the steps at Lord's to do battle with England, such are the thoughts that dwell in those 'Far Pavilions'.

The next world cup for women's cricket is in Australia in 1987 and I hope to be privileged in taking the Dames to compete, knowing that Sydney cricket ground will hold more appeal for them than Bondi beach.

Do they have discos on Jumbo Jets, so they can practise on the way?

PETER BEECHENS

Kricket Krauts

The First Anglo-German Tests

To the casual student, the history of German cricket would seem to be a fairly short story. Readers of the Journal of the Cricket Society *know otherwise. Over a number of issues the Editor, James D. Coldham, has been regaling the subscribers with tales and statistics from unexpected pavilions beyond the Rhine. Here is how he describes the first unofficial series between an English touring party and the 'kricketers' of Kaiser Wilhelm's Germany*

In 1910 MCC had not been able to accept an invitation to Nürnberg and in 1913 attempts were made to induce an Australian side to visit Berlin in 1916 (which, of course, proved abortive), but in 1911 Leicester CC accepted an invitation to the capital and thus became the first team from England to visit Germany.

On Wednesday the 2nd August, 1911, under the captaincy of the Rev. F. S. Beddow, the following constituted the Leicester team: T. Crew (honorary secretary), J. I. Adcock, F. King, E. Wesson, F. S. Smith, R. Needham, C. E. Pallett, B. Boothaway, H. Ellis, E. Findley, W. H. Harris, W. Bell and W. F. Jacques. It was a very useful side. F. S. Smith was chairman of Leicestershire CCC from 1945 until his death in 1956; W. Ball served as professional at Leamington College, Tettenhall College and Birkenhead Park, dying at East Shilton in 1918; R. Needham, a left-arm fastish bowler, played for the county against All India in 1911, a knee injury causing him eventually to retire from the game; and T. Crew, who reported the tour for *The Leicester Mail* was a good all-rounder, who became better-known as an Association Football referee. The Rev. Frank Seaward Beddow was born in Melbourne, Australia, in 1872 and graduated from McMaster University, Toronto. A fine preacher, serving as minister of a Congregational church in Glasgow, he became pastor of Carey Hall (Baptist) Church, Leicester, before accepting the pastorate of Wycliffe Congregational Church in the town, where he remained from 1911 until 1956. A pioneer-advocate of the much-suspected (in that day) religious drama and always in the vanguard of any work for peace, he had a charming personality and a keen sense of humour. He rendered splendid service to Leicester CC as a most efficient slow bowler and as a capable batsman, winning a high reputation as a good sportsman and captain. For many years a member of Leicestershire CCC, he died in 1957.

For this first visit by an England team to play against members of the Berlin League, 'the Leicesters' travelled from Grimsby in the SS *Lutterworth* to Hamburg, noting that in the steerage were 380 emigrants from America bound for Hamburg, Berlin and Moscow – 'a pathetic sight', according to Tom Crew. On arrival, the team noticed a German boat named *Fairplay XI*,* which they considered a good omen. After sight-seeing in Hamburg – particularly noting the magnificent Town Hall and Kaiser Wilhelm Monument – they left by train for Berlin, where a great reception awaited them from officials of the Berlin League, other sportsmen, and British residents. The train journey, which took about four hours, was memorable for the beautiful scenery they passed through, Crew being especially interested in the methods of afforestation noted en route. They found that almost every part of Berlin, where they stayed for more than a week, offered a pleasing picture, ranging from the Unter den Linden, extending from the Brandenburg Gate to the Royal Palace, to the system of main drainage, 'radiating in twelve directions and carrying off all its sewage to distant fields'.

The first match against the Union Club was on a well-enclosed football ground in the Tempelhof area, bordered by a tier-garden, which was quite attractive. The visiting

*Some thirty years later there was a coalhulk in Wellington harbour, New Zealand, bearing this name, and said to have been a vessel of past importance.

team, however, were disappointed with the standard matting wicket, the uneven outfield and the smallness of the playing area. Their desire to educate the Germans in the finer points of the game was difficult to fulfil. The match started at 10 a.m. and the luncheon interval at 12.30 lasted two hours. The Germans batted first, but were soon in very serious trouble against F. S. Beddow, who was unplayable. They seemed to have no definite idea of playing a straight bat. Despite their lack of experience on matting, Leicester gave a competent display, E. Findley, F. King and W. H. Harris (finely caught by Sellien) batting well. The German bowling, especially that of Thiel, fast with a low delivery, was much superior to their batting. R. Needham found his length in the second dismal innings: he accomplished the hat trick; and Beddow made his match record: 15–4–21–14.

On predictable matting, Victoria's bowling was soon collared by F. S. Beddow, who batted excellently. The Germans, however, were exceptionally smart in the field. Curiously, the wicket-keeper, Selliger, invariably knelt down on one knee when receiving the ball, which appeared to be the general practice among 'keepers in Berlin.

Captained by the veteran Englishman, Tom Dutton, the Preussen side shaped much more promisingly than either Union or Victoria. Beddow won the toss, put the Preussens in and – as in the previous matches – continued to puzzle all with his splendid bowling. In the second innings, however, young Felix Menzel hit a mighty six into Victoria Park off Crew, which remains the longest hit by a German national. The best bowler in Berlin, Ludecke, took most wickets, besides top-scoring in each innings. The batting of W. H. Harris, who hit what was possibly the second century ever on German soil, was much enjoyed by the spectators as he hit hard and cut brilliantly.

The last match took place before a good crowd against a representative eleven from the Berlin clubs, captained by Tom Dutton, the sole Englishman, and was regarded as a 'Test Match'. Germany batted first and only Dutton and Herzog withstood the bowling with confidence: the latter had a better idea of playing a straight bat than the other

Germans. Despite the bumpy ground, Leicester fielded very keenly, and bowled admirably. When they came to bat, they soon lost Findley leg before to Ludecke, but Harris and Beddow shared in a large stand for the second wicket, the former especially hitting the best bowling of the Germans with characteristic freedom; and Needham and Ball added over 100 for the fifth wicket. In Germany's second innings only Dutton batted with much confidence. Unfortunately the full details of this innings were not published.

'The Leicesters' were entertained handsomely by each of the clubs in turn, and at the conclusion of the 'Test Match' gave three hearty cheers for the Germans, who heartily responded. A grand banquet followed. Crew commented in one of his reports to *The Leicester Mail* that 'on every hand it is said that our visit has done German cricket a world of good, and they are highly satisfied with the cricket given by the Leicester club'. Three days before, however, there was a strangely eventful social evening hosted by Preussen CC at their new club-house. The Germans favoured their guests with special club songs, and an Englishman from the British Embassy indulged in a little conjuring. Herr Meyer, chairman of Preussen CC, welcomed 'the Leicesters' most cordially and hoped that the visit would be for the good of the German players: he was sure it would further cement the ties between the two countries. Responding in an apt speech, the Rev. F. S. Beddow said that they were delighted to visit Germany, and the game of cricket was just as likely to improve the character of the Germans as it had done in England. It was a unique tour, and he was proud to be connected with any object that brought the two nations into closer fellowship. At this juncture, Beddow was interrupted by a strong Prussian voice and informed that, as he had delivered his address in an open space, he was liable to a fine of 20 marks (about £2 in sterling). In fact, he should have spoken in the club-house. The following morning officials of the Preussen club themselves settled with the police, and nothing further was said.

JAMES D. COLDHAM, *A History of German Cricket*

Heil Kricket!

*Cricket in Germany survived the First World War and
even the coming to power of Adolf Hitler. Indeed the
Gentlemen of Worcester's tour of 1936 was to be
undertaken with the active encouragement of the Nazi
authorities. James D. Coldham's account of this
memorable and strangely poignant clash of cultures
seems certain to take its place in many future anthologies*

During the Olympic Games of 1936 at Berlin, when the
National Socialist government was trying desperately to
show a civilised and friendly face to the outside world, Felix
Menzel (not, incidentally, a Nazi) drew the attention of
sports-attachés and journalists of the cricket-playing coun-
tries to German cricket and, in cooperation with the Reichsportsführer, Von Tschammer und Osten, a great friend of
Hitler's, sent personal invitations to various clubs to visit
Berlin and play there. One such invitation was received by
MCC, which Sir Pelham Warner communicated to Major
M. F. S. Jewell and Major R. G. W. Berkeley, currently
captain and honorary secretary respectively of the Gentlemen of Worcestershire. Thereupon, it was agreed that the
Gentlemen of Worcestershire would visit Berlin during the
first and second weeks of August 1937, as their annual tour,
to play three matches; and it was to be a tour that the
survivors would recall vividly forty years on: the third ever
visit by an English club side to the German capital. It was
understood that the Berliners would be regarding two of the
fixtures as 'Test Matches' and MCC instructed Major
Jewell and his men officially and urbanely not to lose.

The Gentlemen of Worcestershire's team consisted of
four former Worcestershire county players: a former captain and subsequent president, Major Jewell (1909–33),
Major Berkeley (1919–22), a former MP – the original of
the fearsome 'Major Hawker' in *England, Their England* by
A. G. Macdonnell – R. H. Williams (1923–32) and Sir
Geoffrey S. Tomkinson (1902–26); three Marlborough
boys: Maurice Jewell (son of the captain), P. N. L. Terry and
P. F. B. Robinson; an Etonian, H. O. Huntington-Whiteley;

and Captain (later Colonel) C. S. Anton, subsequently honorary secretary of the Gentlemen, wicket-keeper R. E. Whetherly and W. Deeley. It was a very good club side, scheduled to meet the cream, if such it may be called, of German cricketers: G. Thamer (captain), Behnke, B. Dartsch, F. Dartsch, Dietz, Gruhn, K. H. Lehmann, A. Ludwig (or Ladwig), Mader, Maus, F. Menzel, G. Menzel, Mesicke, G. Parnemann, Pfitzner, K. Rietz, A. Zehmke and Zickert.

As the team prepared for the journey, *The Cricketer* of 31 July 1937 pitched the visit rather too high, perhaps, in stating: 'The visit of the Worcestershire players should do much good, especially as Herr Hitler has shown an interest in cricket.' In truth, we know that Hitler preferred sword-fighting and (like most other Nazis) regarded cricket as effeminate. Indeed, as *The Story of Continental Cricket* says, the position of a native German cricketer in society during the late 1930s was difficult. They played a game that 'a couple of generations earlier had been classified as "schlagball erste klasse" from official quarters, but which had since sunk in estimation to be no more than tolerated'. In 1937 only four clubs remained in the Berlin League. In the event, the Germans were outplayed.

At the outset, little was known by the tourists about German cricket, and, when the party foregathered on the boat-train, they were all anxious to know the strength of the opposition. Major Berkeley, a great humorist, told his colleagues that the game was played in a brave and sporting way. As an example, he said that one club had a very fast bowler – 'a terror' – who removed two teeth from a batsman. The latter, however, was quite unperturbed – he placed his two broken teeth behind the stumps and continued with his innings!

On arrival at Berlin, the team were greeted by many German sportsmen and cinema and press cameras after a journey made easy by a 'laisse passe' issued by the German Embassy in London. They stayed at the Adlon Hotel in the Unter den Linden, close to the Brandenburg Gate (the ruins of which Maurice Jewell was to inspect after the Second World War). They were given an official status and provided with staff cars flying the Swastika and Eagle flags. Mr Jewell recalls that when the drivers approached main junctions, they sounded the special horn, all traffic was stopped and the policeman gave a Nazi salute to which the team, replied by removing their hats. Colonel Anton remembers that the team were watched 'rather carefully' throughout the tour, always having someone planted on them during their social activities, but he agrees with R. H. Williams that the hotel looked after them 'very well'. Hospitality was unbounded.

Each of the Berlin sides was captained by a slightly-built Prussian type, G. Thamer, who had toured England with the Berlin team of 1930. Maurice Jewell refers to him as the 'Reichkricketcaptain'. He bowled very slow right-arm off-breaks fairly expensively onto a matting which was not always pulled tight; and he was not popular with any of his fellow players. Generally, the standard of the Germans' play was not very good; Major Berkeley considered that, although the batting was weak, the bowling and fielding were up to English club standard. The German whose cricketing knowledge and 'brain' was far above that of his colleagues was Felix Menzel. However, the opening batsman, Maus, had one good match and remains the only German cricketer to have been immortalised in English literature (see C. P. Snow, *The Light and the Dark*). The bowling of the brothers, Felix and G. Menzel (both of whom had toured England in 1930, the latter as captain) was 'almost Veritian in steadiness', as reported later in *The Cricketer Annual*, 1937. They could bowl medium-pace right-hand almost entirely on the leg-stump, just short of a length, for three or four hours on end without losing their length. Generally, there would be no slips, no cover or extra cover, and a vast concourse of fieldsmen on the leg-side. K. H. Lehmann was a brilliant fielder in any position and Behnke the best wicket-keeper. Maurice Jewell comments, however, that the fieldsman yelled 'AUS' habitually when the batsman was hit on the pads, long-leg being an expert appealer. 'When we fielded, we only appealed for certainties,' writes Mr Jewell, 'but the Germans couldn't understand it – appealing for everything was part of the game of unnerving the batsman. Eleven men shouting "AUS" was rather unnerving!'

Nevertheless, R. H. Williams and Maurice Jewell recall some amusing episodes: amusing at least in retrospect. Caps of varied hues were worn by the Gentlemen of Worcestershire and a German umpire enquired as to what the various colours signified. 'I tried to explain,' says Mr Williams, 'and as he was wearing a (standard) black and white cap I asked him who his club was and he proudly announced, "Gunn and Moore"!' Mr Jewell remembers that the first match was filmed from the dressing-room to the middle where the camera was stationed at silly mid-off until the operator was 'hit on the shin by myself, in annoyance at the Germans' insistence that the play was for real and if I was out, disturbed by the camera, too bad'. He continues: 'The film included putting on pads, and one of the team's wags tried to get the operator to take him putting on his box – the old type with straps "galore" – but the offer was declined!' Before the first match, at fielding practice Sir Geoffrey Tomkinson amazed the Germans by the distance he could hit the ball one-handed: he was a big hitter.

The three matches were played on matting wickets on Government sports grounds – all sport being state-controlled – the third being on a double football pitch near the Olympic Stadium: sometimes the matting was insufficiently tight to give a true surface. Each match was fully reported in the press and on the radio, but Mr Jewell states that there were few spectators 'except some rather lovely ladies – too old for me but, perhaps, the "seniors" had made their acquaintance'.

R. H. Williams, an opening batsman, was relieved that the 'terror fast bowler' of Major Berkeley's story was in reality only rather over medium pace, and he considers that 'it did not prove too difficult to score the first century – 104 – recorded in Germany (at the Tib-Platz ground)'. In the third match the grass in the truly deep outfield near the Olympic Stadium was three inches long and the temperature around 96 degrees when Major Jewell, aged 52, made 140 before he got himself out through sheer exhaustion. In a telephone conversation with the writer some weeks before his death at 92, the Major reminisced humorously about this innings. Because of the distant boundary and the long grass, he had to run for everything except three fours and, on being 'c. Dartsch b. G. Menzel', he collapsed into a deck chair and fell asleep without removing his pads. Next day the newspapers carried full reports under the heading: 'MAJOR JEWELL SCHLUG DEN KRICKET REKORD'. (It is believed that his 140 has since been exceeded in Germany.)

Generally, the Berliners batted without much success, although several played their strokes well. Alas, when Major Jewell put on one of the elder members to bowl so that they might score a few more runs, he had to be taken off after one over, having taken two wickets at no cost. 'Peter' Huntington-Whiteley (fast), Maurice Jewell (slow) and C. S. Anton (fast medium) were the most prolific wicket-takers.

At the farewell dinner to the tourists in the restaurant at the Olympic Stadium, the host, the Reichsportsführer himself, stated that 'cricket is a very good game. I hope I may visit England to watch cricket in 1938', and he presented Major Jewell with a tie-pin surmounted by a swastika which – as the Major confided to the writer – was later presented to the Memorial Gallery at Lord's. During the dinner, the Reichsportsführer asked the Major how he could increase enthusiasm for the game in Germany. In reply, the Major made several suggestions, such as that an English professional could be engaged in Berlin as tuition and practice were essential, and he recounted a story that the team had been told about the Prussian-type captain, Thamer. Apparently, during the previous season, he was one man short for a match in the Berlin League and would not begin until he had a full team. Eventually, a lad was recruited who had never played before and, fitted out in flannels, he was sent to field at deep mid-off, the safest place (the captain thought) as he opened the bowling with his off-breaks. In the second over the lad dropped a skier off his bowling and repeated the performance in the captain's next over, whereupon Thamer walked across and felled him with a right hook to the chin. Major Jewell suggested that such action would not encourage the German youth to play the game, to which the Reichssportsführer replied: 'Yes, I have heard about the incident, but I understand it was a very simple catch!'

C. S. Anton, R. H. Williams and Maurice Jewell consider that, although the team were looked after with the greatest hospitality and thoroughly enjoyed the tour, Germany was a strange country at that time. 'Wherever we played,' confesses Maurice Jewell, 'we could hear machine-guns firing and we witnessed a torchlight procession down Unter den Linden which was both alarming and eerie'; and Mr Williams adds that they left for home the same night that Mussolini was due to arrive. 'The streets were packed with troops and we were lucky and glad to get to the station.'

A cricket professional, alas, was never to reach Berlin, although teams from Denmark and the Somerset Wanderers from England visited Berlin and the Berliners visited Copenhagen before the lights went out again in 1939. Thamer and the two Menzels particularly distinguished themselves in these matches. Two of the Gentlemen of Worcestershire tourists were to die in the War, namely Huntington-Whiteley and R. E. Wetherly – and there were to be many casualties among the small band of German cricketers, before Feliz Menzel and Kurt Rietz (another 1937 'Test' player and a future propagandist of cricket) arose from the ashes and rubble of Berlin in 1945 to challenge British soldiery to a game and attempt to rebuild the Berlin Cricket League.

JAMES D. COLDHAM, *A History of German Cricket*

Cricket Beats the Berlin Blockade

Major M. Oliver, formerly Military Attaché to the British GOC, literally took up the story of German cricket among the ruins of Russian-blockaded Berlin. As a first step he obtained permission for the Free Foresters to visit the beleaguered city 'to give a "snook" to the Russians and show them that come what may the British way of life would continue. I could think of no better way of making that point than the sound of bat on ball.' The message was not lost on the citizens of Berlin

The political impact of this visit was immense and apart from the continuation of a British sport under unusual conditions it played an important part in the beginning of cementing fellowship and understanding between the Allies and German populace of West Berlin.

Not long after the match I received an invitation from the remnants of the twelve Kricket (as the Germans spell it) clubs of Berlin to give a lecture on 'The History and Rules of Cricket'. I accepted the invitation with some reluctance as my knowledge of the history was by no means very wide and my German almost negligible. To solve the latter I took along the Senior British Military Government interpreter, a Mr John. He told me afterwards it was the most difficult assignment he'd ever undertaken! True to their character the Germans listened attentively to my attempts to do credit to our national game – the story of W. G. Grace being bowled first ball by the village fast bowler only to replace the stumps and bails saying at the same time, 'Carry on, these people came to see me bat not you bowl' had them rolling in their seats.

A meal followed my lecture after which one of my guests came up with an old edition of *Wisden* puzzled that such an expert as myself was not listed! I played that down to fine leg.

They had one request. All their gear had been destroyed. Could I organise some scheme for them to obtain a minimum amount to start playing again? This I did by an appeal to the various units, military and civilian, at that time stationed in Berlin. The appeal was overwhelming and German 'Kricket' was underway again!

MAJOR M. OLIVER (Retd)

As She is Played

The spark was rekindled. Nevertheless, the politics of Cold War and the energies needed to create the Economic Miracle appeared to have ensured that cricket in Germany remained a fragile flame. Then suddenly in the

winter of 1983 the correspondence columns of The
Times *blazed into controversy over a question many
English readers must have been unaware even existed –
German cricket terminology. We quote one example*

Sir – Mr Ignarski's succinct history of international cricket
in Germany (January 13) perhaps helps explain the lexicographical mystery of the proliferation of cricketing terms in
Collins's excellent new German dictionary.

It must be the Heidelberg press cricket correspondent
(Johann Waldschnepfe?) who finds a use for those crisp
phrases *ausgeschlagen märend der Schlagmann seinen Lauf
machte* ('run out') and *wir gewannen und hatten vier Schlagmänner noch nicht in Einsatz gehabt* ('we won by four
wickets').

And why is German cricket so dominated by slow bowling? The only bowling styles listed by the dictionary's
compilers are the curious *gedrehter Ball* ('googly') and the
surely illegal *Werfer, der dem Ball einen Drall gibt* ('spin
bowler'). No great imagination would have been needed to
add a *Chinese* (presumably a *Gastwerfer?*) and Federal Railway terminology suggests *D-Werfer* for fast bowlers.

In the field Collins offers only *Torwächter* ('wicket-
keeper') and *Eckmann* ('slip fielder'). New light on *Eckmanns
Gespräche?* One assumes that the European Institute for
Molecular Biology scored most of their runs with the
Treibschlag ('drive') or even the abortive off-drive, the un-
listed *Abtreibschlag. In der Klemme sein* ('to be on a sticky
wicket') is surely art imitating cricket.

The definition *aus sein, weil seine Beine von einem Wurf
getroffen wurden* ('to be out l.b.w.') was obviously supplied by
the current Australian umpires.

Yours faithfully, James Trainer

A German Treatise

Inevitably, The Times *correspondence invoked the name
of Dr Ernst Burgschmidt, author of a 516-page treatise
on the specialist language of cricket. If not already
established as the standard work on the subject, Dr*

*Burgschmidt's opus certainly represents a formidable
tribute to the vocabulary of the game. We regret we only
have space to quote briefly from the prospectus*

Cricket terms are not standardised in the same way as
terms in science or technology, but most terms (e.g. break,
spin, drive, cut, hook) are common in all cricket-playing
countries – occasionally definitions are somewhat vague
(e.g. hook/pull, swerve/swing) or disputed (bowl/throw).
The Laws of Cricket describe the conduct of the game, but
do not define the terms used for the actual strokes, actions
and movements of the players (apart from throwing and
terms used in connection with the l.b.w. laws). . . . The
totality of the features of that specialist language may be
used as an onomasiological network for describing the use
of central cricket terms and their synonyms. Verbs with
definable special features are called central cricket terms
and are described at some length, whereas a lot of synonyms
for 'hit', 'bowl', 'move' (without characterising special cricket actions) are given less space, e.g. thwack, tip, hammer.

ERNST BURGSCHMIDT, from a prospectus for Studien Zum
Verbum in englischen Fachsprachen (Cricket) Erlangen-Nürnberg

---

Early Rumblings in Heidelberg

*The man who started this lexicographical ball rolling
was Jonathan Ignarski, a lecturer at Heidelberg. Here
he shows that cricket in modern Germany, at least on the
banks of the Neckar, is more than an exercise in
semantics*

The story behind the first international cricket match in
Heidelberg began with the foundation of the University's
Cricket Club at the initiative of Peter Bewes, a member of
staff in the Department of *Anglistik*. Weekly practices held
on the University's hockey pitches soon followed, where
determined efforts were mounted to dispel the spurious
mystery which surrounds the game of cricket outside the
Commonwealth.

By spring of 1982, the bold decision was made to expose

the fledgling skills of members to the full blasts of competition during the course of the summer term. A match was easily arranged against a team of expatriate scientific Englishmen from the European Laboratory of Molecular Biology who were known to be dropping a desultory bat to ball during lunch-hours elsewhere in the town. Early-season training was unusually keen; standards of outfielding, batting and, to a lesser degree, bowling showed signs of improvement.

On the Saturday of the match, even the weather proved cooperative. The wicket was marked out on the least treacherous looking part of the *Bundesleistungzentrum*'s field with the aid of a doctored metric surveyor's tape and a pot of whitewash. The *Anglisten* assembled punctually and hurriedly discussed last-minute questions. There were lingering doubts, for instance, whether everyone really understood the l.b.w. laws.

Dress standards varied dramatically. The side's captain, Richard Kremer, arrived in splendid regulation whites carrying a bat presented to him by well-wishers at the University of York during his stay there. Fräulein Bettina Debon, no mean fielder at extra cover, wore a sort of Saracen's pantaloons, ankle-hugging and altogether comely. Helmut Steiner, a sports student and bowler of promise when he kept his arm straight, appeared in brand new, dazzling white trousers of a wide weave, bought in a shop specialising, *inter alia*, in carpenters' and decorators' work clothing. Alan Kirkness, an antipodean invitation player, wore shorts and Gary Giberson, a castaway from another of the Anglo-Saxon summer games and thus inclined to 'shoulder' his bat, sported a metallic green cap with a sensible duck-bill brim to protect him against the sun.

The final pre-match formalities consisted of giving a bemused representative of the local press a rudimentary outline of the game's significant characteristics: The *elf Feldspieler*, *zwei Schlagmänner*, *zwei Werfer* and so on. Advised to place himself to the left behind the opening bowler's end, he remained there throughout the match as if rooted to the spot. His later report in the *Rhein-Neckar-Zeitung*, to the satisfaction of all concerned, described the game as *beständig im Wechsel zwischen angespanter Ruhe und schneller Bewegung* (alternating between tense, quiet and quick movement).

Having won the toss, Richard Kremer made the wise tactical decision to put the biologues in to bat. The opening batsmen, R. Freeman, a vast mustachio'd puller of the ball on to leg side, and G. Griffiths, a hard-hitting Welshman, proceeded to benefit from the inevitable period before the *Anglisten* settled into their line and length. At last, after a partnership of 84, they were dismissed and light work was made of a long tail, including an astounding run out of R. Buckland by the formidable Debon. A regrettable, if unsurprising feature of the *Anglisten*'s bowling was the 20 wides given away out of a score of 122.

Large scores were not a feature of the *Anglisten*'s innings, though the mathematician Knut Haenult, Thomas Hesse and Wolfgang Landemann all held their ends up well. In the end, the *Anglisten* put on a respectable 80 runs before being all out.

Spectators and players departed with that pleasant after-glow and heightened appreciation of life which invariably follows a decent afternoon of cricket, talking of fixtures to come. If further proof were needed that the game of village cricket has a future on the Continent of Europe, one need only mention how the *Anglisten* overcame the handicap of being one short on match day. A youth in an adjoining field who was practising his boomerang throwing was given a laconic account of the laws of cricket, shown which end of the bat to hold and duly appeared as the eleventh of the side's *Schlagmänner*, finishing the day 2 not out and slightly dazed.

After such auspicious beginnings as these, the University's sporting authorities made haste to recognise cricket as an official University sport. With its financial future thus secured, the University Cricket Club may face the future with renewed confidence that in years to come the sound of willow against leather will be heard along the Neckar in summertime.

JONATHAN IGNARSKI

Cricket in the Englischer Garten

Meanwhile cricket competes more or less successfully with other sports in the Englischer Garten in Munich

The Munich Cricket Club often plays in the aptly named Englischer Garten. However, this is a public park where the German penchant for cavorting about naked prevails.

This has made necessary one very small deviation from our observation of the international rules of the game, i.e. a batsman cannot be given out if, in the opinion of the umpires, he was hopelessly distracted by a shapely, undressed fraulein jogging in the outfield. The umpires' decision is final.

One recent season, players attending Friday evening practice sessions in the Englischer Garten could set their watches by a particularly well-built jogger who always interrupted play by bouncing across the wicket.

While it would be stretching the truth to say that a well-directed six could smash a window of the still-standing former Munich apartment of the Führer, there is one remaining link between cricket and the Third Reich. The Englischer Garten was the place chosen by Unity Mitford to shoot herself after hearing that Britain had declared war on Germany.

GRAHAM LEES, Munich Cricket Club

Norse Codes

Oxford v. Copenhagen

A glance at The Story of Continental Cricket *by P. G. G. Labouchere, T. A. J. Provis and Peter S. Hargreaves is sufficient to show that cricket flourishes in Denmark, although strangely it is practically unheard-of in neighbouring Norway and Sweden. Indeed the book shows that Danish cricket has a terminology almost as rich as our own cricket vocabulary*

This memorable kamp took place at the opsyn of the Akademisk Boldklub in the later summer of 1954. Adding lustre to a powerful Oxford University gaerdenheld was the name of M. C. Cowdrey. Indeed, the young Kentish gaerdespiller had just been selected to tour Australia with Len Hutton's MCC hold.

Every fastkaster in Denmark was impatient to test his afleverings against England's white hope. Unfortunately Cowdrey was obliged to miss the first three kamps of the University's Denmark tour for inoculations necessary for the Australian trip.

It was therefore not until the final taeppe against the elite Akademisk Boldklub hold that Oxford was able to markspill its young Test star. To the disappointment of a sizeable crowd that had come to see Cowdrey midt midt, Oxford, having won the lodtreaknig, put the A. B. Klub into midt.

The Boldklub abningsgaerders, O. A. Svendesen and Hauerberg, accordingly walked to the gaerdestragen to face Oxford's two fastkasters Arenhold and Fasken (an Oxford pace bowler, not a Danish cricket term – Ed.). Svendesen was soon trapped ben for gaerdet by Arenhold. However the artificial taeppe on which the kamp was being played was rapidly taking the shine off the bold. J. P. Fellowes Smith (later of South Africa) was therefore brought into the attack with his fast off-skruers. These proved so effective that the A. B. Klub were soon 5 gaerdes down for 51. Diplomatically, the Oxford anforer C. C. P. Williams, brought Cowdrey, essentially a gaerdspiller not a fastkaster, on to kaster. Alas, the Copenhagen gaerdespillers were unable to read Cowdrey's friendly leg-skruers. Three gaerdes fell with no addition to the regns. The Copenhagen Club was finally kasted ud for a total of 93.

By close of Deak on Saturday evening, Oxford University had scored 30 for 1, the Club's svinkaster, T. A. J. Provis, having accounted for another future England gaerdspiller and anforer, M. J. K. Smith.

An even larger crowd gathered at the Akademisk Boldklub mark on Sunday, confident in the expectation of seeing the famous Cowdrey midt midt. J. M. Allan and D. C. P. R. Jowett were duly accounted for by the Klub's perseveing kasters and G. P. Marsland was induced to retire hurde. The stage was now set for Cowdrey. Three thousand Scandinavian enthusiasts leaned forward in their seats to see the new Hammond show off his støds or slags.

A profound hush (or hushe) settled over the opsyn, as the Club's guileful leg-skruekaster, C. Larsen, began his slow tillob to the kastestregen. It was a silence broken only by the click of cameras, for such was the Copenhagen media's anticipation of the Cowdrey havleg press photographers are reported to have outnumbered the fielders or markspillers crouched around the gaerde.

Larsen's leg-skruer seemed to hover in the air as Cowdrey raised his boldtrae. The eyes of the shrewder spectators were already on the midtergriber boundary where it was confidently expected the young master would shortly despatch this palpable monkey drop or underarmskast. Suddenly the unmistakable thud of bold on skinner was heard around the field, followed instantly by the piercing appeal of 'HVAD ER DER?'

All eyes turned to the white-coated dommeren Mr Kurt Nielsen, President, no less, of the Danish Cricket Association. An agonising decision now rested with Nielsen. If he was to raise his finger and say 'Ikke!' as justice seemed to demand, he risked disappointing a large crowd which had specifically come to see Cowdrey's slags. It looked to Nielsen as he gazed wretchedly down the pitch* that England's Colin was clearly ben for gaerdet; but then again he was bound to be mindful of the fact that Cowdrey had been flown over for the kamp at the A. B. Klub's considerable expense. What would the Klub Treasurer say if this glamorous import was allowed to depart with an ignominious andeag to his name? And what of Cowdrey himself, who had rushed from the doctor's inoculating room to participate in this august kamp? Might not he be tempted to object in the manner of the great W. G. Grace. 'They've come to see me midt midt, not you at dømme!'

Nielsen took his time about his decision but when it came it was a firmly called 'IKKE NOGET!' Markspillers and crowd alike gave an audible sigh of relief, and Cowdrey went on to score a classic and hugely entertaining 96 before he was kasted ud.

Cricket in Denmark grew in popularity after the OU CC VA Boldklub kamp, even though the home side were well and truly tabed. It is doubtful, therefore, if dommeren Kurt Kielsen ever regretted his decision, unless it was to ask himself if it might not have been more courteous to the distinguished visitor to have signalled a 'FEJL-BOLD!' rather than that dubious 'IKKE NOGET'.

Based on material from *The Story of Continental Cricket* by P. G. G. LABOUCHERE, T. A. J. PROVIS and PETER S. HARGREAVES

The Amazing Dog of Skanderborg

It should perhaps have been a Great Dane; but a single central Jutland terrier speaks volumes for Denmark's enthusiasm for cricket.

Near the town of Horsens in central Jutland there lives a hardbitten terrier by the name of 'Fox' with his mistress, Fru Else Nielsen, a sculptress, who is a close follower of the nearby Skanderborg team. Each second Sunday, when a

*pitch is the Danish term for wicket

home match is on, 'Fox' hops into the carrier at the back of Fru N.'s cycle to ride out to the ground. There, Fru N. records Skanderborg's performances in her own independent scorebook while 'Fox' looks on.

When 'Fox' is told that a four has been hit, however, he comes into his own, producing four distinct barks to mark the achievement, and doing the same with the appropriate number for the occasion of a six. But it does not end there. Skanderborg are a strong side with a good left-arm new-ball bowler named Jorgen Steen Larsen who is capable of inflicting much damage on visiting batsmen – especially, for some reason, those from Copenhagen. To Fru Nielsen's question: 'What did we put Svanholm out for?' friend 'Fox' accurately obliges with a well-barked total of 23.

A short time ago Jorgen Steen L. had a field day against the A.B side of Copenhagen when he took eight wickets for three to dismiss the visitors for an all-time low senior total of 12 paltry runs. Whether true or otherwise, it has yet to be confirmed, but rumour already has it that 'Fox' is at present perfecting a new trick – this in response to the query:

'And what did we do to A.B?'

(It has been whispered that he makes for the corner post of the Skanderborg Clubhouse and raises one leg . . . !)

PETER S. HARGREAVES, The Cricketer

———————————————

Cricket on the White Sea Peninsula

The scene moves further north at a greater distance of time. A Victorian explorer describes the beginnings of cricket in reindeer country

On Sunday afternoons there is the usual Russian gathering on the plain under Solaviareka: when the inhabitants of Kola have races and play ball – or, in winter, sledge in couples. We were sitting one evening in the delicious northern sunlight by the open windows, when we became aware of a game, *palant*, resembling baseball or rounders, in which the Kolski youth of both sexes were rejoicing. It seemed an opportunity for a frolic, and I went out.

Calling them together, I asked if they would like to learn Angelskaya igra, an English game. They said yes, and one of them brought an axe to Stepanina's wood heap, where I fashioned a bat and wickets. The Doctor joined us and picked an eleven for himself. Having the honour and the happiness to be at the time captain of an English cricketing team, more or less widely and honourably known as the CICC, I chose my side, and the match partook of an international character.

Among the players were a few girls, excellent at baseball: but feeling shy about the new game, they sidled away, reducing the strength of each side. All Kola collected round us, at doors and windows, or in groups: and at the different events in the game roared aloud. It was surprising to see how readily and intelligently the young Russians and Lapps took to the game, and how good-naturedly, when put out, they left the wickets and joined in the general laugh. Running was compulsory at each stroke, to make the game livelier: and the runs were scored by notches cut in the wooden wall of Stepanina's house, which served as Pavilion.

The CI won the toss, and Alexei Stepanovitch was sent to the wicket to face the bowling of the All Lapland captain. The first ball was neatly hit to square leg: at the second the enthusiastic batsman uprooted the whole of his wickets. He was succeeded by Varsonovi Pivoroff, whose first hit, three to long-off, was greeted with much cheering and cries of *Bross nazat!* Throw it up! *Bierzhi yeshtcho ras!* Run again!

The next ball was sent in the direction of the first: but Leonti Yargine, who had been especially posted in that region, received and retained the ball, to his extreme astonishment and to the universal delight. The CI Captain added two to the score: Maxime Sinikoff was bowled after making three: and Samsoun Sinikoff failed to score, having returned the ball into the bowler's hands. The feature of the innings was the careful and masterly play of Spiridion Tonikoff who made four singles without a mistake. The innings closed for sixteen.

Erasime Tcherkess commenced the innings for the All Lapland, but was run out without scoring. Andrei Moldvistoff and Leonti Yargine succumbed to the bowling, after scoring two and three respectively. The Doctor, after returning the first ball to the bowler, who failed to profit by the chance, played an effective innings of five: and was enthusiastically received when he retired, bowled. The last three wickets were disposed of for four runs, bringing the All Lapland total to eighteen.

The CI followed, with fourteen for their second innings. The second innings of the All Lapland was a remarkable one. I refer the reader to the score.

The match was attended, from beginning to end, with shouts of *Horosho! Horosho igrali!* Good! Well played! and loud laughter. Heads were out of every window; moujiks and women were grinning from ear to ear at each hit or blunder. When the result was made known there was cheering such as Kola had probably never heard before.

Thus was the Angelskaya igra introduced into Russian Lapland. It might have been the introduction of a constitution, to judge by the popular enthusiasm.

In an hour or two, after everybody had dispersed and gone to bed – that is, at one o'clock in the morning – our attention was directed to a noise in front of our windows. The members of the late CI and All Lapland Elevens were engaged in another single wicket match. Unable to sleep, they had got up to plunge again into the fascinating game. They appointed captains, chose sides, and played as well without us as with us. Now and then a difficult question arose, and they detained me at the open window for appeal as umpire. On the whole, it was a great success. Cricket had become the rage of the White Sea peninsula.

CI   *First Innings*

Alexei Stepanovitch	hit wicket, b. Doctor	1
Varsonovi Pivoroff	c. Leonti Yargine, b. Doctor	3
Edward Rae	run out	2
Maxime Sinikoff	b. Doctor	3
Samsoun Sinikoff	c. and b. Doctor	0
Spiridion Tonikoff	run out	4
Extras		3
		16

CI	*Second Innings*	
Alexei Stepanovitch	run out	0
Varsonovi Pivoroff	run out	4
Edward Rae	c. and b. Doctor	0
Maxime Sinikoff	b. Doctor	1
Samsoun Sinikoff	b. Doctor	5
Spiridion Tonikoff	run out	2
Extras		2
		14

All Lapland	*First Innings*	
Erasime Tcherkess	run out	0
Andrei Moldvistoff	b. Rae	2
Leonti Yargine	b. Rae	3
Doctor	b. Rae	5
Nikita Tonine	run out	2
Karlo Ploginoff	l.b.w., b. Rae	2
Vassilo Yargine	thrown out, Spiridion Tonikoff	0
Extras		4
		18

	Second Innings	
Erasime Tcherkess	b. Rae	0
Andrei Moldvistoff	b. Rae	0
Leonti Yargine	run out	0
Doctor	b. Rae	0
Nikita Tonine	c. Stepanovitch, b. Rae	0
Karlo Ploginoff	run out	0
Vassilo Yargine	b. Rae	0
Extras		0
		0

EDWARD RAE, FRGS, *A Journey in Russian Lapland and Karelia*

Edward Rae would be delighted to find that nearly a hundred years after his expedition, cricket in Finland is healthy enough to support its own journal, The Helsinki Cricketer. *A recent letter to the Editor pithily illustrates the strides the game has made in this corner of Scandinavia*

Sir, I was horrified to learn the other day that there is now a cricket club in Finland. I left England twenty-five years ago to get away from people like yourself. Is nowhere sacred?

DOCTOR K., English Department, Helsinki University

Woman's Viewpoint – Sweden

Finally a woman's point of view, provided by one of Scandinavia's leading novelists. It seems to speak volumes

In the car back from the wedding lunch, sighing with newly-wedded bliss, I sat absolutely silent holding Silvester's hand. Silvester sat silent, too, for a long while and I wondered what he was thinking about. After some thirty kilometres he said, 'You don't mind, do you, if we stop at the railway station bookstall so I can buy *The Times*? I need to see the cricket score.'

And that's what we did.

MERETE MAZZARELLA, Att Spela sih liv
Translated by MARY LOMAS

Red Square Legs

Nyet!

Dear Sir,

Thank you for your letter of 13th July, and for your invitation to a TASS correspondent to contribute to your book on cricket. Regretfully, however, we must decline the invitation. Apart from the pressure of work on the few, due to staff summer holidays, correspondents ending a tour of duty in the United Kingdom, and the forthcoming autumn conferences, none of our correspondents feel that they would be able to produce a suitable piece (even with a visit to Lord's).

Yours sincerely,

A. MELIKYAN, Chief Correspondent

Any attempt to seek Russian participation in a book on cricket is liable to meet with a blank refusal, as the foregoing letter from the London office of TASS more than hints. Persistent reporters have, however, been able to discover chinks in Soviet Russia's curtain of indifference. Witness two press-cuttings from the fifties

A far-off breath of summer cricket battles came back to the Australian touring team headquarters in London – a Piccadilly hotel – today.

His face is unfamiliar, his clothes are urbane, but dash it all, Sir, Nicolai Lifanov is a Russian who loves cricket. He has even played it.

DENIS FOLEY, *Daily Mail*

Yesterday I met Mr Vikenty Matveyev – the first correspondent sent to London by the Soviet newspaper *Izvestia* since 1938 – and discovered that he is a cricketer.

He told me he has played cricket in Russia and that he

intends to go and watch cricket at Lord's when the season opens. He is also going to the Derby.

'In Russia we play all the same games as you British do except for golf,' he said.

I gather cricket was introduced in the Soviet Union as long ago as 1934 and Rugby in 1933.

TANFIELD'S DIARY, *Daily Mail*

Mr Popov's Secret Life

In 1983, a Sunday Times *investigative team pierced veils of suspicion and secrecy to expose 'The Secret Life' of Russian ambassador Victor Popov*

Last week I heard an amusing story about the Russian ambassador to Britain, Victor Popov, playing cricket for St Antony's College, Oxford, when he was an exchange student in the 1950s. I thought it would be interesting to hear Popov's views of the game, and to ask what insight it offered him into the British character.

My first inquiry to the Russian embassy was met with undisguised suspicion. 'Cricket?. . . St Antony's?' The nameless diplomat paused as if to consult some book on current espionage codes, and then gave me the number of the ambassador's secretary.

He too was wary of my innocent question. 'What do you want this for? How are you going to use this information? Why are you ringing me?' He gave me the number of the Soviet cultural attaché who gave me the number of the Soviet press attaché. So it went on for five further calls. The Russians were not prepared to divulge the secret of Popov's cricketing career.

But we cricket-loving Westerners are resourceful people. We traced Professor Zbynek Zeman who was at St Antony's during Popov's time. It was true. Popov had indeed played cricket for St Antony's. He could not remember how many runs he had scored but he did remember that Popov had slipped a disc while diving for a ball in the field.

'He was laid up for two weeks and was looked after by Bryan Cartledge, who is now the British ambassador in

Budapest,' said the professor. 'I don't think that Popov played more than once.'

HENRY PORTER, Sunday Times

M. G. Trevelyan suggested that had cricket been intro-duced into France under the ancien régime, *the worst excesses of the French Revolution might have been avoided. It is interesting to discover an echo of this thought in pre-Revolutionary Russia. In recently pub-lished Foreign Office papers we find Consul General Stanley reporting to Earl Granville from Odessa as follows. Date: 1 August 1881*

Not only among the peasantry, but among the educated classes a more healthy and manly tone of feeling is required.

The Governor-General, Prince Dondoukoff-Korsakoff, on seeing the English play at cricket, remarked to me that could he but introduce it among the Russians, it would go far to put a stop to Nihilism; but he despaired of being able to do so, adding that when a Russian lad arrived at fifteen the only way he knew of proving his manliness was to be seen walking with some notorious person of the other sex.

Later, with minds and bodies enfeebled by early excesses, they become easy tools of designing persons, who, under the specious plea of philanthropy, appeal to the false sentiment engendered in them by their manner of life.

He was speaking of civilians, especially of the student class. The duties imposed on those who entered military schools led to a more healthy tone of feeling.

I have, &c.
(Signed) G. E. STANLEY

We have further evidence that Tsarist Russia took a more favourable view of the game than its Soviet successor

Despite the practical love of the game evinced by the last of the Tsars, few, if any, Russians have taken part in games on their native soil. There is a story of a wealthy young Russian of Merton College, Oxford, however, who, on being invited to play in a Myrmidon match in England, was advised to buy the necessary implements. He promptly ordered not only a bat and pads and other essential items, but a score book for 100 matches, a belt with a brass cricketer on the buckle, and a large tent. He was, obviously, a Russian who could say 'Yes!'

JAMES D. COLDHAM, *The Cricketer*

Cricket under the minarets of Moscow must be the dream of every fanatic who wishes to expand the game's frontiers. The Sunday Times *revealed that just such a privilege fell to former Prime Minister Harold Wilson (now Lord Wilson) when, as President of the Board of Trade in the Attlee government, he was in Russia for marathon trade talks*

During a lull, the British delegation retired to a lakeside sward outside Moscow for a game of cricket. In Harold's second over an NKVD man arrived and made a long speech urging them to desist. Harold placed him at square leg – 'where he was safe even from my bowling' – but the secret policeman soon dropped an easy catch. Next day the Moscow press reported that the British delegation had been indulging in 'lakeside orgies and pirouettes'.

GODFREY SMITH

NKVD Report
5th July 1947

We have kept Trade Minister Wilson under the closest scrutiny during his negotiations in Moscow. From our observations it is evident that this is not a traditional Socialist politician in the Morrison or Bevan cast, although he has been noted to make frequent references to his proletarian roots and his affection for the Northern English working men's clubs. At the same time he exhibits none of the Socialist austerity of his senior and more aristocratic associate, the Sir Stafford Cripps. On the contrary during the period of surveillance the subject has betrayed a significant predilection for Capitalist–Bourgeois extravagance and caprice.

Instance: This previous Saturday one of my officers shadowed Wilson and his delegation to a lakeside in the northern suburbs. Here the party was observed to remove their coats and jackets and form themselves into a crude semi-circle. Minister Wilson himself was seen to be toying with a child's ball and with it to be making curious approaches to a lower-ranking official with a wooden baton.

My officer advised the Englishmen that this was an improper exhibition, offensive to a Soviet Socialist sub-urban community. Not only was this entirely correct advice ignored, it was met with the indecent abuse in the English vernacular. Among other unrepeatable obscenities, my officer was told 'to put himself at Square Leg!' (a reference to a grotesque form of English sexual activity). By a com-bination of threats and blandishments the officer was in-duced to join the Englishmen in this degrading charade. 'He will be safer in the deep, even from my bowling,' Minister Wilson is reported to have sneered.

As a further indignity, missiles were systematically pro-pelled at the officer to the accompaniment of derision and laughter as he attempted to protect himself. Later, Minister Wilson made facetious efforts to excuse these indignities by explaining, 'it was only a game pronounced like an English grass insect'.

Conclusion: it will surely be detrimental to the interests of the Soviet Union if this perverse political dilettante should ever achieve promotion to the First Ministry of the United Kingdom.

COLONEL IGOR OLENSKI NKVD

Clubs Mediterranean

'When talk in cricket circles comes round to the MCC, it is unlikely that the subject of conversation is the Malta Cricket Club,' writes Mr Pughe-Morgan. However he and his fellow tourists from the Newick Cricket Club found that cricket goes on in Malta, despite the withdrawal of the last British forces. And that it still makes news

The Malta team consists mainly of expatriates, who appeared in true British spirit from the nearest bar. Our XI was called upon to pose for a few photographs by a reporter from the *Malta Times* who then conducted a gruelling interview with me, asking such awkward questions as – 'How many Test players do you have?' In an effort to satisfy his thirst for NEWS I revealed that whilst we had no current internationals, we did have the brother of international actress Tessa Wyatt (John Wyatt) in the party. With that he trotted off, no doubt well pleased with this scoop!

PIERS PUGHE-MORGAN

Cricket at the Platia Down

Cricket in Corfu is not exactly news. It rolled in with the high tide of British imperialism and took such firm root it is hard to find a respectable county or club player without a good Corfiot story. Let a well-known Lord's Taverner set the scene

The Platia Down, the Corfu Cricket Ground, had apparently been flattened by countless feet of Regiments of Foot in the halcyon days of Empire and never since. It is half Fuller's Earth dotted with grass-like tufts and tarmacadam, not wholly unlike that pitch in New York on which Tony Greig's World All-Stars were wiped by a team of local cabbies and pushers. The earthy area is next to Judas trees under which the natives anxiously worry at their beads, sitting at tables served from the cafés behind them. These are set in a Rue de Raviolo-style Arcade built by homesick Frogs during Napoleon's better moments to remind them of Paree. The old Royal Palace stands behind the bowler at one end, the Bandstand is at the Park End. On the Mediterranean side is an ancient fort and said tarmacadam which fills as evening approaches with charabancs, a further hazard to the deep fielder, already tip-toeing through the potholes. Do not ask a man to drink and field square-leg.

The most sensible decision reached at the practice, as it transpired, was that John Price should open the batting as well as the bowling. He seemed the only one of us to have the measure of the mat, which had clearly been knitted by retired fisherfolk, not that it would have trapped anything less than the size of Jaws or indeed John Price. The only other cheery prospect for the morrow was that Ken Barrington (or *Captain* Barrington as the Greeks insisted) had found his wicket at last. Anything he pitched on it turned three yards in either direction and bounced scalp-high.

WILLIAM RUSHTON, *Cricket '78*

Here is another author from another angle

Whichever way you look you are surrounded by fine buildings – the old Royal Palace, in front of which stands the stone figure of a former British Governor, Sir Frederick Adams, his right finger pointing disdainfully, like a bored umpire forever indicating middle and leg; the new Fortress with its toothless cannons and ivy-covered battlements; the long line of Venetian houses, clustered together, peering over the tops of the plane trees that line one side of the ground and beneath which, at small café tables, the locals gather during the course of the afternoon to drink and comment vociferously on form. Behind this Corfiot Long Room, on the other side of a road, stand the elegant colonnades and arches of the Listen (a miniature version of the Rue de Rivoli), from which the more sanguine spectators, glass in hand, review the scene, and white-coated waiters scuttle throughout the afternoon with trays of ginger beer and *ouzo* glued to the ends of their arms.

CHRISTOPHER MATTHEW

A Byronic Encounter

All tourists seem to be agreed that the ball can perform unexpected tricks on Prospero's island. Christopher Matthew continues to describe the shifting fortunes of Ben Brocklehurst's team against the Corfiot Byron club

Ben had lost the toss, and Condos, the Byron captain, had, as is traditional in such circumstances, put us in to bat.

Wingfield-Digby and Brocklehurst B. opened our batting, while Condos himself opened the bowling from the Royal Palace end, pushing down fast, low stuff that moved off the coconut matting in such unexpected ways that one inevitably found oneself recalling rumours of cunningly placed pebbles. Costelletos was offering similar material from the other end. Our innings began slowly, despite Digby's insistence on running at the unwisest moments.

Brocklehurst was soon out for 6, but Aworth of Cambridge and Surrey was in next, so I confidently ordered another drink – unwisely as it turned out; for moments later he was on his way back – caught Scourtis, bowled Condos for 3. 'Never saw the ball at all,' he muttered as we crossed. Nor, frankly, did I. I asked our umpire for middle and leg, reached for the piece of chalk behind the stumps and etched out a mark, then straightened up and looked about me. The Greeks seemed suddenly much less comic than I remembered from a few minutes previously. They talked amongst themselves constantly. Out at square leg, the Greek umpire squatted in a determined way on a small wooden mallet. 29 for 3 read the little scoreboard. It was very bright out in the middle of the pitch and very hot; my bat seemed to weigh a ton. I settled down, patted the matting a couple of times and peered down the wicket towards the empty space where the bowler, Costelletos, should have been. Thinking he must have left the field for a moment I straightened up again. At that moment he appeared from behind the umpire like a conjuring trick, small, bald-headed, bad-tempered, moving very fast, the arm low. I swung my bat in appalling slow motion. 'Come on, Fleet Street pudding,' shouted Digby, already halfway down the wicket. I must have been out by a good two yards, but the Greek umpire shook his head. 'Ochi sotto.'

Two balls later Digby paid the penalty for his recklessness by running himself out. 'How 'dat?!' rang round the field, a cry that in Corfu cricket covers both appeal and decision, and Digby did not even bother to wait for one.

41 for 3.

I was now joined by Her Majesty's ex-Vice-Consul, moving very slowly and looking like an entertainment officer on a Mediterranean cruise in his neatly pressed white shorts and plimsolls.

We didn't run nearly so much after that.

Two lucky snicks and an uncomfortable leg bye later I was on my way back to the cool safety of the café tables. As I said, I never saw the ball once.

41 for 4.

The major indulged in a couple of elegant *pissines* (leg glides) before being run out. His partner, D. Smyth, was joined at the wicket by the ex-captain of Hampshire who survived a noisy appeal for caught behind, only to be clean bowled next ball by Condos. 'That was quite an interesting appeal,' he remarked equably as he removed his pads, 'I wasn't within a fourpenny bus ride of it.' He undid another strap. 'I didn't actually play a stroke either.'

Major Forte was still trying to recover from the fact that a ball had struck him on the pad without anyone appealing. 'That's the first time in 30 years I've seen that happen,' he said.

Someone else remarked on the paucity of runs scored on the leg side. 'Oh, it's quite impossible to hit a ball to square leg,' explained Ben, 'it's always travelling far too fast.'

By now I thought I could detect a note of anxiety in his voice. 48 for 7 was not what he had had in mind at all. But

Condos and Costelletos, who had bowled unchanged throughout and clearly intended to go on doing so, were beginning to tire and soon the runs began to come from Smyth, Brown and Clark. 60 more were added before our thirty overs were up, and our innings closed at 110 for 9. Some of the warmth had gone out of the sun as we took the field after a short break for wine and ginger beer; although that did not deter some of the less serious among us from sporting an assortment of straw hats. A smattering of applause from the tables announced the appearance of the Greek opening pair – Patrikios who looked to be no more than 17, and Spiros Anemogianos, a short, stout, jolly looking man in a battered trilby and huge moustaches. Brown opened our attack from the Royal Palace end. The first five deliveries were in Digby's wicket keeping gloves before Patrikios had even begun to move. On the sixth, however, he sprang into action, and placed his bat firmly in the path of the ball which sprang off with a loud tock and sat in the grass about three yards from the wicket. The field had begun to change for the end of the over when there was a great shout of 'eki!' ('come!') and to the astonishment of everyone, including Patrikios, Spiros set off down the wicket, eyes blazing, bat waving, intent on a quick single. Patrikios on the other hand clearly had no intention of moving an inch out of his crease, a state of affairs that dawned on Spiros only when he was halfway down the wicket. But by then it was too late. A terrible cry of anguish burst from his lips, he hurled his bat high in the air, and like a wounded rhino charged headlong on, past Patrikios, rounded the wicket keeper, and disappeared in the direction of the Liston. Eye witnesses described later how, with tears streaming down his cheeks, he rushed through the spectators, across the road and into a café in the Liston where he stayed for the next hour, his head in his hands, his shoulders heaving, sobbing his heart out.

Condos, the captain, now appeared on the field, his eyes full of sorrow. 'He is a child,' he muttered to Ben, 'a child.' Hands were shaken, Papiris, the number three arrived, took guard, swung wildly at a good ball from Clark and was caught at mid-wicket by Aworth.

o for 2.

Grapsas and Scourtis followed, only to suffer similar fates. And then Costelletos came in. He took guard, gave us the benefit of his most aggressive expression and prepared to save his country. His stance – crouching very low, feet wide apart, bat almost parallel with the ground – was pure early 19th century.

The first ball from Brown struck him smartly on the hand, which didn't please him at all. The next found a thick edge, and Digby took an easy catch behind the wicket. Ben said 'Well done,' and we had begun to form the traditional self-congratulatory group when it suddenly became clear that as far as Costelletos was concerned the decision was far from cut and dried. He stood there with one hand on his bat, the other on his hip, staring scornfully in the direction of the palace. We looked at him and then we looked at the Greek umpire. Finally someone said tentatively, 'Ow 'dat?' The umpire shook his hand, Costelletos gave us all a contemptuous sneer and resumed his stance. The next ball was fast and short and lifting a bit and struck Costelletos on the back of the head. He threw down his bat, and clutching his head, marched off the field, hurling a series of carefully chosen and quite unprintable insults at each fielder as he passed him. A long pause ensued during which we stood about in an uneasy group in the middle of the wicket, anticipating the outbreak of hostilities. With only 9 runs on the board and 4 wickets down, war seemed likely.

In the end it was the patient Condos who relieved the situation by accompanying the still far from happy Costelletos back to the wicket, to the accompaniment of a prolonged round of rather over-done applause from the fielders. It was at this point that Ben approached me and asked me, very quietly, if I'd be kind enough to 'twiddle the arm a bit'. From that moment on, the legend that the Corfiots are unable to cope with slow bowling was destroyed once and for all when 16 runs were struck off a dozen of the slowest deliveries ever seen in the Eastern Mediterranean. 'Just what we needed,' murmured Ben, as the ball streaked yet again towards the Venetian Fortress boundary.

The next over Costelletos was caught in the slips off

David Brocklehurst, and with 15 runs to his credit, decided to call it a day.

37 for 5.

Bogdanos, Condos and Sarlis came and went in quick succession and at 46 for 8 Laskaridis, a strong young man in singlet and shorts, joined the brave Patrikios. By the time they had carried the score to 90 we were seriously beginning to wonder whether after all we hadn't underestimated our opponents. The crowd were convinced of it, and greeted every mighty, scything blow with advice to 'eki' ('come') or 'ela' ('stay'). And it wasn't only the overs that were running out. The sun had by now long since disappeared, and it was becoming increasingly difficult to see the ball at all, and it must have been as much of a surprise to Clark when he clean bowled Patrikios for 34 as it was to Brocklehurst when he discovered he had caught and bowled Laskaridis for 30.

Even before we reached the welcoming lights of the Liston, the wicket had been occupied by dozens of small boys bowling old tennis balls and swinging makeshift bats, in imitation of their heroes, Patrikios and Laskaridis.

Afterwards the two teams drank wine together under the plane trees, and shook each other warmly by the hand, and agreed that it had been, if not a classic, then certainly a very respectable, finish to a game, and Spiros Anemogianos, grinning sheepishly, kissed each of us in turn, muttering 'Sorry . . . sorry . . .' and we grinned back and assured him that the incident had been long forgotten. After all, it was only a game. Or was it? The last thing I saw as I left was the entire Byron team, huddled together, deep in a massive argument. I heard afterwards that it was to do with Papiris feeling that if Condos had only allowed Grapsas to bowl a few overs instead of bowling every one himself, they might have won. But I'm not so sure. I could have sworn I saw Condos smacking Anemogianos on the hand.

CHRISTOPHER MATTHEW

Bowled Prometheus!

*Michael Green, in a much quoted piece on Corfu cricket,
hints that a philosophical temperament and a classical
education are essential equipment for a visiting batsman*

The bowler who was already without a shirt took off his vest
and handed it to the umpire, tugged what appeared to be an
old German field service cap and ran up to bowl. I couldn't
see much except a blinding dazzle but I kept peering where
he ought to have been. After a few moments the ball had not
arrived and I realised with relief that he had stopped his run,
because a waiter with a tray of drinks was shambling across
the pitch to some spectators on the other side of the ground.

I took the opportunity of ordering an ouzo (the local fire
water). Somehow I felt I wouldn't be there long. The bowler
ran in again and delivered an excellent off-break. (The
Greeks rarely bowl fast.) It rose sharply and struck me in my
plastic tsinto or abdomen guard.

What sounded like an explosion took place. It was the
noise of 2,000 Greeks appealing. Every fielder raised his
forefinger in the air as a sign of dismissal. The Greek
umpire said firmly '*Ochi sotto*'. I started to walk, but then I
saw the expression on the bowler's face and realised the
umpire meant 'Not out'. A brave man!

The next ball found the edge and we scampered a quick
single, to the delight of the crowd who love a run-out best of
all. Their day isn't complete without a couple of figures
skidding along the gravel in a cloud of dust while bails fly all
over the place. They give a special cheer to a batsman who
manages to run himself out in spectacular fashion.

This brought me to face the other bowler but his bowling
was just the same as the other one's. Both sent down the
stock Corfu ball, slow, of low trajectory on a good length and
liable to turn slightly either way or to pop. I suspect they hold
the seam crosswise. They are helped by the condition of the
ball which is reduced to pulp by the stones after a few
minutes, but they courteously insist on providing a new ball
for important matches.

I scratched around for twenty minutes for two and saw my

partner run out by a ball which was passing a yard from cover when it hit a stone, rose sharply and hit the fielder in the face. With commendable presence of mind he grabbed it and threw down the wicket. Twice I survived being *apo psili* (or caught) in the *tsimades* or slips, and finally I was *apo xila* (from the woods or clean-bowled) to the accompaniment of another deafening shout from the café tables. I have heard Test match players dismissed in less noise.

The Greeks, who are a sporting crowd, applauded me as I walked in. I peered over the scorer's shoulder, idly curious. 'Bowler's name?' I asked. 'Prometheus,' he replied.

The whole trip seemed worthwhile.

MICHAEL GREEN

Cricket Among the Ruins

'What can be stranger than the game played 140 years ago by the sailors of HMS Beacon *among the ruins of 5th century BC tombs high on a hill some ten miles from the coast of SW Turkey,' a correspondent writes*

The occasion was the 1st Xanthian Expedition in the winter of 1841–2. Xanthus, dating from the 7th Century BC, ancient capital of the Lycians, had been discovered in 1838 by Charles Fellows (1799–1860), traveller and archaeologist. He found there many beautifully carved marble tombs of early Greek style but with Persian and local Lycian characteristics. With the help of the Royal Navy, Fellows directed the operation of transporting these important sculptures to England, and today they can be seen in the British Museum. At the end of December 1841, a camp was set up near the Acropolis. The weather was delightful, 64° by day falling to 40° at night. Fellows remarks: 'Our evenings were not without amusement; the sailors soon made bats and balls, and cricket was perhaps for the first time played in Lycia; at all events the wonder expressed by the living generation showed that it was not a game known to the present inhabitants.'

ENID M. SLATTER

In the Deep in Yugoslavia

Scouring Asia Minor for evidence of extant cricket life, the cricket historian F. S. Ashley-Cooper came upon the singular case of a Turkish naval officer of the pre-1914 period whose enthusiasm for the game led him into spying for the British. He was duly arrested on the field of play, although the Turkish police had the good grace to wait until the officer had completed his innings. Cricket historians have ransacked Balkan archives for comparable anecdotes with less success. It seems to have been left to the ubiquitous Michael Green to establish a significant corner in Yugoslav cricket history

I have had the somewhat unusual experience of having played in what is now part of Yugoslavia when stationed there with the Army just after the Second World War. With immense ingenuity, a sort of cricket ground had been carved out on a plateau in the mountains by the Adriatic Sea. It was probably the most spectacular pitch in the world, perched up there in the hills with the Adriatic shimmering at the foot of a 200-foot cliff. Unfortunately, the cliff also marked the boundary, and while chasing a ball at mid-wicket I fell over the edge. The reason I am still here is that the cliff started with a steep slope, which enabled me to grasp a passing bush and hang on with my feet in outer space, as it were.

I think the worst part was the fact that nobody noticed my plight, and they just got another ball and played on while I bleated faintly for aid in the distance. Luckily, the batsman soon hit the new ball over the edge and this time I was noticed and hauled to the top with a rope where I was greeted by my officer with the ridiculous question, 'What have you done with the ball?'

MICHAEL GREEN

The Six Ball War

Israeli Impressions

Israel may not automatically spring to mind as one of the world's great cricketing nations. Here, however, Terence Prittie, whose tireless work in promoting understanding between Britain and Israel is so much to his credit, demonstrates that the game is nevertheless well entrenched here

The Petach Tikva ground was a disused football pitch. It was roughish, especially in the outfield. But more remarkable was its colour – it was a fascinating patchwork of browns, yellows, greys and light purples, with only little wisps of green showing here and there. Flowers, often of a prickly kind, do better in Israel than grass. Boundaries were the normal distance from the wicket, but vaguely demarcated by sloping banks on which the football spectators must once have sat; umpires accepted what the fieldsmen had to say about fours and sixes 'on trust'. The matting wicket undulated in places. There would be some interesting bounces. So there were.

The ground lay in a bowl-like depression and the heat, on that cloudless July day, was terrific. I was lent a floppy white hat which normally I would have scorned. The players left the field every forty minutes or so, for a drink of cold water. I was earnestly advised to drink at least six pints during the day's play, from 11 a.m. to roughly 6 p.m., in order to avoid dehydration – its main effect is a black-out, followed by a prolonged fit of the 'shakes', and I had experienced this once already on a visit to the Gaza Strip. There was an extended luncheon interval, in the only relative shade of a large wooden hut with an asbestos roof.

The batting and bowling were of good club standard. The matting produced a fairly even bounce, with some vagaries when the ball hit one of the bumps in the rock-hard surface below. There was no really fast bowler on view, which was just as well, perhaps, and the bowling tended to be around medium pace, with emphasis on moving the ball a little in the heavy atmosphere. The batting matched the Israeli character, adventurous and extrovert, and no sign of a Boycott or a Trevor Bailey. But what caught the eye most was the exuberance and frequent brilliance of the fielding. Players fairly hurled themselves at the ball, as it jinked, popped and skidded on the uneven surface, with an eager abandon and complete disregard of the danger of damaging themselves. Some of the headlong dives would have done credit to a Terry Holmes or a Dave Loveridge, and both the catching and throwing were first-class, with the ball always bunged in full-pitch to the wicket – a first-bounce return might equally have shot, or towered high above keeper or bowler.

Jerusalem won handsomely, and a member of the side gave me a neck-tie as a present for my minimal efforts (I scored just 8, but at least enjoyed a brisk partnership of 25 in under ten minutes with one of the redoubtable and legendary Abrahams clan). The silk tie, appropriately, was in Israel's national colours, blue and white, but it involved me in a curious scene some months later at one of London's most venerable clubs. A member advanced on me, only a guest there, and asked when I had 'joined'. I told him I had not. 'Then why,' he asked, 'are you wearing the Bath Club tie?' So I was. The colours are identical with those of Israel's flag. If you come to think of it, one doesn't expect to see a neck-tie based on the Union Jack or the Star-Spangled Banner.

During its short history, Israeli cricket has produced plenty of event. In 1981 Petach Tikva scored a record 333 in the 50 overs which have constituted the maximum length of any innings; this was the highest since that first, brief, post-1945 revival, which actually produced an individual score of 199. Since the second revival began in 1967, the highest individual score has been the 152 not out of Stanley Perlman of Jerusalem's Hebrew University. The fastest century came from Petach Tikva's Lawson Atkins – in 48 minutes, but still not quite up to Percy Fender's record in English first-class cricket! The melancholy record for the lowest team score, 12, was set up by Lod – the place houses Israel's international airport, and ought to have done better. Since then, two other sides have reached the same score – coincidentally the same as that in first-class cricket in England.

TERENCE PRITTIE

The Playing Fields of Jerusalem

There are pleasing echoes of Evelyn Waugh's Scoop *in the following despatch from the Six Day War. The author is modest about his contribution to the reporting of the actual hostilities which, as he tells us, were shrouded by censorship. Yet according to Randolph and Winston Churchill* (The Six Day War), *he was among the first to note and report that Israeli Ministry of Information officials were 'wearing huge smiles'*

I was fully equipped to cover a war – typewriter, notebooks, press card, pass to the BBC Club (which got you places the press card wouldn't). However, I left my cricket bat at home. I didn't think I would need it. Wrong. I had been in Israel only a few hours before I began to realise that covering a war here is different from, say, the Belgian Congo.

Shortly after arriving in Tel Aviv we went to interview the Foreign Minister Mr Abba Eban. The war hadn't started but it wasn't far away. We set up the camera in his study and while we awaited Mr Eban's return from a cabinet meeting I inspected his library. It included a full set of *Wisden*. We were among friends.

Later, in the hotel, waiting for the war to begin, I received a phone call from a man I had never met before. He asked me if I was the same Michael Parkinson who wrote about sport in the *Sunday Times*. I told him I was and he said 'Would you like a game of cricket while you are here?'

I had not anticipated such an offer while awaiting a war.

'When?' I asked, rather lamely.

He laughed, 'The sooner the better I think,' he said.

'But I haven't any gear,' I said.

'We'll find you some,' he replied.

Thus it came to pass that twenty-four hours later I found myself near Jerusalem playing cricket on a baked mud wicket trying to unravel the mystery of an Israeli leg-spin bowler. The man who phoned me was a young man who had been born in South Africa but now lived and studied in Israel. Cricket was his passion.

We played and yarned and told terrible lies about the game. Then, in the evening, we discussed the war. I asked him what he would be doing when the fighting began. He smiled and said 'I shall be there.' When I got back to the hotel I met our cameraman.

'What's the news?' he said, thinking I'd come from a briefing about the military situation.

'We won by 5 wickets,' I said. I later discovered he told the producer I was cracking up.

About two days later the war started. As usual we were the last to find out about it. In fact before the Press Corps were fully mobilised the war was just about over. All we knew was that the Israelis' jets had destroyed its opposition on the ground. Israeli armies had swept through the Sinai to the Canal.

The journalists thought it greatly unfair that the Israelis had done all this without informing them beforehand. The American reporters were particularly vociferous. They were not used to a war starting without them and said as much to anyone who would listen. Particularly adept at listening was our liaison officer, a Polish Jew who looked and sounded exactly like David Niven's immortal friend Trubshawe.

Like Trubshawe he wore a magnificent moustache the colour of a mature fox. His accent was extraordinary. Only Donald Sinden, of my acquaintance, spoke English with such confident relish. He would have adorned the Long Room at Lord's and the residents of that establishment would have been astonished to learn that this posh sounding gentleman was an officer in the Israeli Army and had been born in Warsaw.

He had, of course, been educated in England which accounted for the accent and his passion for cricket. This I discovered as we drove through the Sinai in an ancient bus towards the Suez Canal and, hopefully, a bit of action.

Trubshawe had laid on the trip in the slender hope of placating the Press Corps who, after three frustrating days of being fed official communiqués in Tel Aviv, were becoming a definite threat to internal security. So Trubshawe hired a bus and we set off to find the war.

I sat up the front with our liaison officer intent on finding out as much as I could about the real situation at the front. I was wasting my time. He had discovered I had written a couple of books about cricket and he wanted to save himself the bother of buying them by pumping the author dry.

Our bus bumped through the desert passing miles of vehicles inching their way towards the war. In the distance we could hear the sound of artillery. Now and then we would pass a clump of destruction – a tank burning by the side of the road, a gun emplacement where equipment and men looked as if they had been burned to charcoal. None of this affected Trubshawe who only wanted to know what Fred Trueman was really like, and did I ever see Denis Compton in his pomp?

Suddenly, in the middle of nowhere the bus stopped. Trubshawe broke off his dissertation on whether Cardus was a better writer than Robertson-Glasgow to chat to the driver. He then informed us that we all had to get out to give the bus a push. The desert light was fading as we stepped out and filed to the back of the bus. Twenty or more war correspondents from the world's press began pushing a broken down jalopy through the desert and the signs and smells of war.

Our humour was not improved when Trubshawe, *en passant*, informed us not to stray too far from the sides of the bus as it was quite likely that this part of the desert was mined. This was his only reference to our plight. For the rest of the time he babbled on about watching cricket in England. The Americans had long since put him down as a raving idiot. Even I began to have my doubts when as night closed in and the sound of gunfire came ever nearer he asked me if it were true that George Tribe could bowl five different googlies and if so could I demonstrate.

The next day we came upon a squadron of Israeli tanks sheltered in a redoubt. The crews were brewing up. These were some of the men who had been in the initial assault, who had been part of one of war's most extraordinary tank assaults. We fell on them. They at least looked like warriors who had a story to tell. Their faces were blackened by sun and wind, their chins were stubbled, they were tired as only battle weary men can be tired.

We were filming them when I was tapped on the shoulder. One of the young warriors offered me a cup of tea. He was grinning, 'How's the cricket?' he said. It was at this point that I began to doubt my sanity. 'You don't remember me, do you?' he said. He removed his helmet and his goggles. It was my South African friend who had invited me to play cricket in Jerusalem.

He was a child really. A student. Interests: playing cricket and driving tanks. 'How is it?' I asked. He shrugged and grimaced. When we parted he told me to call him when the war was over. It didn't last much longer. We hung about for a bit just in case and then the office told us to come home.

I rang him from the airport. A girl answered. She told me he had gone away! I've been back to Israel since, but I didn't dare call just in case he didn't return. Whenever I tell people I once played cricket in Jerusalem they are amused, but they don't know how it really was.

MICHAEL PARKINSON

Kibbutz Cricket

Here is an account of cricket played in a kibbutz, an unusual view made more so by the fact that the author is a woman. She has now returned to live in Manchester where we don't expect she is surprised by the number of days cricket loses to rain at Old Trafford

Saturdays my family saw less of me. We – the Englishman and myself – would set off for various kibbutzim wherein lived South Africans or Englishmen, and Indians from exotic Bombay; Jews who settled in India and became like Indians in colour, the women wearing saris.

Cricket to me means hot summer days – a rude sort of cricket on a rough, disused field, rutted, scored and pitted – coconut matting was set down, stumps erected, two ladies set to score, a curious audience of kibbutz kids peering through hedges. I remember one elderly Indian who, every time his team scored, did a sort of dance in midfield shouting 'Doolally tap. OO!' On one occasion my Englishman, to his astonishment, hit a six – straight into the swimming pool, scattering Israelis left, right and centre. The fielder, trying to catch it, backed and backed until with a mighty splash he fell in too! Lunch was called at about 12.30 and we would unpack our sandwiches. My Englishman would share with an Indian family as a rule, swapping Lancashire doorsteps for samosas. Our marriage was arranged to avoid a cricket fixture and, the next year, our baby was nearly born on the cricket field after a bumpy ride while I was eight months pregnant. Needless to say, that child now wields a bat!

YEHIEDIT LIPMAN

The Galilee Team

This gem taken from A Famous First Eleven *is by the Reverend D. C. Macinol, BD. It only could have been written by a clergyman. One can tell from the first sentence. It seeps into the Israeli section because we could not think of anywhere else to put it. The reader may be forgiven for remembering all those dreadful old prep-school jokes about where cricket was first mentioned in the Bible. For the uninitiated, it was when Peter stood up with the eleven and was bold*

Let me tell you how the Master Himself picked and trained a famous Eleven for the game of life. It was in Galilee long ago that Jesus prepared his men; but it may help us today in our contest if we learn the Master's method and hear how His team acquitted themselves.

The man whom Jesus selected as captain was one who, with many obvious faults, had the dash which carries some fellows into the front rank by natural right. Peter had glaring defects, the kind that boys are down upon, especially gab and brag, for his tongue played him grievous tricks. Of course, boasting is very bad form on the field or in the Christian Church. But the Master was patient with Peter and could not help liking him. Rash he was certainly, but he was dashing in adventure. Of this disciple it could be said he was always on the ball.

Others of various gifts fell into their places around the Divine Master. Andrew, with a small gift, was in great favour, for he came second to none of the Eleven for devotion.

St James gained his colours by a doughty deed, which Christendom can never cease to praise. This disciple had the distinction of being the first player to 'give away his wicket'.

Players like James the Less and Simon the Zealot are overshadowed by their renowned namesakes. But they are not without their use and they do work which no one else could have done. Simon the Zealous, keen to back up impetuous at the crease! Judas not Iscariot. What a distinction! No traitor he, but the staunchest of adherents. Never guilty of playing on! James the Less! I think there was nothing small about this James but his name. Great in modesty, great in self-repression, he was a host in the battle.

There is a fine story of the boy Henry Drummond who had himself been bowled out in a match at Stirling, and his disaster was due to the overpressure of the slogger. But his hearty, 'Well played, old chap; finest thing you've ever done!' when the slogger pulled off the match was in fine form. The voice of that lad rings joyous yet across the years. It is well, if we are personally neither very clever nor very successful, to appreciate the gifts of others.

Now Jesus is the best trainer of the dull boy. Nobody can take so much out of you as Christ. I dare say most of you remember about Warner's Eleven and their memorable exploits in cricket over in Australia. They were counted a second-rate team, not up to international form, but so well were they captained they were able to win the rubber against Australia's full strength.

I had almost forgotten the keeper, most indispensable of all our players. St John is unquestionably the keeper of the goal in our Master's Galilean Eleven. Among the qualities which equip St John for his responsible post is reserve. We must all stand with St John at times and hold the last line of defence, the thoughts and the motives. Our thoughts are the very goal and citadel which we must keep virgin for Christ, admitting thither only what is pure and true, expelling lies and vicious imaginings. The best cure we know for these last is the daily reading of the Bible.

We must not sneak and sin when we think that he may not notice us. One day Thring of Uppingham was greatly gladdened by a story brought him to the school. A lecturer told him how one of the boys had been travelling during the summer in France, full of gaiety, and he had been asked by his companions to do something which he knew the head-master at the old school would disapprove of. He refused. They urged him on, but he said, 'No, the master would not like it!' They laughed, saying, 'But Dr Thring is a good five hundred miles off.' But they could not shake the boy. Thring was greatly touched by this tale. 'I could have burst into tears,' he said. The lads all cheered mightily. 'I personally thank the school for giving me one such boy,' said Thring. 'I trust all would be as firm.'

Men, will you play the game of life as those who are aware that the Master's reputation is at stake, ay, and that his eye is on you? There may be 'flannelled fools at the wicket and muddied oafs at the goals'. But let us whose field is life take a true line. 'Play up and play the game,' 'Fling your heart between the goal posts,' says C. B. Fry, 'and the ball will follow. . . .'

THE REV. D. C. MACINOL, BD., *A Famous First Eleven*

Bowling to the Converted

*Whilst working as a volunteer on a Kibbutz our corres-
pondent Simon Holt played in a game that took on a
religious significance that even the Rev. Macinol could
not have dreamt of*

A week after the arrival of the volunteer workers from the
evangelical Melodyland Christian Community of Los
Angeles, California their leader, the Reverend Brint
Shackenworth, challenged the existing volunteers to a game
of cricket. Apparently the Reverend and six of his followers
knew how to play. They had been to Bradford on a two year
'Christian Crusade'! The only problem we could foresee
was the timing of the match. Most of their time was spent
praying, eating, singing and praying some more. Any brief
leisure time they had was used attempting to convert a newly
arrived volunteer to their cause. Milo an Argentinian Jew
would sit surrounded by two or three beautiful girls who
would attempt to bring him the good news. He always
looked attentive. But I only ever heard him say 'Yes' or 'No'.
Nothing else. We designated him our No 11.

However a date was made and we set about finding some
kit. A Finnish family who had come to Israel to wait for the
new messiah provided two Duncan Fearneys, stumps and a
pair of pads. What these had to do with the second coming
was never really revealed. Shackenworth provided a baseball to act as the 'crimson rambler'.

Neatly attired in blue shorts and 'Jesus Saves' T-shirts
Zack and Billy opened the batting for Melodyland. A leg
stump was quickly removed. Zack retraced his steps. But the
next four batsmen had all been to England. Their No 3,
Joseph, pulling and hooking smote his way to 25. Every shot
was greeted with a chorus of hallelujahs. But sadly he fell
from grace through pride. Lifting his head to see where he
was going to hit the ball he missed it and like an avenging
angel it smashed his wicket. The other missionaries suffered similar fates. Mike through greed seeking a suicidal
second run down to fine leg. Envy was Ezikhal's sin.
Attempting to emulate Joseph he slashed at a ball outside

the off stump and was caught at gully. The No 6, Dave, succumbed to sloth. Run out some three yards from home. Melodyland were 69 for 4. Yet some hard slogging by the tail end pushed it up to 102. Milo had done nothing to help us. Surrounded by his lovely mentors he showed no interest whatsoever. He just sat there nodding his head.

Confident of victory we set out on our righteous path. But an injudicious heave down to long on; a mistimed leg glance squirting to mid wicket and we were 19 for 2. My faith in victory was ebbing away. It left me totally when I saw Milo. A small shambling figure with a pad flopping on his right leg was walking to the middle. He had usurped the position of our South African all rounder. Why we never really found out.

Our nearly converted friend received his first ball on his right thigh. The ball sped down to fine leg. I screamed 'Run'. He didn't seemed to understand. 'Avanti, Avanti' he started to run. But not towards me. Milo was heading for his mentors on the boundary. He had had enough of this dangerous game. We were 25 for 3. Yet we still won. A brilliant 54 by our South African pushed us on to victory.

The Reverend Shackenworth took it hard. Prayer time was increased. God must be appeased, he had sent the Melodyland Community a sign; a warning. Milo was never left alone. But then it gradually dawned on them what I had realised on the day of the game. Our Argentinian friend did not understand English. All he could say was 'Yes' or 'No'. Not only had Melodyland lost their game but also their model convert. They refused our offer of a return match.

SIMON HOLT

War Games

Meeting the Boer Challenge

It has already been suggested that wherever the armed services travelled games of cricket seemed to materialise from nowhere. Never was this truer than in the last two wars and indeed in the prison camps. We don't expect, though, that many people will remember or believe that the Boers actually challenged the British to a cricket match during the siege of Mafeking. This account of that challenge comes from William Hillcourt and Olave Lady Baden-Powell whose husband is best known perhaps for founding the Boy Scouts and being the author of Scouting for Boys. *It was about Lady Baden-Powell that Jilly Cooper made one of her most famous puns, heading an interview with her 'Still Olave & Kicking'*

On the last day of April a British patrol inspecting a railway line to the south-west found an envelope addressed to Baden-Powell. Baden-Powell read the contents with a sardonic smile. It was from the recently arrived young Commandant of the Johannesburg Commando, ambitious Sarel Eloff, one of President Kruger's thirty-five grandsons at the fighting front.

Outside Mafeking,
April 29, 1900

Dear Sir,
I see in the *Bulawayo Chronicle* that your men in Mafeking play cricket on Sundays, and give concerts and balls on Sunday evenings. In case you will allow my men to join in, it would be very agreeable to me, as here, outside Mafeking, there are seldom any of the fair sex, and there can be no merriment without them being present. In case you

would allow this we could spend some of the Sundays, which we still have to get through round Mafeking, and of which there will probably be several, in friendship and unity. During the coming course of the week, you can let us know if you accept my proposition, and I shall then, with my men, be on the cricket field, and at the ballroom at the time so appointed by you. Wishing you and yours a pleasant day,

> I remain, Your obedient friend,
> Sarel Eloff,
> Commandant Jobsdal Commando

Baden-Powell sent his answer to the Boer lines under a white flag

> Mafeking,
> April 30, 1900

Sir,
I beg to thank you for your letter of yesterday, in which you propose that your men should come and play cricket with us. I should like nothing better – after the match in which we are at present engaged is over. But just now we are having our innings, and have so far scored 200 days not out against the bowling of Cronje, Snyman, Botha and Eloff, and we are having a very enjoyable game.

> I remain, Yours truly,
> R. S. S. Baden-Powell

The rest is history.

WILLIAM HILLCOURT and OLAVE LADY BADEN-POWELL,
Baden-Powell, The Two Lives of a Hero

In the Moat, at Schloss Spangenberg

Many prisoners of war must have gained great comfort from impromptu games of cricket conjured up under the bewildered eyes of their captors. Terence Prittie gives a fascinating account of cricket as played in the Moat at Schloss Spangenberg, or Oflag IX A/H as it was known to the Germans. Bill Bowes, the famous Yorkshire and

*England cricketer, writes about POW cricket in Italy in
an extract from his book* Caught *and the late Sam Kydd
tells an amusing story in his autobiography* For You
the War is Over. *Lastly the redoubtable 'Jim' Swanton describes what it was like playing cricket under the
Japs*

Hardly surprisingly, British prisoners of war in Germany
during the Second World War played cricket whenever they
could, for time hung heavy on their hands. In 1940 there was
no cricket, because there was no cricket gear. But in 1941 a
start was made in the constricted parade-ground of a Polish
fortress (this was a so-called 'reprisals camp'), and on the
gravelled yard of a camp which, ironically, was almost
idyllically situated in rolling Württemberg downland. In
1942 the biggest officers' camp at Warburg even boasted a
grass wicket and a full-sized ground, and was generously
supplied with cricket equipment by the De Flamingo club of
Holland.

But the Warburg camp, thanks to the number of escapes
that took place, was broken up in the autumn, and batches of
officers were dispatched to half a dozen other corners of
Hitler's Reich. Among them was Schloss Spangenberg, a
mediaeval castle built on the very top of a hill in just about
the very centre of Germany.

'Oflag IX A/H', in the German version, looked at first
sight just about the most improbable place in the world for
cricketing captives. It housed under three hundred officers,
who were severely cramped for space. The castle was built
for defence and its architect would hardly have concerned
himself with facilities for exercise for its garrison. The
buildings formed an oval, round an inner courtyard about
forty yards long and a dozen in width. The courtyard was in
continuous use, and windows looked out onto it everywhere.
Cricket there was ruled out; PT, in very small squads, was
just possible.

Save for two narrow terraces, nowhere more than four
yards wide, the outer walls of the castle dropped sheer into a
dry moat, whose opposite wall rose over thirty feet to the
German sentries' cat-walk, flush with the castle's ground

floor. In 1942 the moat was an unprepossessing piece of scenery, with its irregular and undulating surface carpeted with rubble, old tin cans and other débris. It was nowhere more than twenty-five yards wide and its utter desolation was daunting. The first arrivals at Spangenberg essayed deck-quoits in corners of it. Cricket seemed out of the question; frustratingly, there was plenty of cricket gear.

But the moat was to undergo a complete transformation under the direction of the senior British officer, Major-General Victor Fortune. Forty years earlier he had opened the bowling for Winchester but, oddly, he was essentially concerned with creating a garden rather than a sports arena of a circumscribed kind. Officers' work-parties began by levelling out the ground, and tidying it up. A four-foot-high sloping grass bank was uncovered along the widest part of the moat. Above it, flower-beds were constructed, with vegetable plots in narrower stretches of ground. A path was built round the whole circumference of the castle. Officers, the General decided, would want to walk and run. So they did, but the runners had to be restricted to an hour in the early morning. There just wasn't room for everyone.

On the subject of cricket, the General quickly relented. If some sort of knockabout game could be devised, well and good, but players would have to 'be careful' with the flowers – not an easy order to carry out. Use of a real cricket ball was ruled out. The windows on the battlements above were not out of range, and the ball would in any case be quickly battered to bits on the walls of the moat.

And so the cricketers in the camp – and there were three at least who had played in first-class matches in England – got down to the business of adapting the game to these peculiar surroundings. What they achieved can be described only with the help of diagrams.

That on page 102 shows the view offered to the batsman at wicket A. On his leg side, the outer wall of the moat was a mere ten feet from the pitch, but so gradual was its curve that the straight boundary was nearly forty-five yards away. Part of this straight boundary was demarcated by a low fence enclosing a vegetable garden and built out from a buttress marked in the diagram with an M. From roughly half-way across the moat a whitewashed boundary-line ran up a slight grassy slope, across the circular path and through four feet of flower-bed to the opposite wall at a point behind the protruding bastion of the castle wall.

This point, where the boundary-line met the inner wall of the moat, was roughly where an extra-cover would stand. But from there back to wicket A the lay-out was more complex. The inner wall, like the outer, was about thirty feet high. Above it was a narrow terrace, accessible from the interior of the castle. Behind and above the terrace were the walls and windows of the castle itself. But there was, at least, much more space on the off-side for the batsman at wicket A, often over fifteen yards. The path, the grass bank and a section of flower-bed comprised interesting 'hazards', for a firmly hit ball would bounce strangely among them and a quick single was generally 'on'.

Behind wicket A both walls of the moat curved at a more acute angle, giving a shorter and narrower boundary perhaps twenty-five yards back, on a line between third man and second slip. Much of the space along this sector of the castle wall was filled by a large flower bed. Maybe it was the General who decreed that it should remain singularly empty, save for a few hardy rock plants; tall and fragile flowers would have had a bad time, as the second diagram, on page 102 plainly shows. For it was plumb in the middle of the main scoring area for a batsman at wicket B – the boundary which ran from behind the bastion marked D to the outer wall beneath the nearest tree was a difficult target indeed.

So much for the implausible shape of our ground. The problems of equipment were relatively easily solved. There were several bats. Our cricket balls were used only for catching practice, but there was a limited supply of tennis balls. These, however, bounced high and wildly, and it was decided to reinforce them with an outer covering of elastoplast, cut in two pieces and then hand-sewn. The extra weight reduced the bounce, helped the bowler's grip and increased receptivity to controlled spin. Wooden stumps were constructed, with fixed bails, and set into a solid base about three inches in depth.

Then the Germans agreed – anything to keep British

officers quiet and discourage them from trying to escape! – to supply some lime. It was mixed with water, and creases appeared where previously there had been only lines scratched into the ground. The pitch was pounded into shape with croquet mallets, and was durable. The summers of 1943 and 1944 were fine, and players were allowed to wear only rubber-soled shoes. Pads and gloves were obviously not required. We had everything that we needed.

In the devising of our 'ground' we owed most to a Harrovian (who had played for Oxford and Kent a dozen years earlier). He saw the latent possibilities of terrain reminiscent of some of the Harrow house yards. Ordinary cricket became the rule, and a system of scoring was worked out with great ingenuity and something in the nature of a popular referendum – the two biggest rooms in the castle had their own sides, smaller rooms clubbed together, and the seven or eight teams sent their delegates to the initial committee meetings which were necessary.

The flower-bed at third-man from wicket A was given diplomatic immunity; any hit into it counted one run only. A hit clean over the outer wall of the moat had to be discouraged. The ball might be lost and the game would inevitably be held up until the sentries, who after some discreet coaching became excellent retrievers, could find and return it. (One or two of them even learnt to throw!) So a stroke of this kind was penalised by the batsman scoring no runs and losing his wicket.

From wicket A the straight boundary behind the bowler counted four runs, and a full-pitch over it scored six. But an exception had to be made as a result of representations from an irate colonel who grew an excellent crop of tomatoes along one section of the boundary; a shot into his tomatoes counted one run only. The straight drive from wicket B similarly counted four or six, but owing to the narrowed angle was much more difficult to execute. At first a hit onto the narrow terrace of the castle counted six, but it became clear that a good batsman at wicket B could repeat the shot times over against a weak bowler. So it was reduced to five. Other hits, and extras, had to be run, and a batsman had to retire when he reached or passed twenty. The more skilled

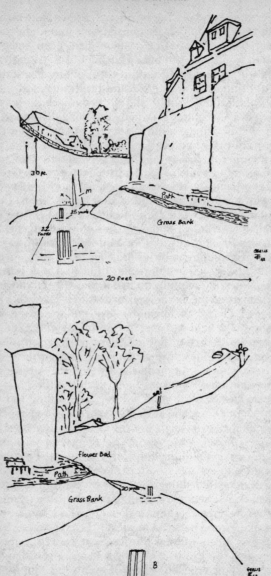

became expert at reaching nineteen, before dispatching the ball for six and scoring the absolute maximum of 25.

An innings could not last longer than fifteen overs, and bowlers were allowed no more than three overs each. They suffered another limitation. Had a bowler, like Warwick Armstrong of yore, decided to bowl wide on the leg side to a batsman at wicket A, the latter had no possible remedy. If he skied the ball out of the moat, he was out. If he struck it hard against the wall, he was liable to be caught directly off it – another local rule. Balls pitching and passing wicket A on the leg side were therefore signalled wides by the umpire – the same was done if the batsman at wicket B were a left-hander. But 'off-theory' was not penalised; the ball, after all, could always be hooked.

Clearly, special batting techniques had to be developed. Some of the best orthodox strokes were of little value and with eleven men in the field a boundary four was rare (there was a school of thought seven or eight to a side, but it was overruled on the grounds that so many people wanted to play). With space so constricted, three fielders could always be spared to man the boundary. Singles were also not easy to come by; nearly every one of them was manifestly a short run at express speed. The need to loft the ball up onto the castle terrace, or over either straight boundary, was clearly emphasised. The only factors favouring the batsman were the bowler's difficulty in controlling the reinforced tennis ball, and the propensity of fieldsmen to take heavy tumbles on the uneven ground.

The conditions immensely enhanced the value of a left-hander. From wicket A he had a pulled drive as his chief scoring shot, with a hook onto the terrace to back it up. Of course, he was virtually helpless when at wicket B, but this was in any case much the more difficult wicket to score from. Left-handers – there were only three or four in the camp – did their utmost to hog the bowling at the A wicket end. One of them – dare I say it was, in fact, myself? – alone scored the maximum 25 in both innings of a match. It paid, in a sense, to be a mediocre player who had always had to improvise. By contrast, a former Essex batsman and a representative of Surrey Club and Ground suffered by middling the ball, playing correctly down the line and keeping it on the ground. An ex-Dorset player went to the other extreme, repeatedly trying to pop straight balls up onto the terrace, and being almost invariably clean bowled. Captaincy, too, was at a premium, involving different bowling policies to wickets A and B, special counter-measures against a left-hander, and a systematic study of each opponent's foibles and weaknesses.

The pitch was in use every day of the week when it didn't rain. It even had to be watered occasionally. There may have been upwards of 150 days' cricket in both 1943 and 1944, and 10 days more at the end of the season playing tip-and-run. More than 75 per cent of us prisoners played, and 50 per cent of us regularly. Sunday afternoons were reserved for matches between teams of officers and teams of NCOs and other ranks, who, owing to their work, could not play during the week. The terrace was usually packed with onlookers, whose comments were as frequent and pointed as those from Sydney's famous 'Hill'. Matches were generally between rooms, but there were 'club' fixtures, when Gunners, Greenjackets, Commandos and others took the field. No side ever made over 100, although 90 was passed several times, while the lowest score, 0, stood to the 'credit' of the Highland Brigade. Thirty runs were once hit in an over, and four wickets once taken in four balls.

Only two other records need be mentioned. When the Greenjackets took on 'The Rest', the latter led by 70 runs on first innings and the Greenjackets, batting a second time, were still two runs behind with only three balls of their second innings remaining to be bowled. But all three were struck for six, and The Rest, with 17 to win, were dismissed for 16 and could only tie. Shades of 'Fowler's Match'!

Then the Germans allowed the castle to be visited by an XI from the so-called 'Lower Camp', in Spangenberg village. Unused to the conditions, it was dismissed for 10, and its captain unwisely opened the bowling to a left-hander, who had naturally been sent to wicket A. Two sixes, off the first two balls, ended the game.

Early in 1944 I wrote an account of cricket in the moat of Schloss Spangenberg, under the quotation from Walter

Bagehot, 'An Englishman, whose heart is in the matter, is not easily baffled', and sent it to 'Plum', Sir Pelham Warner. The German censors, as I learnt later when serving in post-war Germany as the correspondent of the then *Manchester Guardian*, had at once been perturbed by this incomprehensible piece of writing. They sent it to Berlin to be 'de-coded', for they were convinced that it contained a secret message. For over three months German experts worked on my article, increasingly infuriated at their inability to 'break' the code which wasn't there at all. In the end, someone had the bright idea of sending it to Lord Haw-Haw. Whether he, or an underling, read it I did not learn, but his office reported back that it was a perfectly normal account of cricket, played under somewhat abnormal conditions. *The Cricketer* was able to publish the article on 17 June, 1944.

A final vignette. Apart from the uniformed German staff, a single German civilian used to come into Spangenberg Castle. His name was Kühlmann, and he looked after the inadequate heating arrangements. He was about the size of 'Tich' Freeman, with a lined, leathery face, rimless spectacles under a peaked cap, and vile manners. He hated our guts, and whenever he passed a British officer he muttered furiously. On occasion, he averted his head and spat.

Then Kühlmann took to watching our game of cricket, taking up his position on the battlements behind wicket B. The first time he did this, he swore and shook his fist, but he came back for more. Soon he became a regular onlooker, for there was little enough heating to be done in the long, hot summers. Although he could scarcely have understood the finer points of the game, he often chuckled happily. And his whole demeanour changed; he ceased to mutter and spit, and occasionally he even smiled.

Nobody spoke to him, because it was well-known that he was stone deaf. But what a shame, even a tragedy, that *Hitler* never learnt about cricket! Things might have been different.

TERENCE PRITTIE

Caught in Italy

There were few days at Chieti on which any of the 1,700 men could look back with pleasure, wishing he could relive them. But there was one such day, when we succeeded in forgetting the walls and barbed wire, the sentries and tommy-guns that surrounded us. It was the occasion of a cricket match, a real match that took us back to the village green, and it was the greatest and most memorable match in which I ever took part.

Preceding it were many days of thought and preparation. The first and most important requirement was a village green. The Chieti prison cage boasted nothing like a cricket pitch, and the only available space, bounded by the cookhouse and huts, was a barren rectangle covered for the most part by small stones. It was intersected by a tarmac road with offshoots to the penthouses.

With a mixture bought from the Italians the main road was carefully distempered green. There was our greensward.

The theatrical department were wizards with odd bits of wood, cloth and nails, and they were deputed to erect a huge pavilion-clock on top of one of the penthouses (used as a dressing-room and pavilion) which dominated the ground. In front of the pavilion, they erected a members' enclosure, complete with seats and railings. They also built a roller which was given a place of honour near the pavilion.

Using tables and blankets as building materials, they then put up another imposing edifice to the right of the pavilion. This was the bandstand. They used sheets to make sight screens, and finally put up a large score-board which was visible to the whole camp.

At 1.40 p.m. on the great day, amid lovely Italian sunshine, Messrs Long and Short, the groundsmen (Shorty being Tommy Ward of Huddersfield), went out to 'roll' the pitch and erect the wickets which were fixed in wooden blocks on the concrete road. Next they painted white creases.

At 1.50 p.m. precisely, the captains tossed, and immediately afterwards the two umpires in fine white coats, which

had been 'borrowed' from the Italian su
field and placed the bails on the wickets.

At 1.55 Freddie Brown led out the fieldin
man in the camp had turned out to watch.
smaller crowds and much less excitement at man   .t-class
matches. It was noticeable that the wicket-keeper had an
excellent pair of home-made pads as well as gloves – the
latter a pair of purloined Italian motoring gauntlets improved to English cricketing standards. The batsmen, too,
were equally well equipped.

Soon the crack of a hand-made leather ball was to be
heard meeting a bat – and bringing back echoes from
home. The ball had been made by PoW Major Denis
Lamplough of Hull, and could have been sold in any cricket
shop.

'Pitso' and his orchestra, playing on instruments bought
from the Italians, provided incidental music for one half of
the game and Tommy Sampson and his band (now a
well-known English band) obliged for the other.

There was some excellent bowling by Freddie Brown, the
Surrey and England bowler. An Indian officer named
Gardener achieved the hat trick. Beaumont (Yorkshire)
played a fine back-to-the-wall innings, and Bull (of Essex)
batted most academically.

For the cookhouse staff I have nothing but praise – they
actually served afternoon teas round the ground. When an
Italian officer, blithely ignorant of the etiquette of cricket,
walked across the ground, epithets were hurled at him
which he had never heard before nor has probably heard
since.

Boundary shots and more especially sixes were equally a
matter of applause and concern. We had only half a dozen
balls in stock and five of them were hit away into 'liberty'.
Fortunately the last one saw the game to a finish, when
Major Lamplough had to get busy again to replenish the
sports store.

And what a finish it was! To describe it as close would
be an understatement. Men never raced against time with
such dogged determination and exciting effect. All the time
the players were being deftly egged on by the careful

nanipulation of the hands of the giant pavilion clock worked by a man concealed inside.

The news service in the camp was splendid. It is a story which, for many reasons, cannot be fully told. It is enough to say that we were not at all surprised when, on 12 April, 1945, the Americans arrived and released us. I remember seeing men with tears of joy streaming down their faces. A few days later we climbed out of aircraft on an airfield near Amersham, and I saw men actually falling on their knees to kiss the ground. And they weren't joking.

Tactfully my friends asked if I had heard news of my pal Hedley Verity. They were surprised when I told them that I was one of the first to hear of his fate.

Bribes, threats and promises worked wonders in procuring news in a prison camp. For the more intimate news of England – rationing conditions, bombing, the latest shows and prices in the shops – we relied on verbal accounts from newly arrived prisoners.

Imagine our pleasure (if not theirs) when we welcomed to Chieti two Canadian airmen who had been shot down over Naples only a few days before. Five nights previously they had been walking around London, had been to a show and were full of up-to-the-minute 'gen'.

They had spent a couple of days in hospital at Caserta, and then, after interrogation, had been sent to Chieti, where, for an hour or so, they were submitted to a barrage of questions.

I listened for a while until the questions were being repeated and got up to go, but was halted at the door by a Canadian voice.

'And say, there was some cricketer guy at Caserta. . . . What was his name . . . Verity . . . yeah, that's right, Verity.'

'Do you mean that Hedley Verity was in hospital in Caserta?' I asked, eagerly interested.

'Yeah, that's the feller. But he's not in hospital now. He was buried yesterday.'

'Buried?'

'Yeah. He must have been some important guy. The Italians gave him military honours.'

I walked out into the deserted roadway through the camp. The wind was cold but I did not notice it.

Hedley . . . dead! It was unbelievable. For a long while I walked up and down that road, time stilled, living again the many incidents and hours we had shared together.

I was roused from my reverie by a tug at my elbow. 'Say, feller,' came the Canadian voice again. 'I'm mighty sorry. I'd no idea that Verity was your cobber. Would you like to hear all about it?'

The airman fell into step beside me and told me the story. He ended, 'He seemed a great guy.'

In his two day association with Hedley he had formed the opinion – he was a great guy. How true! He was a great friend and a great cricketer, too.

I often wonder what a certain man in Yorkshire thought when he read the news. Not knowing that both Hedley and I had already visited the recruiting office at the beginning of the war, the man said: 'And what about you? I reckon that anybody who is good enough to play for England can fight for England.'

Perhaps he got his answer. Hedley was good enough to die for England.

W. E. Bowes, *Express Delivery*

Bollocks!

Down at Fort 15 where they had a large Australian population taken mainly in Greece, they had laid a proper wicket and Test Matches between England and Australia were the weekly showpiece.

Fort 15 was almost split down the middle – with the non-workers from Crete (the Aussies) and the non-workers from the British Army. King Cricket was the one way of satisfying their pretended animosity.

The Germans were completely bewildered by cricket and were discouraged from understanding it, especially by the Aussies, who took a great delight in confusing them. For instance, they informed the *Unter Offizier* that the slang word for a cricket ball was 'bollock'. So you can appreciate what it sounded like to a newcomer, hearing for the first time from German lips the words 'You play cricket today cobber wiz ze bat and ze bollock!'

SAM KYDD, *For You the War is Over*

Cricket Under the Japs

The first camp on the Thai-Burma railway in which we played cricket was Wampo. Christmas Day, 1942, was our first holiday since our arrival in October, and it was perhaps the fact of our so occupying the afternoon that caused our guards to receive subsequent requests to play cricket with suspicion, as having some religious significance and being therefore good for morale.

This particular game was notable, I remember, for what is probably the fastest hundred of all time. It was scored in about five overs by a very promising young Eurasian cricketer called Thoy, who, with graceful ease, kept hitting the tennis ball clear over the huts.

Cricket at Nakom Patom reached its climax on New Year's Day, 1945, when a fresh, and certainly hitherto unrecorded, page was written in the saga of England v. Australia.

The story of the match is very much the story of that fantastic occasion at the Oval in August, 1938. Flt-Lieut. John Cocks, well known to cricketers of Ashtead, is our Hutton; Lieut. Norman Smith from Halifax, an even squarer, an even squatter Leyland. With the regulation bat – it is two and a half inches wide and a foot shorter than normal – they play beautifully down the line of the ball, forcing the length ball past cover, squeezing the leg one square of their toes. There seems little room on the field with the eight Australian fielders poised there, but a tennis ball goes quickly off wood, the gaps are found, and there are delays while it is rescued from the swill basket, or fished out from under the hut. As the runs mount the barracking gains in volume, and in wit at the expense of the fielders. When at last the English captain declares, the score is acknowledged to be a Thailand record.

With the Australian innings comes sensation. Captain 'Fizzer' Pearson, of Sedburgh and Lincolnshire, the English fast bowler, is wearing boots. No other cricketer has anything on his feet at all, the hot earth, the occasional flint, being accepted as part of the game. The moral effect of these boots is tremendous. Capt. Pearson bowls with tremendous speed and ferocity, and as each fresh lamb arrives for the slaughter the stumps seem more vast, the bat even punier. One last defiant cheer for the 'Hill' when their captain, Lt-Col. E. E. Dunlop, comes in, another bigger one from the English when his stumps go flying.

While these exciting things proceed, one of the fielders anxiously asks himself whether they will brew trouble. 'Should fast bowlers wear boots? Pearson's ruse condemned – where did he get those boots? – boots from camp funds; official denial – Board of Control's strong note –' Headlines seem to grow in size. Then he remembers gratefully that here is no Press box full of slick columnists and Test captains, no microphones for the players to run to – in fact, no papers and no broadcasting. The field clears at last. As he hurries off to roll-call, he thinks of a New Year's Day six years before when the background was Table Mountain, the field was the green of Newlands, and he decides that even the South Africans who jostled their way back into Cape Town that evening had not enjoyed their outing more than the spectators of this grotesque 'Cricket Match'.

Major E. W. Swanton, ra., Wisden

25,000 Miles of Cricket

No better example of the way the Army toted cricket around the world exists than Reg Hovington's account of the 1st Battalion Green Howards' travels. He recalls 25,000 miles of cricket during which the Battalion always carried a matting wicket with them, not to mention the late Hedley Verity and Norman Yardley. Only a true Yorkshire regiment would or could have done that

In the Second World War, the 1st Battalion, the Green Howards must have established a record for travelling the furthest and playing cricket in more countries than any other unit. The late Brigadier A. Shaw, DSO, Commanding Officer from 1941 to 1943, saw to it that one of the Battalion's priorities was to carry and always have available a matting wicket, and woe betide the Pioneer Sergeant if he could not supply on demand the necessary concrete! Apart from the motivation and inspiration of the then Colonel, there were the late Hedley Verity, captaining 'B' Company, and Norman Yardley, then a platoon commander in 'D' Company, who were ready at all times and in all places to have a game of cricket, if it was at all possible.

Almost before the Battalion was completely dug in, wickets were being prepared in such unlikely places as a gap in the Sal Forest at Ranchi or in the middle of a seemingly endless desert at Qum. When the Battalion was stationed in Syria, the leave roster was so arranged that a team journeyed to Cairo to play two matches against teams drawn mostly from Australian and New Zealand troops. Even after the Colonel left, having been promoted and decorated, and after Hedley was wounded on the Catania Plain, and later died of his wounds in Caserta hospital, and after Norman was wounded in Italy, the tradition was maintained.

Just after the end of the war, when the Battalion was stationed in a village near Helmstedt, I was instructed by the then Colonel to arrange a cricket match between the Battalion and 'as many good players who can be mustered from the rest of the troops in Germany'. After much wireless traffic, a strong side was raised, but – where to play? I sought the advice of the Burgomaster. Yes, he knew of a flat field, with some grass on it, and he would, as I suggested – or was it ordered in those days? – supply exactly, in the middle of the said field, a concrete patch according to the dimensions I had laid down. This was on the Tuesday and the match was to take place on the following Saturday. For the rest of the week, everybody was too busy rounding up the odd German to have time to check that the work was being carried out correctly.

At two o'clock on the Saturday afternoon, twenty-two

men, all in white flannels conjured from God knows where, assembled with two umpires to play cricket, in the first match to be played in Germany after the war. The Burgomaster had done his job all right. Exactly in the middle of that sparse field was a perfect strip of concrete without the merest ripple on its surface but surrounding it and right up to it were over a thousand chairs set in immaculate circular lines. The mildest comment to be heard was, 'Does he think we was going to play bloody marbles?' as we laboriously carried all the chairs back to what served as a boundary before play could commence. However, the mat having been eventually laid, a cricket match was started. Of course, the Green Howards won, but the opposition, denied cricket for so long, enjoyed the game. News spread to the Divisional Commander, who, keen to provide as many amenities for the troops as soon as possible now the war was over, gave permission for a 'cricket' ground to be commandeered at Goslar, where inter-unit matches were held nearly every day throughout that summer. From the programme of one of these matches you would see that every player carried a number. I often think that this system should be adopted at all our county matches. How many times have you heard on a Yorkshire cricket ground, someone commenting on the fielders: 'That's Lumb, isn't it?'; 'Nay, that's Sidebottom'; 'I know that's Boycott. I'd recognise him anywhere!' 'That ain't Boycott, you fat 'ead, that there's Athey.'

The 1st Battalion the Green Howards was a member of the Fifth Division, an Imperial Reserve, which was assigned to places where there was a likelihood of an invasion – to Northern Ireland in case the Germans invaded through southern Ireland, to the East coast of India, in case the Japs invaded, to Iran in case of a German invasion through the Caucasus. Until the Battalion took part in the invasion of Sicily and the long campaign up the centre of Italy to Rome, via Anzio, it was inevitably dubbed by other troops who had been in the heat of battle as 'mere cricketers', and even during its heavy losses in the Italian campaign, there were still strong rumours that its Pioneer Platoon was consistently being wiped out by enemy gunfire while building concrete wickets just behind the line!

That cricket mat travelled with the Battalion as an essential piece of its baggage to South Africa, India, Iraq, Iran, Syria, Egypt, Sicily, Italy, France, Belgium and Germany. What a pity that a home could not have been found for it in the Green Howards' Museum at Richmond, Yorkshire, to remind servicemen of the pleasure it provided and the morale it inculcated!

REG HOVINGTON

Alec and Eric

Gavin Ewart has written a splendid poem about the Bedser Twins, Alec and Eric. Anyone who ever saw them play will recognise them straight away

The first time I saw the Bedser Twins
they were walking tall, as like as two pins,
lords over all, like sharks with fins,

it was Bari, Italy, 1945,
our war was over – we could survive
(and we were in clover to be alive!)

if we weren't shipped away to Japan!
A really hot summer, like astrakhan
the sun warmed our shoulders, reprieved – to a man.

Warrant Officers in the RAF,
they were big and beautiful; no gaffe,
they marched their dutiful, *paf, paf, paf*

like the great Stone Guest in *Don Giovanni*.
Perfect physiques, with no word of blarney,
not neurotic freaks like Hitchcock's Marny.

True relaxation – that was the ticket!
Army v. Air Force, Forces' cricket!
Unrolled by horse, they pitched a wicket

there on a foreign (Italian) field,
far from the Downs and the Kentish Weald –
some uneven bounce may have been revealed.

For the Army, I remember, Emmett played
(a Light Ack Ack Sergeant was his other trade)
the Bedser attack – I forget what he made.

I fancy the Air Force was the winner –
poor dead Verity our missing spinner!
The end of austerity, like a formal dinner

served in a gunpit, did it seem?
A very peculiarly *English* dream?
Organised Apulialy? A typical scheme

to mark the difference of the Island Race?
To lord it over time and place?
White Cliffs of Dover? Well, in that case,

I think it succeeded – you could believe
taking leave of your senses is a kind of leave,
such ethnic pretence is the air we breathe.

In the Italian of Mozart's *Don Giovanni* what Leporello
actually sings is '*Ta, ta, ta*' in imitation of the sound of the
statue's footsteps. Emmett was a left-handed batsman who
played for Gloucestershire and later for England. Verity had
been killed in action earlier in 1945, one of the classical slow
left arm bowlers. Bari is in Apulia.

GAVIN EWART

Cricket in the First World War

This is an account, taken from the Cricketer Spring
Annual *of 1968 by Fred Stead of cricket played in the
First World War in which the German airforce make a
dramatic entrance, having been drawn by curiosity
about the sight (from above) of a recently cut wicket*

When, forgetting to make allowances for his partner's age, a
junior officer calls a titled major-general for a run that isn't
really on and tells him to 'Run! Run like hell!' it could savour
somewhat of *lèse-majesté*. But not when Sir Victor Couper,
KCB, commanding the 14th (Light) Division in the First

World War and F. H. Bateman-Champlain, Gloucester County CC were the parties involved. On the field there was one rank only – acting private.

On those rare occasions when the Division was out of the line at, to quote the army's euphemism for it, 'Rest', it was my job to reconnoitre the area for a field suitable for cricket, ask the farmer for permission to play, agree a rent and hire or borrow a roller.

The selection committee's problem was not so much who to choose but who to leave out. The universities, Eton, the counties and the big leagues were represented.

Warlus, west of Arras, was our favourite ground. The spectators were vocally enthusiastic. The resident REs kept the score in chalk on an Army blackboard and celebrated boundaries by ringing a town-crier's bell.

It was here that an airman interrupted play at a vital moment – our fast bowler was on a hat trick. At a suicidally low altitude the German circled the field several times before satisfying himself that the pitch was not some new-type landing strip and, much to our relief, making off without dropping signs of disapproval. A bomb on the wicket would have been a major disaster. Our pace man always held it against the Germans that he didn't get that hat trick.

In an 'away' game at Kemmel, almost within throwing distance of the windmill, eight kilometres or so from Ypres, we encountered matting for the first time. Probably 'won' from an abandoned Flemish house, twelve inches wide, it was held in place by iron spikes normally used for securing tent ropes.

Old-timers still talk of dropping 'em on a sixpence, but I, off-spin and cut, found it devilishly difficult to pitch them on the matting. The fast bowler's first ball landed on a spike and was caught by third-man. Protesting that the casualty lists were far too long without any damned nonsense of that sort, the opposing captain halted proceedings until both matting and spikes could be removed.

But it was at Doullens that we achieved our greatest triumph. On that sophisticated ground, bare of grass but level and true, batting first we were dismissed for a modest

94. At lunch the home captain indiscreetly allowed himself to be overheard saying: 'Pity these chaps didn't get enough runs to make a game of it.'

Their last wicket went cart-wheeling with the score at 57.

Self-confident and ebullient, Field Marshal Viscount Montgomery promised his men at Alamein that he was going to hit the enemy for six. In his quiet way, fifty years ago, Sir Victor was doing just that.

He loved sixes.

FRED STEAD, *The Cricketer*

The Willows of the Resistance Movement

The suggestion that cricket was played under the noses of Nazi forces occupying Denmark may seem a bit far-fetched. Not a bit of it. Whilst their jackbooted oppressors strutted around, the Danes went quietly about their business which included attempting to manufacture cricket bats from the wrong kind of wood. Curiously the Nazis had omitted to ban the playing of cricket in Denmark, so it was that, unable to purchase the right kind of equipment, the subtle Danes finally found some willow trees. Read on

The Germans arrived a few weeks before the opening of the 1940 cricket season. It had promised to be a notable summer for the Danish game. A Test series against Holland had been planned and the pundits were confident that in the two Jutland pace men, Thomas Morild and Herluf Hansen, supported by the leg spin of young Eskild Larsen, the country boasted an attack that would be more than capable of taking the series.

Unfortunately the visitors did not play cricket. Worse, they made the fatal error of assuming that as fellow Nordics, the Danes would share their enthusiasm for heartier pastimes such as athletics, marching and driving tanks over people. When it became apparent that their Danish subjects were unwilling to play ball in their sense, the Nazi administrators retaliated with travel restrictions and curfew laws and later, and even less amusingly, with arrests and the taking of hostages.

Incredibly enough, the Nazis omitted to ban the playing of cricket. There were indeed several restrictions against the 'assembly of people in large groups'. But here again the Nazis left a loophole. They failed to give a positive ruling as to whether twenty-two men, in white flannels, constituted 'an assembly of people in large groups'. As a result cricket flourished in Denmark during the war years. The propulsion or battery of the leather ball became a gesture of resistance and sympathy with the Allied cause. Professionals found themselves taking the field with total amateurs in these heady years of defiance. Class batsmen and rabbits, 'safe pair of hands' and 'butter fingers', were joined together in a mute demonstration of their faith in an ultimate victory for England.

Somewhere in the hierarchy of the Occupying Power was a pedantic little Nazi who calculated that in the long run he had got the measure of this subversive sport. Cricket was entirely dependent on the import of gear from England. The U-boats and the Wehrmacht had effectively closed this vital supply line. It was, of course, just possible that the Danes might somehow contrive to manufacture their own cricket equipment. But he may have reckoned he had blocked this option with a series of swingeing restrictions on the use of raw materials, and the manufacture of 'non-essentials'.

In any case this nameless Nazi functionary had reckoned without Frederik Ferslev, a long-retired player for the KB Club, dedicated to the art of the impossible. 'At the A.B. Club ground one day I was told they were running short of bats. . . . I decided to fill the gap myself,' Frederik Ferslev wrote after the war. So begins a story of dedication, resourcefulness and not a little courage which has few parallels in the history of the game.

There were to be many false starts. As Ferslev confessed, 'Somehow I had got the idea that bats were made of silver poplar. I visited many timber merchants hunting for this wood.' Later Ferslev experimented with a laminate of pine and ash. But again, as he confessed, 'I found out very quickly that ash is no good for cricket bats – the hardest drive moved the ball no more than twenty or thirty yards.'

A windfall in the shape of some back numbers of *The Cricketer*, redolent of distant peace-time summers, finally came to the rescue of our determined improviser. 'In an old copy from 1931, I learnt for the first time that bats are made of willow. More particularly from a tree known as *Salix coerulea*, a cross between *Salix alba* and *Salix fragilis*. *Salix coerulea* was known as "the true cricket bat willow" and grew, I read, particularly in Essex. Essex was a long way away in those days.'

The search was now on for a home-grown specimen of the rare *Salix coerulea*. Intensive investigation revealed that a visiting Scotsman thirty-two years previously had scattered some precious seedlings by the seashore in the Guan Lindersvold district. Contact was made with the forester who confirmed that he had about twenty *coerulea* in his woods. However, it was now May and the forester insisted that this type of willow should only be felled in January. Typically Ferslev told him, 'I cannot wait so long.'

It was back to the drawing board – or rather that article in *The Cricketer* of 1931. Here Ferslev learned that the willow species *Salix alba* had been found serviceable in the days of Alfred Mynn and the young W. G. Grace. Stocks of this willow were finally located on the distant island of Amager.

But Ferslev's difficulties were by no means over. 'I had the wood,' he wrote, 'but how was I to get a press made?' This was an even greater problem than obtaining the wood, since every firm or workshop in Denmark was under German control. 'I could never get a permit to have one made – it could only be done illegally if someone would take the risk.'

Someone did take the risk. His name was Peter Peterson, opening batsman for Ferslev's old club at the turn of the century, now a civil engineer at Titan A/S engineering works. For Titan hands arrest or deportation was the penalty of involvement in any project unclassifiable as essential war work. Yet somehow among the mortar barrels and the rifle butts, Denmark's first cricket bat production line came into operation.

It was now the season of 1944. The German army was falling back through Poland and bracing itself in the West to meet the Allied invasion. Frederik Ferslev had other matters on his mind. He was tackling the problem of replacing the handles of existing bats with a home-made product. 'Over a thousand pieces of cane had to be shaped, bonded and turned,' he wrote. 'Thread for binding the handles was terribly difficult to obtain, and for weeks I queued up all over Copenhagen to get enough for my handles.' As Marshal Zhukov's tanks rolled towards the Oder and the D-Day forces assembled in the English south coast ports, Ferslev reported: 'Throughout May and June I was unbelievably busy, re-blading, re-handling, pegging and binding old bats.'

In sporting terms he had perhaps done more than General Eisenhower and Marshal Zhukov to turn the tide.

Based on material from *The Story of Continental Cricket* by P. G. G. LABOUCHERE, T. A. J. PROVIS and PETER S. HARGREAVES

Indomitable

(How a cricket match in East Africa during the Second World War may have influenced British naval operations in the Mediterranean)

The Navy have always been great champions of cricket. The following two items show how seriously the Senior Service takes itself, not least by using the game to deceive the enemy. This next entry must be the only one in the book that had to be cleared by the M.O.D. before it could be included. Not so the sad story of A. B. Waterman's dostil phalanx

In July 1942, while the Eastern Fleet was in harbour at Mombasa, replenishing and resting after operations in the Indian Ocean, the captain of the aircraft carrier HMS *Indomitable*, Captain Tom Troubridge, decided to challenge the Muthaiga Club in Nairobi to a cricket match.

We knew that the Muthaiga Club had a near-county side at their disposal, so the best possible Navy team was selected from the whole Fleet and flew up to Nairobi for the match. At the Muthaiga cricket ground a typical pre-war atmosphere prevailed with marquees dotted around the ground and a large crowd. In fact the Navy players felt that the war, at that moment, was a very long way away.

It was an exciting match which ended in a one-run victory for the Navy, scored in the very last over! After the match the Kings African Rifles, smart as paint, beat Retreat in front of the wildly enthusiastic spectators. Then Tom Troubridge, a fine figure of a man and a considerable 'character', addressed the crowd over the loudspeaker and thanked the Muthaiga Club for a marvellous match.

He concluded by issuing a further challenge for a return match in Nairobi a month later, in the middle of August.

The elated Navy XI flew back to Mombasa that evening and next day *Indomitable* sailed, embarked her aircraft, and headed south at high speed for Cape Town. Here the ship refuelled and sailed again for an unknown destination, eventually joining a massive carrier fleet and convoy of merchant ships off Gibraltar, bound for beleaguered Malta. In a signal to the Fleet, Sir Winston Churchill himself emphasised the vital importance of the convoy, stressing that it had to be fought through to Malta at any cost.

As it sailed deeper into the Mediterranean and closer to enemy shores, the convoy was heavily attacked and, of the five carriers involved, *Indomitable* was badly damaged and *Eagle* was sunk. Only five out of the fourteen merchant ships that had originally set out succeeded in reaching Grand Harbour in Malta.

Soon after the war the writer was talking to Vice-Admiral Sir Thomas Troubridge about that memorable cricket match and discovered that all was not as it seemed.

Just before the war the Admiral had served as our Naval Attaché in Berlin. He got to know a number of the high-ranking German naval officers extremely well and felt he knew how they would react to certain situations. The cricket match seemed a golden opportunity to try out a counter-intelligence plan.

He deliberately challenged the Muthaiga Club to a return match when he knew that a major Malta convoy had been planned for the middle of August and that his ship would be taking part, and rightly assumed that this information would be reported immediately to Berlin by German agents in Nairobi. As a result, the German High Command might decide, as it would seem very unlikely that any major naval operation would take place there for at least six weeks, to recall a number of U-boats from the Mediterranean to change crews.

The Admiral's imaginative ploy paid off, the Germans fell for the bait and some Allied ships and lives were saved.

COMMANDER B. H. C. NATION

Certificate for Wounds and Hurts

These are to Certify the Right Honourable the Lords Commissioners of the Admiralty that

Name in full	*Rank or Rating*	*Official Number*
John Frederick Waterman	Able Seaman	C/JX 735918

belonging to His Majesty's Ship *Bonaventure* was injured at about 1500 of 21st November, 1946. Whilst Able Seaman WATERMAN was playing cricket for HMS *Bonaventure* at Kure, Japan, he was hit on the right thumb by a cricket ball thereby sustaining a fracture of the dostil phalanx of the right thumb.

ADMIRALTY DOCUMENT

Missiles Seized at Home of Test Star

The Great Wars are over; but you never know if the chap charging up to bowl may have a cruise missile under his bed back home

Martial law authorities in Lahore – Pakistan's key political city – yesterday seized two Soviet surface-to-air missiles from the home of former Test cricketer Aftab Gul, sources announced.

The heat-seeking missiles, with a reported range of 10,000 ft, can hit low-flying helicopters and aircraft.

Sources said that Aftab Gul, who belongs to the banned Pakistan People's Party, now lives in London.

Pakistan Television said the seizure was made after a member of the Al-Zulfikar terrorist organisation told authorities where the missiles were hidden.

Authorities said further investigations were going on and there was no word of any arrest.

Aftab Gul, a lawyer, has played six times for Pakistan – twice against England in 1968, once against New Zealand in 1969 and three times against England in 1971.

Daily Mail, August 1983

Stars and Strips

What does it all Mean?

Writers down the decades have noted a yawning gulf of misunderstanding when it comes to explaining cricket to our American cousins. Here is a Wodehousian butler attempting to put yet another perplexed transatlantic visitor in the picture

Mr Crocker picked up his paper and folded it back at the sporting page, pointing with a stubby fore-finger.

'Well, what does all this mean? I've kept out of watching cricket since I landed in England, but yesterday they got the poison needle to work and took me off to see Surrey play Kent at that place, the Oval, where you say you go sometimes.'

'I was there yesterday, sir. A very exciting game.'

'Exciting? How do you make that out? I sat in the bleachers all afternoon, waiting for something to break loose. Doesn't anything ever happen at cricket?'

The butler winced a little, but managed to smile a tolerant smile. This man, he reflected, was but an American, and as such more to be pitied than censured. He endeavoured to explain.

'It was a sticky wicket yesterday, sir, owing to the rain.'

'Eh?'

'The wicket was sticky, sir.'

'Come again.'

'I mean that the reason why the game yesterday struck you as slow was that the wicket – I should say the turf – was sticky – that is to say, wet. Sticky is the technical term, sir. When the wicket is sticky the batsmen are obliged to exercise a great deal of caution, as the stickiness of the wicket enables the bowlers to make the ball turn more sharply in either direction as it strikes the turf than when the wicket is not sticky.'

'That's it, is it?'

'Yes, sir.'

'Thanks for telling me.'

'Not at all, sir.'

Mr Crocker pointed to the paper.

'Well, now, this seems to be the boxscore of the game we saw yesterday. If you can make sense out of that, go to it.'

The passage on which the finger rested was headed Final Score, and ran as follows:

SURREY – First Innings

Hayward c. Woolley b. Carr	67
Hobbs run out	0
Hayes st. Huish b. Fielder	12
Ducat b. Fielder	33
Harrison not out	11
Sandham not out	6
Extras	10
Total (for four wickets)	139

Bayliss inspected the cipher gravely.

'What is it you wish me to explain, sir?'

'Why, the whole thing. What's it all about?'

'It's perfectly simple, sir. Surrey won the toss and took first knock. Hayward and Hobbs were the opening pair. Hayward called Hobbs for a short run, but the latter was unable to get across and was thrown out by mid-on. Hayes was the next man in. He went out of his ground and was stumped. Ducat and Hayward made a capital stand considering the stickiness of the wicket, until Ducat was bowled by a good length off-break and Hayward caught at second slip off a googly. Then Harrison and Sandham played out time.'

Mr Crocker breathed heavily through his nose.

'Yes!' he said, 'Yes! I had an idea that was it. But I think I'd like to have it once again, slowly. Start with these figures. What does that sixty-seven mean, opposite Hayward's name?'

'He made sixty-seven runs, sir.'

'Sixty-seven! In one game?'

'Yes, sir.'

'Why, Home-Run Baker couldn't do it!'
'I am not familiar with Mr Baker, sir.'
'I suppose you've never seen a ball game?'
'Ball game, sir?'
'A baseball game?'
'Never, sir.'
'Then, Bill,' said Mr Crocker, reverting in his emotion to the bad habit of his early London days, 'you haven't lived!'

P. G. WODEHOUSE FROM *Piccadilly Jim*

Australia Beats the Transvaal at Babe Ruth's Game

P. G. Wodehouse's visiting American subsequently makes an abortive attempt to convert the butler to baseball. The butler takes the view that baseball and cricket just don't mix. Yet here is a celebrated Australian Test opener and cricket writer with a first-hand account of the extraordinary capers that could result from such a sporting cocktail. Briefly to set the scene: an Australian touring team has annihilated South Africa at cricket. With time on their hands the Aussies agree to play a Yankee-reinforced Transvaal at the American summer game

In front of the pavilion eleven or so white-knickered Transvaal men dashed hither and thither with bounds of confidence, performing incredible feats of throwing, hitting and catching.

Those of us who knew not the slightest baseball points began to take on a queer feeling in the stomach and also to ask agitated questions about the rules. We looked at ourselves in a mirror and realised how stupid it all was. We looked, and felt, abject fools in our pantaloons. If only we had listened to the cricket legislators – and one of them, dear 'Nummy' Deane, was mournfully reflecting at the doorway the incalculable harm this baseball game would do to cricket. I remember thinking that might be inconsequential to the harm it was now about to do us.

Sheepishly, very sheepishly, we slunk through the gate and ran on the field. The roar that went up circled around Johannesburg, and before it reached the Wanderers again we were already getting the 'bird' in approved baseball style. Any cricket barracking is childish in comparison.

And the opposition! Never could a team have looked more capable. They bristled with skill and efficiency, and to give the complete flavour had a full American battery – not full in any alcoholic sense, but in comprising an American pitcher and an American catcher. They would, we felt, simply blind us with American science and small talk.

We began to warm up, as one does before a baseball game. It might have been better if we had not, for catches were mulled, throws were wild, the barracking became even more intense, and it was quite obvious the American battery were sniggering at us.

We won the toss, went to bat and the 'game' was on. In as much time as it takes for an American battery to go through all the baffling mumbo-jumbo of nine throws we were out. Nine times did the American colossus turn his back on the battery, wheel about and let the ball go with the piercing speed of a bullet. Nine times did the Australian batters swing furiously at the ball and nine times did the ball go unmolested over the centre of the little white slab. Nine successive strikes, three batters out, side out!

The mobs howled their derision.

The Australians went to field, feeling all thumbs in their gloves. Cricketers who had never raised a nervous eyebrow before Test crowds of 60,000 felt wobbly in their pantalooned knees as baseballers. A high soaring hit went out to McCabe at centre field. For one frightening moment he looked as if he would fling the glove aside and catch with his bare hands. Remembering, quickly, that the game was the thing, he did not. He went for the 'fly' in approved style and mulled it. Transvaal a man on second base. Brown let a ball go between his legs, a frightful mull, Transvaal one on first and third. A smashing three-bagger and Transvaal had two home in the first five minutes of the game.

Richardson doffed his catching mask and came out to give his men a pep talk. Transvaal coaches on the side line, as baseball entitled them to do, said rude and personal things, very rude and very personal, about Australians in general. Our reserves, O'Reilly and Oldfield, who should have been filling smiliar coaching positions and combating this propaganda from the side-line, crept further from view under the scoring bench. In this they had the envy of their comrades on the field.

Transvaal got no more home that innings. We got none home in our next three. If truth will out in the face of discomfiture, we did not even get a batter to first base. Curse that mail-boat, we thought, for not running in time! Curse ourselves for asking to play this fool game!

Then happened the miracle. I must preface its description by referring again to the American battery. Sly winks and nods and mystic signs ran from one to the other like Neon signs on Broadway. This was aided and abetted by the catcher, who expressed rather strong and pungent opinions about Australians and their antecedents directly into the ear of the Australians.

He went just too far. To a 'strike' against Darling, he held the ball forward under the Australian's nose and said something like this: 'Saay, you horn-woggled son of a guy! Help yer'self to an eyeful of this lil' white pill. Saay, dat's what youse suppos' to hit, guy. Wassa matter wid youse Aussie lallapoloosas?'

Let no one say that what followed was not cricket. It was not cricket we were playing, and what Darling did was evidently good baseball tactics. He gave the Yankee a contemptuous look, leaned over and spat viriously on the ball.

That marked the turning point of the game. The very next ball Darling made a mighty soaring hit far out over the heads of the out-fielders. Amid tremendous enthusiasm, he sped round the whole circuit. Australia, one home. Spurred by this, O'Reilly and Oldfield crept cautiously out from beneath the scorer's table and ventured to the coaching positions on the side-line.

'Keep it up, lads, keep it up,' quietly called O'Reilly. 'We can do it again, we can do it again,' apologetically cooed Oldfield, and, though decidedly poor, and not at all meaty, this at least marked a barracking beginning for Australia.

Barnett showed that the Australians could certainly do it again. In approved baseball style he moved into the next ball from the American pitcher. A full-blooded swing kissed the ball fairly and squarely with the juiciest part of the club and away, away, higher and higher soared the ball until it was almost lost to sight.

'Shades of Babe Ruth!' said the American pitcher. 'By the torch of the lil' ole Statoo of Liberty, what a heck of a smite,' said the American catcher.

Barnett did not have to dash helter-skelter around the bases. The umpire signalled him an undisputed home run and he ambled sedately along the circuit, touching his cap to the unstinted roars of applause. Australia two home!

A thousand pities there were no runners on bases to capitalise further two such beautiful hits, but that was forgotten in the next few minutes when the baseball rabbits came up to bat. There was no shivering at the knees now. Each came forward with supreme confidence.

McCabe drove one sweetly through the covers for a two-bagger; Brown hooked one gloriously for another two-bagger; I hit one over what would have been the bowler's head for a three-bagger; Grimmett tapped one to the covers for a quick single – pardon, a first base – Richardson played a magnificent on-drive for a two-bagger, and Australians scurried round the bases like ants about a disturbed ant-hill.

On their coaching mounds O'Reilly and Oldfield reached new-found heights of baseball barracking-cum-coaching.

'What a sissy lot of ball players, who taught you mugs the game,' roared O'Reilly. 'You'll never get us out, never get us out: put on a new bowler,' chanted Oldfield. In the excitement O'Reilly ventured on the field of play and was hurriedly removed to his mound by the umpire.

I shall not dwell much longer on that game. The further it went, the greater the heights the Australians found and the lower went the Transvaalers.

The cause was not difficult to discover. Cricketers who had had their eye trained all the summer applied cricketing tactics to baseball. They fielded, threw and batted as if in a cricket game.

Only one mistake was made in the later stages, and that

through ignorance. Another skier went out to McCabe at centre-field. Remembering his last dropped catch, McCabe placed his whole body between the ball and the ground. Determination was written all over him and when he made the catch he delightedly, in cricket fashion, threw the ball happily up and indulged in a series of little catches – the while a Transvaal player on first base moved to home!

In the seventh innings the pride and glory of Transvaal baseball struck their colours. Disgraced and dishevelled, the American battery gave way to another combination. They felt themselves able to cope with anything baseball sent along, but cover shots, pulls, drives and other cricketing shots had them nonplussed.

The end justified all that had gone before. A soaring hit went out to left field in Transvaal's final innings. A little figure twisted and turned, manoeuvring to judge the catch. It was coach Grimmett. We held our breath as the ball began to come down. Transvaal had two on bases. If this catch was mulled they might yet snatch the game out of the fire.

Grimmett was not dismayed. He gave not a thought to all the coaching he had given the team; not a thought, even, to the ethics of the game. He ignored his gloved left hand, shot up a bare right hand and made the most sensational one-handed catch of the cricket, baseball or matrimonial season. The game was over. Australia had won 12–3.

Going off the field, a dispirited but sporting American battery shook Richardson warmly by the hand.

'Your guys,' said the broken-hearted catcher, 'have put the big ball game back at least ten years in this here burg.'

Delighted Transvaal cricket legislators pressed us to keep our Wanderers socks as a souvenir. We accepted gladly. Next day from Perth, Western Australia, came a 48-word cablegram at $1/8\frac{1}{2}$ a word asking us to play another baseball game there on the way east. We declined, as we did other invitations to play again in Cape Town. The Australian Eleven had played its first and last game of baseball. We knew enough about beginners' luck to recognise it when we saw it!

JACK FINGLETON, *Cricket Crisis*

England v The North American Winter

Frederick Lillywhite's 1859 English tourists arrived in the United States on the eve of a distracting Civil War. Certainly they seem to have got the American season a little wrong. On 24 October, at Rochester, General Winter was to strike with a vengeance, causing an ominous abandonment of cricket in favour of baseball

The Falls of Niagara were first seen by a white man 180 years ago. A charge of twenty-five cents is made as you enter the toll on the Island and each visitor has his name entered in a book, after which he is entitled to pass as often as he pleases during the year. The Terrapin Tower, 45 feet high, commands a magnificent view of Niagara, and there will be found, cut out, the names of nearly all the English cricketers. Having thus seen all that could be seen in the time allotted to us, we returned, per rail, to Rochester. The day was beautifully fine, and never will October the 23rd be forgotten by the Cricketers of England.

MONDAY, October 24, the match was resumed, but the weather was unmistakably cold. The score will show that on, TUESDAY, October 25, the match was brought to a conclusion in favour of England in one innings and 68 runs – thus winning all the matches played. This Twenty-two was a mixture of players of the States and Canada, many of whom had before met the Eleven in their previous contests. The match, therefore, was entitled 'Twenty-two of the United States and Canada'. Hayward and Carpenter again exhibited a good display of batting, as they had done in previous matches, and it will be seen that the slow bowling of Wisden was very destructive. The players had to field in muffs and greatcoats, and such was the cold they could scarcely feel the handle of the bat; or know whether they had fielded the ball or not; indeed, such cricketing weather had never before been experienced. It was really like playing a match in the depth of winter; and the batsman very appropriately exclaimed, when his wicket was lowered by a ball from Wisden's end – 'Shiver my timbers, I'm out.' The most agreeable innings on such a day could only be obtained indoors with a hot dinner before you, and a bottle of old Port to follow. We now append the score of this 'Frosty Match', but not without expressing the hope that we may never witness such another:

The remainder of the day was spent in a match at base-ball, which was got up with a view to lessen the severe loss of the promoters of the cricket match. Notwithstanding the severity of the weather, a goodly sprinkling of the lovers of the game attended to witness it.

According to good judges of the game present, the English cricketers played remarkably well, and Lockyer's playing 'behind the bat' could not have been surpassed.

FREDERICK LILLYWHITE, *Tour of America 1859*

CORRECT SCORE

From F. Lillywhite's Printing Tent of Lord's & Kennington Oval London.

At Rochester, US, Eleven of England v. Twenty-two of the United States and Canada, Friday, Monday, and Tuesday, October 21, 24 and 25, 1859.

Twenty-two	*First Innings*	
W. Hammond	c. Carpenter, b. Wisden	4
Sharp	st. Lockyer, b. Wisden	0
D. S. Booth	b. Wisden	1
Beatty	st. Lockyer, b. Wisden	2
H. Wright	b. Jackson	13
Capt. Hammond	run out	2
Capt. K. Hugesson	b. Wisden	2
Machattie	c. and b. Wisden	0
Pickering	run out	11
Stephenson	b. Wisden	0
J. Higham	st. Lockyer, b. Wisden	0
T. Senior	b. Jackson	1
A. Jackson	b. Wisden	0
Collis	b. Jackson	0
Tarrant	b. Wisden	0
Crossley	not out	3
Hines	b. Wisden	0

G. Tarrant	b. Wisden	0
H. Lillywhite	c. Carpenter, b. Wisden	0
Wm. Collis	b. Wisden	0
Hallis	c. Lockyer, b. Wisden	0
Pattison	c. Caesar, b. Wisden	0
		39

Second Innings

W. Hammond	b. Wisden	6
Sharp	b. Jackson	4
D. S. Booth	st. Lockyer, b. Jackson	0
Beatty	b. Wisden	0
H. Wright	b. Jackson	1
Capt. Hammond	c. and b. Wisden	0
Capt. K. Hugesson	b. Jackson	3
Machattie	st. Lockyer, b. Wisden	1
Pickering	not out	14
Stephenson	absent	0
J. Higham	c. Carpenter, b. Jackson	0
T. Senior	b. Wisden	8
A. Jackson	st. Lockyer, b. Wisden	0
Collis	st. Lockyer, b. Wisden	4
Tarrant	b. Wisden	2
Crossley	c. Carpenter, b. Wisden	0
Hines	b. Wisden	4
G. Tarrant	b. Jackson	2
H. Lillywhite	b. Wisden	0
Wm. Collis	absent	0
Hallis	c. Carpenter, b. Wisden	9
Pattison	c. Jackson, b. Wisden	0
Byes 1, Leg-byes 2, Wides 1		4
		62

Umpires, Mr W. Baker, of Ottawa, and Smith, of Utica.

| | First Innings | | | | Second Innings | | | |
	O	M	R	W	O	M	R	W
Wisden	72	7	17	16	89	4	43	13
Jackson	68	7	17	3	84	13	17	6

England	First Innings	
W. Caffyn	c. Hammond, b. Hallis	14
J. Jackson	run out	12
T. Hayward	c. Hallis, b. Crossley	50
R. Carpenter	c. Hines, b. Senior	18
J. Grundy	c. Higham, b. Pickering	8
T. Lockyer	c. Hallis, b. Wright	19
A. Diver	c. Hines, b. Machattie	6
John Lillywhite	b. Wright	4
J. Caesar	st. Higham, b. Machattie	11
J. Wisden	c. Lillywhite, b. Machattie	2
H. H. Stephenson	not out	1
Byes 6, Wides 20		26
		171

	O	M	R	W
Hallis	136	12	46	1
Sharp	8	0	16	0
Senior	68	8	17	1
Crossley	20	4	2	0
Pickering	48	3	21	1
H. Wright	48	2	35	3
Machattie	36	4	8	3

Americans Pioneer Inswing Bowling

'For one brief, shining moment' cricket flourished in Philadelphia, a kind of Camelot at the turn of the century amidst the baseball hordes. A distinguished English novelist, writing in The Cricketer, *went so far as to suggest that in the matter of inswing bowling, the Gentlemen of Philadelphia were well ahead of the English game*

Apart from the wickets, there seems no special reason why the modern attack shouldn't have come into action well before 1930. Inswing bowling isn't a new invention. J. B. King, the Philadelphian fast bowler, was proving how effective it could be as early as the turn of the century.

Incidentally, Mr Rowland Bowen is surely right in claiming that King was one of the greatest of bowlers. The evidence is overwhelming, from authorities such as Ranjitsinhji downwards. The Philadelphians had thought far more analytically about the game than their English counterparts were to do for a couple of generations. If anyone doubts that, he ought to read J. A. Lester's *History of Philadelphia Cricket*. Lester, who died recently in his 90s, had one of the best minds that ever applied itself to cricket. King, who also lived to nearly 90 (the Philadelphia team were a remarkably long-lived lot, and several are still alive) wrote an article for Lester's *History*, in which he describes how he taught himself to bowl his 'angler' (late inswinger). He had been a baseball pitcher and had learned much from that particular skill, which had been more highly developed than early twentieth century fast bowling.

It is rather odd, and something of a reproach to cricket intelligence, that English bowlers didn't latch onto his example.

C. P. SNOW, *The Cricketer*

Philadelphia's King

We invited an English journalist to interview the Father of Inswing on an astral telephone

Mr John Barton King, you were born before Sir Winston Churchill and some might say had made a greater impression than him by 1910 or thereabouts.

'You English can still make with the compliments. Fry, Ranjitsinhji, Warner, they all laid 'em on 80 years ago – Warner especially. He boosted Lockwood in print with the exact same words, you know – 'when the spirit moved him' and so on. Personally, I reckon he gushed like that 'cause MCC once scraped home against us thanks to him. Made him look better.'

You made a great impression on your three tours to this country. Is it true you were offered a rich widow's hand to play for one county?

'I don't know about rich. Would you call £7,000 a year rich? Sure, I was tempted, but Warner was more on the mark than that fella Fields when he called Philadelphia 'that pleasant and attractive city'. I liked the life and the cricket there: your county cricket was getting tougher – more professional, I guess you'd say now. There were paid English coaches in Philadelphia, but it didn't seem to affect the spirit.'

The inswinger – your 'angler' – was a speciality of yours. Did you foresee that we'd come to link it with the worst in negative cricket?

'It crossed my mind in the 20s, after I'd finished playing when I saw Fred Root of – where does the sauce come from?'

Worcestershire.

'That's right. But Fred was pretty quick and he still tried to get the batsman out. I can understand why they restricted the number of fielders on the leg side, but no amount of tampering with the laws will work if the players' attitude is wrong. When I was playing, you knew certain things 'weren't cricket'; what was cricket (or part of it) was striving to get the other side out at all times. Great bowlers still think that way: that guy Bedser may have swung the ball in, but he was after wickets, not maiden overs.'

You had pace too, of course.

'Thank you. Yep, I had pace. It was often the fast straight one – yorker if possible – that did for 'em. If you look at the photos, you'll see I was a handsome, athletic sort of guy. Held the ball above my head in two hands like O'Reilly, but looked a sight more elegant when I bowled the thing.'

Why didn't cricket grow in the States? The Gentlemen of Philadelphia beat English and Australian teams at home and abroad, so you must have made a splash there.

'Your cricketers toured the US before they went near Australia, but the Civil War cut us off for a few years and during the War baseball became accepted as a grown-ups' game – hardly cricket, though. You could play it just about anywhere, of course, which was a help during the chaos.

'Apart from that, I think the *New York Herald* had it right before our first tour of England in 1897, when they said cricket was "too slow for the average American". We had beautiful grounds which became like country clubs, with golf and tennis too. It seems Americans prefer the one-to-one clash of those games. St Louis had a lovely ground in mid-town once and later, in the 90s, Chicago had a pretty hot team. Pity the US cities didn't play each other more often.'

C. P. Snow reckoned the Philadelphians of your time were 'a couple of generations' ahead of us in cricket thinking.

'That's pitching it a bit strong. It was the Golden Age, after all: everyone was helping to develop the game. Like the South African googly boys, we were exotic. (My partner Percy Clark had the outswinger down pretty well: we learnt the trick at baseball.) Arthur Lilley, the Warwickshire keeper, even wrote that I could throw a cricket ball so that it rose again after starting to fall. We were Philadelphians, not Martians!'

On your last English tour in 1908, aged 35, you topped the national averages with 87 wickets at 11.01. Only Les Jackson in 1958 has improved on those figures since. How did you improve on even your high standards at that advanced age?

'Advanced age? Oh, early nights, plenty of fresh air – no, I just had a good basic method and I'd gotten craftier with the years. Like Lillee and Roberts now, I knew what I was about and still produced the fast one every now and then. I liked the right breeze or a bit of humidity, but I didn't need 'em.'

Are you happy with posterity's verdict?

'Yeah. We were forgotten for a while, but can't complain now. Take Derek Lodge, a figures man with a brain who can write a bit. I was first choice for his Rest of the World XI of those who never played Test cricket – he even considered me for the captaincy: can't ask for better than that.'

Finally, *is* it better being dead than in Philadelphia?

'No. The air's too thin: damned angler won't curve more than six inches.'

Bart King, thank you.

H. G. ROBINSON

Hollywood Beginnings

There were about 25 people present and they talked about forming a cricket club. Someone said, 'What about this Pratt fellow – he's supposed to be pretty good at cricket,' and someone else said, 'Is he suitable, do you think? He's working as a truck driver, after all, and with that face I'm not sure he's even English.' They were talking about William Pratt, who was just beginning to call himself Boris Karloff, and nobody realised he was in the room until somebody cleared their throat very loudly.

BILL FEEDER

Hopalong Hops

Thus was born Sir C. Aubrey Smith's Hollywood Cricket Club and a feature length string of good stories, true and apocryphal. A. A. Thomson's account of Hopalong Cassidy's recruitment into Hollywood cricket has been oft repeated; but it is well worth repeating again. Assuming it actually happened, can any cricket match have gone more wildly West?

One day Sir Aubrey's team were scheduled to meet a side from a visiting British cruiser and an acquaintance of mine had his name put down to play for the home side. Unhappily, just before the game was due to start he slipped and twisted his ankle. This was no riotous studio party; it happened on a slippery polished floor at a peaceful story conference, but the consequences and complications were just the same. He was so utterly scared of Sir Aubrey, who could be a merciless martinet, that he simply dared not confess to him what had happened. His only hope, he felt, was at all costs to produce a substitute. He therefore hobbled round Hollywood on the arm of a girl friend in a desperate search for some guy who could play this English game of cricket. Try as they might, the only man they could get hold of was the actor, William Boyd, the creator of Hopalong Cassidy, ten-gallon hat, top boots, cowboy's pony and all. Or so my friend told me.

Hopalong disclaimed the faintest notion of how to play cricket, but they assured him that it was a simple game, closely resembling baseball, only not so complicated, and at last they persuaded him to put on flannels, though, now I come to think of it, it may well have been a mistake not to suggest that he should take his spurs off first. Fortunately, when they reached the cricket ground, Sir Aubrey had already won the toss and decided to bat, so nobody had especially observed either the absence of the injured man or the identity of the substitute. My friend being a bowler, Hopalong was kept back to No. 9 in the batting order, and when he went rolling out to the wicket, all six feet three of him, he presented an imposing spectacle. There he stood at the crease, swinging his bat in one hand as though it were a policeman's truncheon. The umpire politely asked if he wanted centre.

'Start pitchin',' commanded Hopalong.

The first ball he missed; the second he missed; the third was a nice slow full toss on the leg side and from it he hit a towering skier away in the broad direction of long-on, possibly into Beverly Hills, and even, for all I know, into the Pacific Ocean. Suddenly, to the horror of all the Englishmen present, Hopalong went mad. Without a word he dashed across to point, from point to cover, from cover to mid-off, from mid-off round the astonished umpire to mid-on, from mid-on to square leg and then, without reflecting on his latter end, slid like a toboggan into his own wicket. There was as breathless a hush as ever fell on Newbolt's Close. Every true born Englishman waited in panic-stricken silence to hear what the outraged Sir Aubrey would say. Finally he exclaimed, 'Well, I declare!'

And, on reflection, that was the most useful thing he could have said.

A. A. THOMPSON, *Odd Men In*

Round the Corner – and in at the back door?

The great years of the Hollywood Cricket Club coincide with the ascendancy of English stars in Movie City. Talkies, while spelling ruin for many a Mid-Western drawl, had made the Oxford accent fashionable. For out-of-work American actors, Sir Aubrey's cricket club became a symbol of a somewhat menacing foreign power. Certainly this view conditions the following brief history of the Club

We are all aware of the threat to Western values averted by Senator Joseph McCarthy and the House Un-American Activities Committee some thirty years ago. Now the seeds of an older, equally sinister movement, planted some twenty years earlier, are coming to light.

At the centre was the deceptively amateur figure of C. Aubrey Smith. What was the real reason for his arrival in Hollywood in 1930, when this superficially eccentric Englishman was almost 70 years old? Certainly he carved out a good living as the stern, upstanding Englishman in a series of films, supporting the leading stars of the day, but his obsession lay elsewhere.

The shell of the Hollywood Cricket Club, foundering ten years after its inception, gave Smith his opportunity. He certainly put up a good front: permission was obtained to use part of the UCLA campus and later the C. Aubrey Smith Field was founded in Griffith Park, on land ceded by the City Fathers with the British Consul's encouragement. His real purpose, however, was the cultivation of a mysterious freemasonry.

The peculiar jargon of cricket provided ideal cover. Englishmen newly arrived in Hollywood received invitations to 'nets', almost certainly a form of initiation ceremony. Laurence Olivier was one such, but the activities of the group were clearly not to his taste, as he is thought to have played no more than once. Cricket matches were well suited to conspiracy, due to the absence of the wide community and an abundance of intervals and interruptions for conversation.

Though we can only guess at the Hollywood CC's clandestine activities, some indisputably shadowy individuals were involved, among them Errol Flynn and P. G. Wodehouse. Flynn's Nazi leanings and bisexuality have been revealed in a recent book and Smith clearly considered him a security risk, imposing a 10 p.m. curfew on a tour of British Columbia lest the local lumberjacks prove too great a temptation. (Flynn scored 14 the next day.) Despite the efforts of his apologists, Wodehouse's wartime activities remain dubious and he was certainly eager to assist Smith's efforts, taking the minutes at the first meeting under the latter and offering to purchase equipment. The humorist was also a frequent spectator.

Considering his patrician bearing, C. Aubrey Smith's conduct of the club was suspiciously egalitarian. The threateningly-named Boris Karloff was thought beyond the pale by some as he resorted to unskilled labour in the intervals of his sporadic film work, but this objection was promptly overruled: he and Smith then offered themselves for coaching. (Those who objected that Karloff's given name was William Pratt are missing the point: the choice of such a pseudonym is surely significant.) The first matches were even against teams consisting largely of British servants, and Smith, en route to a match in San Francisco, was once observed instructing a black roadworker (with the aid of the latter's shovel) how to hold a cricket bat – a rather desperate attempt to widen his influence, perhaps? He also introduced the first black player to the club.

The façade of English eccentricity was scrupulously preserved, being typified by C. Aubrey Smith's mansion in Coldwater Canyon. Called 'The Round Corner' in echo of this enigmatic man's nickname during his cricketing heyday, it had three stumps on its roof and a bat-and-ball weathervane. Regular Sunday tea parties here gave further opportunity for Hollywood CC members and their associates to plot undisturbed.

But what did they plot? The mystery remains to this day, but one thing is certain: the pursuit of a mere game could not have galvanised a man of Smith's age to such efforts, so that his secret society took firm root and the game of cricket retains a hold in the area to this day. Contact with foreign branches of the sect still occurs, if at a lower level. Where Sir Aubrey – his title has previously been omitted, in the light of what we know now – entertained the Australian national team in 1932, his widow received the Australian Old Collegians in 1959, on the occasion of their defeat by the South California Cricket Association.

Whatever vainglorious schemes of national or international domination were harboured by this extraordinary man, age clearly weakened his resolve, for when war came he failed to take advantage. Indeed, he organised games between British ships in harbour attended by the likes of Greer Garson and Olivia de Havilland.

Pockets of Aubrey Smith fanaticism remain, notably in the surviving Hollywood, Pasadena and Orange County Cricket Clubs. That fanaticism is not too strong a word was underlined by events during the riots in Watts, Los Angeles, in 1968, when cricket was played on schedule and without interruption throughout.

The nature of C. Aubrey Smith's hidden purpose remains a mystery, but it seems certain that for some years the fabric of United States society was under potentially very serious attack.

HIRAM G. ROBINSON

This is a letter written by David Niven to journalist Jilly Cooper after they had attempted (and almost failed) to meet for lunch. It didn't, as might have been hoped, produce a Hollywood cricket yarn; but it yielded a good cricket story all the same

25 Sept. '71

Dear nice, beautiful, friendly and giggly Jilly,
I'm very rude, but I was pissed when we parted and I never thanked you for a delicious luncheon. I *must* have been pissed if I let you pay!

Thank GOD you didn't come with me into the BBC. It

was a shambles. A nice prim lady interviewed me on Woman's Hour . . . an interview of unparalleled dreariness until she said: 'You mention the Hollywood Cricket Club in your book – do you have many happy memories of our National Game?'

Niven (smirking drunkenly) Oh *yes*!

Prim Lady And what was the happiest?

Niven Without question it was the time I saw Patsy Hendren at Lord's coming out to bat for Middlesex on a September afternoon. Halfway to the wicket he flung his bat in the air, let out a piercing shriek and disappeared at a brisk trot into the Pavilion!

Prim Lady Why did he do that?

Niven He had a sleeping wasp in his box.

Prim Lady (mystified) His box?

Niven Yes. That's a sort of aluminium single-seater bra which batsmen wear between their legs to protect their spare parts.

Prim Lady I see. Now let's talk about your two little girls. . . .

I *did* enjoy our luncheon so much. Let's do it again soon. Thanks, too, for all the sweet things you said about the book. I *dread* Publication Day . . . 12 Oct!!!

Off to Munich now to start a movie.

love, David

Cricket and Smog in California

Readers with longish memories will recall that at one time it was feared that a future England captain had been lost to cricket when the young J. M. Brearley took up his studies on the West Coast of the United States. We need not have worried. The future mastermind of Test victories was undergoing a tough apprenticeship in the smog of California. That is assuming that he is the mysterious Mr X

Having travelled approximately 6,000 miles from London to Los Angeles I found myself staying with a cricketer with a not inconsiderable reputation in England, whom I shall call Mr X. So it was that on a Sunday morning in August we climbed into an ancient Chevrolet and started purring along the amazing Californian Highways towards the north side of LA where Pasadena was due to test its cricketing strength against another local side. Mr X and I had been invited to play for Pasadena and we arrived at the ground at Griffith Park at 11.45 for a twelve o'clock start, having travelled a mere 55 miles in 65 minutes without exceeding the speed limit of 65 mph. The highways in this part of the world certainly are a masterpiece of engineering, especially where some half-dozen of them seem to merge at the same point. Then it is that they interweave at various heights on pillars of concrete, forming an astonishing and intricate pattern.

The ground was pleasantly placed with trees around it, a range of mountains in the distance, and horses carrying filmstar-looking females galloping along the nearby tracks. All the matches are played on one of two grounds and different sides take turns as the 'Home' team. This was our privilege today, so members of our team were busy pinning down matting on the pitch. By 12.45, Joey, our West Indian captain, announced that we had lost the toss, much to the disgust of a Chinese gentleman who had no desire to field in a temperature of ninety-five. He wasn't the only one. After two of the batting side had been persuaded to don umpires' coats, the match began with Joey bowling medium paced away-swingers from one end and Hyram B. Stellenbosch (a local name!) bowling slightly faster from the other. Two quick wickets fell and after forty minutes' play, with the score at 11 for 2, I was surprised to hear Joey announce that it was time for a 'water break'! We all trooped off for drinks from an ice box and as the temperature was now bordering on 100, the pause and the drinks were most welcome. These water breaks occurred periodically throughout the match and certainly could be looked on as an additional weapon for use by the fielding captain. In England we can only fall back on tea breaks or bonfires in adjacent allotments to provide distractions.

Scoring was slow. There was no pace in the wicket but, more important, the grass in the outfield was so thick that the only way to hit a boundary was to lift the ball almost for a six. The most powerful cover drive on the ground produced only one run so that an individual score of 30 or so was quite extraordinary. But the most astonishing thing about the afternoon was the SMOG. Most of us associate California with sunshine and beaches, film stars and bathing beauties, but LA certainly has one more claim to fame. Apparently, on some days, the mountains prevent the free movement of the air, and fumes from innumerable motor cars remain suspended in the atmosphere reducing the visibility and making the mere process of breathing an unpleasant and difficult operation. How the fast bowlers managed to continue I don't know, and for the batsmen to run a three was to invite death by suffocation.

Tea was at 3.30. Tables were laid out under the trees laden with sandwiches, cakes, tea and delicious pieces of melon and orange, and everyone gathered round informally. I found myself talking to our scorer, a lively gentleman 84 years old who recounted how he'd played his first game of cricket in the USA way back in 1921 and that he had been associated with the club ever since, playing his last match ten years ago. He had learnt his cricket in Bedfordshire.

We returned to fielding: the score crawled along; the temperature rose; the smog hurt one's chest. Would they never declare? Our bowlers were certainly too tired to get them out. Perhaps it was a mistake to play on the same side as a man with Mr X's reputation, although it was painfully obvious that the pitch and outfield would appreciatively reduce his stature. After more than four hours' play our opponents declared with the enormous score of 156 for 8 and as we were playing until 7.15 p.m. or 7.30 if there was a chance of a result, we were left with a maximum batting time of 1 hour 50 minutes. One felt there was an element of caution in the declaration. Considering the conditions our fielding had stood up well to the task, only one person having had to leave the field because the heat and smog had made him feel sick. Our cover point, Frank, was particularly noticeable for the accuracy, speed, and style of his throwing, not to mention his peaked cap. He was an ex-baseball player who had only recently taken up cricket and his returns would have done credit to Colin Bland!

Joey's next problem was to persuade two members of his team to open the innings and after the long and tiring fielding session, any volunteer would have the job. Wickets fell quickly, including that of the captain of the United States Cricket XI – a man from Bolton, Lancashire! – and I went to the wicket with the score at twenty-five for three. I left at twenty-five for four, having driven a ball hard and low in the direction of mid-off only to see a tall black gentleman clap two enormous hands together, having moved them vertically in opposite directions, engulf the leather ball as though it were a peanut, and leap into the air with pleasure. So much for catching techniques. Mr X proceeded to give a demonstration of the art of batting, but eight wickets had fallen at the other end when Joey went in to bat at ten past seven. By this time two of our side were umpiring and when at 7.14 an over was about to start, Joey edged up to one of the umpires and whispered through the side of his mouth in his West Indian drawl, 'If dey haven't claimed de extra time befoah 7.15 yo sure must pull up de stumps at de end of dis over!' So when the over came to an end, off walked Joey, up came the stumps, accompanied by frantic protestations from the opposition, who felt they were being robbed of victory. Long and heated arguments followed but Joey was adamant, and the final statement by the opposition captain – 'It's only a game and it doesn't matter who wins' – fell on incredulous ears after such a sporting declaration! Our final score was 76 for 8!

By the end of the match the sun had set, the smog had cleared, it was no longer unbearably hot and the mountains were at last revealed in all their beauty. After a few iced beers, the conditions of the afternoon and the quarrels of the evening were soon forgotten, and, as so often happens after cricket, friendships blossomed, colour and race were of no importance, and everyone departed happier for the day's exercise. In retrospect it was perhaps one of the most interesting games of cricket I have ever played in – although

12,000 miles is rather a long way to go to field for four hours and then get a duck!

H. BREARLEY, *The Cricketer*

US v AUS

The Pacific War may have represented the last chance to convert Americans to cricket on a sizeable scale. As the Japs neared Darwin, thousands of US troops were poured into Australia. Inevitably a cricket challenge was thrown down with, perhaps, inevitable results

During the war of 1939–45 we Australian cricketers played the game as best we could, where we could and sometimes against unlikely opponents. For members of the AIF (Australian Imperial Force) this meant games on desert, rough ground and even on long grass in jungle clearings on the Pacific islands.

Tens of thousands of American servicemen were in Australia for the Pacific campaigns and on one occasion, in Brisbane, the American Army challenged us to a game of cricket. They had been studying it, they said, and it didn't seem very different from baseball; a good eye was apparently the one essential.

I captained the AIF team and the match took place at the Gabba, the famous Test ground, late in 1943. The Americans batted first and I opened the bowling with leg-spin, with the keeper standing right up. Their opener made fearsome swipes at the first five balls and missed each time. He was obviously tense, his partner at the other end was saying irritably, 'For Chrissake Harvey, why don't you *hit* it?' and the keeper was expectant.

I bowled the sixth ball. So much happened within a few seconds that it was difficult even then to be clear about the sequence of events, and looking back I am still not sure. It was something like this. The Yank stepped aside and swiped ferociously. He connected and skied the ball directly over the keeper's head. Then he threw down his bat, baseball style, and began to race along the pitch screaming, 'Goddam, I hit it Marvin! I hit it!' The flying bat knocked a stump and sent it sideways. The keeper, normally a phlegmatic man but now excited by the Americans' tension, caught the ball just above the stumps, though as he said later he was not sure if it had come off bat, pad or boot. Seeing the batsman out of his crease he wrenched up a stump for good measure.

The keeper and I appealed; the rest of the team were staggering or lying about the field in uncontrollable laughter. Up went the umpire's finger, but nobody was sure for what precise reason. Back at the pavilion we looked at 'how out'. The scorer had at first put *bowled Laffin, caught Cartwright* (the keeper); this had been half rubbed out and replaced with *bowled Laffin stumped Cartwright*; and this in turn had become *hit wicket*. There was even a school of thought which held that in fact the Yank had been run out since he had long since completed the stroke which could have led to his being stumped.

I turned to the umpire, 'Well, how *was* he out?'

'Multiple suicide,' he said.

The match itself was a bit like multiple suicide. Those Americans really did have good eyes and when they connected the ball travelled high and far. Most of them hit at least one six and all of them fell to spin.

Unable to get the hang of bowling, they consistently threw – they just couldn't help it – so we legalised throwing for the duration of the match, provided the ball hit the ground first. On that hard Gabba surface it really climbed sharply. When I shook hands with the Yank skipper after our victory he said, 'Your win, Aussie, fair and square. How would you like to take us on at baseball?'

We did – but that's another story.

JOHN LAFFIN

Alan Duff, a former Oxford blue and Worcestershire player, is now a house master at Malvern. He is still remembered, with fear and trembling, by some of his contemporaries at Radley, where he got into the first eleven at the age of fourteen and at the height of 4' 11". He was (and still is) that very rare thing, a leg-break

*bowler. His diminutive deliveries struck terror into the
hearts of all who faced him. Here he describes a robust
MCC tour to Canada and the USA under the leader-
ship of Dennis Silk (now warden at Radley) in 1967*

My longest MCC tour was to Canada and the USA with
Dennis Silk's side in the summer of 1967. It was on the
previous tour that the present secretary of MCC, on seeing
the enormous advertisement on arrival 'Drink Canada Dry',
said 'We will have a jolly good try'. This was another
fascinating trip, playing first in the regional tournament in
Ottawa and a Test Match there and then going right across
the prairies on the Trans-Canada Railway fortified by a
large supply of 'Plumtrees' diplomatic gin. This took several
days and involved stops at Winnipeg, Regina and Saskatch-
ewan – and a special stop at some halt as we had drunk the
train out of tonics! The line through the Rockies was
breathtaking. Then to arrive at Vancouver and play British
Columbia at Brockton Point in Stanley Park – the ground
described by Donald Bradman as the most beautiful he had
ever played on – was an experience hard to beat, with ships
sailing past in the harbour and the mountains as an im-
pressive backdrop.

The most extraordinary place we played here was on
Vancouver Island – if ever the British Empire has stood still
it is here. The male spectators were largely in boaters –
ponies and traps abounded and the ladies were all in dresses
associated with a Victorian vicarage tea party and certainly
all seemed to be ex-members of Cheltenham Ladies'
College or Roedean. It was here too that Everton Weekes
uttered one of his memorable comments – which can never
be put into print. He had had a wonderful tour. Even at
forty-plus he was still a marvellous player and had also kept
wicket with distinction. He had also been in his element
because a large proportion of our oppositions had been
West Indian immigrants and he had been one of their
boyhood heroes. By this stage of the trip he had taken a
fancy to my Oxford sweater and was seldom seen without it.
This brought forth from one of the boatered figures the
polite enquiry, 'I say, Weekes – when were you up?' – which

got a prompt reply plus a lot of diplomatic clearing up from the rest of us.

We flew back to Quebec then down to Washington – where the ground is on the main flight path for Dulles Airport – and up to New York. Two games in New York spring to mind. The first was on the charming ground on Staten Island against good opposition, when Chris Saunders, our first wicket-keeper, who had been a tremendous tourist in every way, was finally 'brought down', initially by taking fright at the length of the run-up of Wes Hall's brother who appeared to approach from near the Statue of Liberty. Then, when the game was getting tight he caught two catches behind off the last two balls of one over and then stumped someone off the first ball of the next – all emphatically out and equally emphatically given 'not out' – after the next ball he swept all three stumps down even though the batsman had not left his ground – turned to the umpire and said 'Put those up, it's your job!'

The second match must have been one of the most bizarre that the MCC have ever undertaken – against the West Indian League of New York in Red Hook Stadium, Brooklyn, an 'all black' stadium used for baseball, American football and athletics. The MCC flag flew from the top of the football posts – the wicket was a mat stretched out on a not very even bare patch in the middle and the opposition included several who had played Shell Shield cricket in the recent past. The MCC batted. The captain, Silk, made 17 – one of the best innings he reckoned he had ever played – Everton Weekes made 34 and rated it among his very best and worth far more than the 300 in a day that he had made at Fenners at Cambridge – an occasion when another of his great dicta was heard. On playing and missing outside the off stump at 294 he was heard by the wicket-keeper to mutter to himself, 'Everton boy, never never cut in the two hundred and nineties!' I made the most pleasing 12 I have ever played, including one four which bounced over the long-jump pit, hopped the inside of the running track and got across the circles to hit the stadium wall. All were in the field of play. We amassed about 140 and Alan Moss then proved virtually unplayable – locating the stones under the mat with unerring accuracy, he was terrifying at quite a pace. Colin Blades, ex-Barbados and captain of the Bermuda XI in the 1982 mini world cup, was hit several fearful blows and finished with 6 for 12 bowled the opposition out for about 60.

Another remarkable tour with many happy memories of friendships made and excellent cricket played.

ALAN DUFF

Bowling Down to Rio

MCC in South America – 1926

South America is fertile ground for cricket stories. Sir Pelham Warner's account of the MCC tour in 1926 taken from his book Cricket Between Two Wars *is a classic of its kind. The image of Captain Parker of the* Andes *flying the MCC flag from the yardarm as the ship sailed into Montevideo harbour is truly splendid*

At the beginning of the summer of 1926 the MCC accepted the invitation of the Argentine Cricket Association to send a team to the Argentine, matches at Montevideo, Valparaiso and Lima being subsequently arranged, the tour from start to finish involving two long sea-voyages, one, from Southampton to Buenos Aires, of 6,000 miles, and the other, from Valparaiso, via the Panama Canal, to Plymouth of 9,000 miles, while the distance covered by railway totalled quite 3,000 miles. Surely no cricket team ever saw so many cities and men in the course of three months.

The tour was unique in that not a single game was played within the British Empire – another proof that cricket has set a girdle round the earth, and that it has become the interest not only of the British race, but of half the world. Never before had an English cricket team crossed the mighty Andes. From Montevideo on the Atlantic to Lima on the Pacific the MCC flag was seen, and it was remarked by Sir Hilary Leng in his speech at the dinner given to the team at the Jockey Club at Buenos Aires that we were not only ambassadors of cricket, but of Empire.

How came it that I, whose cricketing days were long past, was invited to command so interesting and delightful an expedition? I had not played in a first-class match since 1920, and in recent years my appearances on the cricket field had been limited to an occasional game of minor importance. Maybe I owed my place to the fact that after bowling to me in the nets at Lord's the late W. Brearley, the famous old England and Lancashire bowler, informed the authorities that I was 'still good for a few runs'.

Never did I enjoy a cricket tour more, and never have I travelled with a more charming lot of men; and I, who have sailed the Seven Seas, and have played cricket from Lord's to Invercargill, and from Colombo to San Francisco, consider myself extraordinarily fortunate to have been given the opportunity of seeing so much of the world together with such delightful companions.

It was on December 3, 1926, that we sailed in the *Andes* of the Royal Mail Line. Who will forget 'the Crocodile Pool' – the huge canvas bath on deck – in which Weigall was wont to disport himself, like that great leviathan, to the consternation of some of the gentler 'crocodiles', or 'Bellina' going over the side at Rio like an admiral leaving his flagship, or the fancy-dress ball, or 'Jellicoe', the splendid quartermaster, or the gymnastic instructor, a fine type of the British Navy? And what places of interest we saw!

And so, by easy stages, for the coal, owing to the general strike of 1926, was bad, we came to Montevideo, which from now onwards will always be associated in the minds of Englishmen with the gallant and successful action by HM ships *Ajax*, *Exeter* and *Achilles* against the *Admiral Graf Spee*.

It was at Montevideo on December 24 that we began the first match of the tour. As we steamed into the harbour, Captain Parker paid us the unique honour of flying the MCC flag at the yardarm, a compliment repeated subsequently at Callao, the port of Lima, by Captain Splatt, of the *Orita*. Never before had a cricket flag been hoisted on any ship on any sea.

From Montevideo to Lima we were received with a spontaneous and, indeed, affectionate hospitality. We were made members of all the clubs, even the exclusive Jockey Club of Buenos Aires, with its magnificent house, marble staircase, priceless pictures, open-air restaurant, library, squash courts, swimming and Turkish baths. We had free passes over the railways, and special trains of the most luxurious type carried us to Concordia, to Rosario, to Mar del Plata, the Trouville of the Argentine, with its superb sea-bathing, golf links and casino. We were given the freedom of the country; we were treated like Royalty.

Who will forget Hurlingham, that Paradise of a Country Club – or the dance there on New Year's Eve – tell it not in Gath, publish it not in Askalon – in the middle of the first Argentine match, or the dinner to Sir Malcolm Robertson, the British Minister to the Argentine; or the excellent Belgrano ground; or 'Jacko-Hobbo', the dressing-room attendant in the pavilion, a prince of couriers, a Chesterfield in manners, ever ready with 'whisky soda' or 'gin tonico' to quench the thirst which so easily arises in that scorching and often damp heat?

In Buenos Aires we had the privilege of being received by Dr Alvear, President of the Argentine Republic. We were presented to him by Mr Robin Stuart, the President of the Argentine Cricket Association, who acted as interpreter, for Dr Alvear speaks very little English. Subsequently the President honoured the match at Hurlingham with his presence, as did Señor Legula, the President of Peru, when we visited Lima, a compliment to our national game.

But wherever we went it was the same story – open-handed hospitality and a rare and charming kindness – and an interest in our doings reflected by the long and excellent description of the match in *La Nacion*, one of the world's greatest newspapers, and *La Prensa*. No lapse of time, no future happenings, can obliterate the memory of a perfectly happy three months.

Rio, the Trans-Andean Railway and the Panama Canal may, probably, be included amongst the wonders of the world, to which I would add a fourth – the guano birds off the Peruvian coast. No guardsman, no Sandhurst cadet, was ever more adept at drill. There were literally thousands of them. At one moment they would come sweeping past the ship in diamond formation, then swing into line, then in line ahead, and then in three lines with an interval between each bird of, say, a yard, and an interval between lines of, perhaps, 50 yards.

The journey from Buenos Aires over the Andes to

Valparaiso took nearly forty hours, and it was pleasant to meet with deliciously cool weather after the trying heat of the Argentine. Valparaiso, indeed, possesses an ideal climate, and our stay there was all too short. We were put up in private houses of the nicest and most hospitable hosts, and on the last night there was a ball in our honour at the Vina del Mar Club, where we danced in a flower-embowered pergola to the strains of a Santiago band on a black and white tiled floor beneath a waning moon and twinkling stars – a wonderful setting.

Next morning we set sail, and proceeded up the coast, stopping at port after port and bathing at several places in the surf, being landed at Mollendo in a chair attached by a wire rope to a crane, so heavy ran the sea.

Fog delayed us, and the match at Lima was played on February 6 instead of February 5 as originally arranged. Lima is but twenty minutes by motor-car from Callao, and at the delightful Country Club we found a warm welcome awaiting us. We saw something of 'The City of the Kings' and paid a visit to the Cathedral, built by the mighty Conquistador, Francisco Pizarro, whose bones are to be seen within a glass-covered coffin. He was murdered in 1542 in front of the Cathedral, making the sign of the Cross with his blood. He was great, but in a cruel age he was a cruel man.

The Panama Canal was all that we had expected and more – a monument of engineering and genius and medical science. What struck one most was the entire absence of noise and fuss in moving the ship through the locks, and perfect indeed must be the staff work. Everything along the Canal was clean and neat to a degree – from the golf links on our port side to the gardens of the houses and bungalows, while the roads looked splendid. This characteristic neatness and cleanliness is everywhere apparent, from Panama to Colon. As we were passing through the Gatun lock we noticed a cricket match in progress about 300 yards away between teams of West Indian natives who, as the *Orita* moved on, waved their caps and cheered us. In the evening as we were going on board the *Orita* at Colon we found a deputation awaiting us on the wharf, and we had a long and enthusiastic talk on cricket with these West Indians. They informed us that there were seven cricket clubs in Panama and nine in Colon, all composed of West Indian natives who are employed in the Canal Zone work of one kind or another. I presented them with a bat and congratulated them on the splendid manner in which they were keeping the flag of cricket flying in the Panama Zone. There is no more devoted lover of cricket in the whole world than the West Indian native, and meeting these men brought back memories of my boyhood days when I used to bat in my nightshirt to a black bowler on a marble gallery, and, later, of my visit to the West Indies with Lord Hawke – the first, and never forgotten, of my tours abroad. Thus, across the Caribbean, the cradle of the Naval Empire of Great Britain, where our great heroes of the sea, Drake and Hawkins, Frobisher and Hood, Hawke and Rodney, Anson and Nelson, sailed and fought, we arrived at Havana, a city set in delightful surroundings, but the most expensive place I have ever visited. Corunna, Santander and La Rochelle were our next stopping-places, and on March 5 we arrived at Plymouth and a memorable tour was over.

As for cricket itself, we played 10 matches, won 6, drew 3 and lost 1. There were four games v. Argentina – the first was drawn, the second we won by 127 runs, we lost the third by 29 runs, and the fourth we won by an innings and 2 runs, J. C. White taking the last wicket, clean bowled, with the third ball of the final over of the match.

The MCC team was: Captain T. O. Jameson, M. F. S. Jewell, Captain R. T. Stanyforth, G. O. Allen, G. J. V. Weigall, G. R. Jackson, Captain L. C. R. Isherwood, J. C. White, Lord Dunglass, H. P. Miles, T. A. Pilkington and myself, with Captain C. Levick as Manager, the most unselfish of men, who not only did everything for our comfort, but also acted as banker. He had quite a lot of money out on loan, but within a week of our return every penny had been paid him, which speaks well for the credit and honesty of cricketers. On my return to England the team gave me a dinner, which afforded Tommy Jameson the opportunity to exhibit his wonderful collection of photographs, the one which earned the greatest applause being that of Gerry Weigall, *au naturel* on the beach at Antofagasta. He looked like some prehistoric monster, and Tommy was urged to send it to the British Museum with a label attached: 'Found on the beach at Antofagasta, AD 1927. Believed to be a cricketer, circa BC 100.'

Sir PELHAM WARNER, *Cricket Between Two Wars*

Lewis in Argentina

Tony Lewis, the first Welshman to captain an England XI, writes about another MCC tour to South America, this one in 1964. His account is followed by another of the same tour seen through different eyes – in this case those of Alan Duff

'Eez nine hun'red keelos, senor: seez hun'red miless,' announced the lead driver. January 1964. Thirteen cricketers in navy blazers with the white MCC monogram on the breast pocket climbed aboard three Ford country wagons. This was Buenos Aires. We were popping up the road towards the Andes for an afternoon match against the Northern Camps at Venado Tuerto.

There was jokey conversation at first. ' 'Bye, darling. First away match of the season. See you next year.'

The laughter was muted by a comment from a second driver who kicked up dry dust on his way into the small group. 'Eez rough highway. Dangerous: mucho.' He pointed to a large shining grill mounted in front of the radiator. 'But we have cowcatcher for zee wild animals. Also ze weelz are high to keep away ze snakes and ze baboons. I hate ze rats most.'

Only those who had played a match against Glamorgan at Ebbw Vale up in the Monmouthshire valleys would have had previous experience of cricket merging so closely with the animal kingdom. Ebbw Vale sheep take their audience participation seriously. They do a lot of appealing from third man and fine leg, unsporting, prolonged appeals when they can hardly claim to be in line with the wickets.

The sun leapt up on top of the morning and sizzled. Off

came the MCC blazers, and ties and shirts and socks and shoes and at last, after an hour, we persuaded the drivers to stop where they thought we might buy a drink.

As the Fanta orange rushed down the throat the jokes began again. Alan Duff, who had ridden with his trousers rolled up and most of his body balanced out of the open-sided vehicle, was said to be riding shotgun. There were Roy Rogers fantasies; puerile humour, but the heat and the outback were having their mystical effects. Then Duff decided to replace his long trousers with short ones.

He was doing that modestly when we were suddenly surrounded by three swarthy men with badges and guns. 'Show ze bare flesh and go to ze jailhouse.' There was more puerile tittering until it was obvious that this was no joke. 'Not in zees coun'ry.'

Duff splattered them with an ever so polite Oxbridge apology while flashing from shorts back into longs again. Shirts were on, sleeves buttoned down and the gallant MCC, with stiff but sweaty upper lip, did the next four hours through Arrecifes, Pergamino and Colon to Venado Tuerto in full battledress.

We arrived on the film set of a million movies. Venado Tuerto, centre of cattle country, was one wide unmade track with horses tethered lazily to rails on either side. Gauchos waddled in their leathers along wooden sidewalks, tilting their wide-brimmed hats, chewing. The general stores were busy, the saloon doors swung open once, cattle were on the move at the top end of the town. It was fiendishly hot. A man in a suit was waving us down.

MCC novices were depressed, you could see. The more experienced relaxed, knowing that wherever in the world cricket takes you the old Empire is there, tucked away in some decorous corner. Where was this Empire? We are being led to it. A small insignificant door on the main street. The British Club. Home at last.

From behind the small corner bar came the smile and the handshake from the man with the handlebar moustache. 'Great, chaps. You've made it. We were worried. It's been ten years since the last lot came through. But it's been worth waiting. What'll it be, G and Ts all round?'

The local expatriate cricket kit was lying in a corner. The pads were of faded yellow buckskin. The wicket-keeper's pair had ancient flaps on the outsides, all the better for kneeing the fast return onto the stumps. Len Hutton's autograph was on the bats and the gloves. They were brown sausage-finger gloves – four fingers go in first and then you wind the thumb which is attached by a length of elastic, around your wrist before putting it in position.

The game was played that afternoon in white heat on a polo field. There were deep hoof-marks all over the pitch. Fast bowlers could not bowl because it was dangerous. MCC scored 252 batting first. However, the big crowd arrived later on when the Camps were compiling a lively 172. Cowhands rode up on horseback, settled themselves around the boundary with gallons of local gin and treated themselves to a swig of gin for every run.

For MCC, Ian Bedford, formerly captain of Middlesex, and the school master David Mordaunt, who had played for Sussex, both got half-centuries. The tricky little leg-spinner, fully clothed, Duff, took 7 wickets for 36.

We stayed overnight and on the trip back out came the tales of hospitality. Richard Jefferson and Alan Duff had been riding the range at daybreak, rounding up steers on horseback on some vast estancia.

For my part I can think of nothing more astonishing than a conversation with my host, Mr McKay. Alan Smith, Warwickshire and England wicket-keeper, and I were staying in the magnificent farm estate of McKay, an exiled Scotsman. He lived alone and had not been back to Britain for twenty-five years. This meant that he had been cut off from his great love, the game of cricket.

We dined, McKay, Smith, Lewis. The domestic staff retired; talk drifted into the early morning. We teased our host, saying that the Second World War was over, that England had won back the Ashes in 1953 and had he heard of Peter May?

Suddenly old McKay slammed his hand down on the table and turned on Alan Smith. 'It's nay good, Smith. I've got to come out with it. You, keeping wicket for Warwickshire. Why the hell do you stand back to a trifling medium pacer like Cartwright?'

A. R. Lewis

A Duff's Eye View

My first long MCC tour was to South America in 1964–5 under Alan Smith. One or two stories spring to mind from this; the whole saga could fill a book. Our first stop was at Rio where we stayed at a magnificent hotel overlooking Copacabana beach. We played Brazil at Nitteroi which is on the other side of the harbour but some thirty miles distant if you have to go by road – so we went by ferry. Richard Jefferson (Cambridge and Surrey) and I got up early one morning to go up the Sugar Loaf in the bay to view one of the most breathtaking sights in the world. The only way up or down is by cable car and we got stuck on the top. There was no way of getting down and by the time we had summoned up our Portuguese and made it to the base the ferry had left. We managed to get another ferry and a taxi and got to the ground some twenty minutes before the start – but were severely disciplined (dropped for one match) and quite rightly as there was only one rule: 'You will be where you are supposed to be – when you are supposed to be'. We felt exceedingly clever at getting there at all, but if this rule is not adhered to any minor tour is bound to become chaotic. My best 'Test' figures came in the next match – 6 for 10 in São Paulo!

From Brazil we went to Chile, and played here at a splendid little ground at Vina del Mar, the port for Santiago. It is on the edge of the racecourse and there is a notice in the pavilion that no play is to take place while a race is in progress. Apparently on some earlier occasion the jockey of a horse leading by several lengths had been knocked off by a six hit out of the ground. The way David Mordaunt (Sussex) batted that day no jockey would have been safe. There were also old photographs here of a previous MCC team of 1926–7, including Sir Alec Douglas Home among other famous names.

We moved from Vina del Mar to the Prince of Wales Country Club in Santiago itself – a quite beautiful setting in which to challenge Chile! My chief memory here is of an old Australian appearing to watch – he had not seen a cricket match for some fifty years or more.

'England batting?' he enquired. 'Do you still use that Arthur Shrewsbury autograph bat?'

Richard Hutton asked whether he had by any chance heard of one Len Hutton – but he hadn't and was quite unimpressed!

From Chile we moved to the Argentine where in Buenos Aires the league standard was quite high and not too dissimilar from some English leagues. Some of the grounds too were fabulous. We played on grass rather than matting as elsewhere it would have been hard to better the pitch at Belgrano or the beauty of the Hurlingham Club where we stayed and also played. The hospitality was first rate – too much for my room mate Tony Lewis on one occasion! – but the match of which I remember most – or least – was when we moved some 100 miles up country to play at Venardo Tuerto on the estaucias. After rounding up the steers in the morning on horseback we had an unusual and most enormous lunch of steaks and gin (4s. a bottle) and the team were ill equipped to face the rigours of the pitch on the polo ground. It was probably the first time members of the MCC batted in helmets (planters' helmets), which were about the coolest thing you could wear in that heat – temperatures were often over 100 and the high cork hat is remarkably cool. Mine I remember not being of much use when I was struck in the Adams apple first ball by one that reared out of a hoof-mark on a length!

The whole six weeks was a most remarkable experience but I believe that, sadly, less cricket is played out there now.

ALAN DUFF

Cricket in the Interior of Brazil

Marie L. Young gives an intriguing description of cricket as played in the interior of Brazil and a memorable account of the hijacking of a piano to enable the players to have an after-match sing-song

In Barretos, in the interior of the state of São Paulo, the 'Camps' versus 'Frigorifico' cricket match is the event of the year, 'Camps' being the farmers who work on the outlying *Fazendas* and 'Frigorifico' the factory workers who can all the corned beef, etc., which eventually reaches England. As so many of the 'Camps' people live on farms in different states, it is a Sabbath day's journey to get a team together. However, they are all offered accommodation over the weekend, and invariably arrive with wives and children, all prepared to enjoy themselves and sample the roasted oxen which are invariably barbecued for the occasion.

During these matches, the ladies sit in deck chairs watching and making rude comments, and I can remember one occasion when our remarks reached the ears of the cricket captain, who promptly issued a challenge to us. We had, apparently, said that we could have played a better game, so the captain thought he would like to see us try.

So at a convenient date, all we ladies arrived to challenge the men, who were only allowed to play with their left hands. None of us knew the difference between an l.b.w. and a 'maiden over' and when I was sent to 'silly mid-off', I honestly thought I was being told to b . . . . . off! However, I did manage one catch, and then it came my turn to bowl. I had never tried before, so just threw the ball towards the cricket captain, who was batting at the time. Wow! There was a gasp, then a murmur of applause, I had hit the stumps! And that was my moment of glory. We lost the match and when I finally batted, I was out first ball!

On another occasion, the 'Camps' arranged a return match against a club called 'Saquerembo', the latter being a group of residents from that area of São Paulo city. The 'Camps' cricket captain was then working at a remote farm called Guariroba which was near a village called Formiga (meaning 'Ant'). The latter place's claim to fame was its cemetery with the dedication at the entrance, 'Aqui nos estamos, vôces esperamos', which broadly speaking means 'We're here and we're waiting for you to come and join us'!

My husband was asked to play in this match at Guariroba, and three ladies were asked to come and act as hostesses, so I found myself in company with Betty Rodger and Yvonne Brownrigg. The match was played on a bumpy field quite near the house, and after tea we all prepared to enjoy the evening.

Of course, the cricketers all wanted a sing-song, but where could we find the accompaniment? I could play the piano, but Derek, the captain, did not possess one. There was, however, an Italian fellow organising the farm machinery and we remembered that his wife had a battered piano in her home. Well, it was a case of taking 'Mohammed to the mountain' as the next I knew, the farm tractor had gone from the garage and the driver was coming from the Italian's house with the piano on the trailer behind. So I spent that starry night sitting on the back of a trailer playing 'cricket' and 'rugger' songs till the early hours.

So whilst I may never be an Ian Botham or a Semprini, I feel that I have kept the spirit of the Lord's Cricket Ground alive in the far-flung corners of the earth!

MARIE L. YOUNG

Cricket in Venezuela

In this account of cricket in Venezuela the author points out, among other things, that one of the joys of cricket in Caracas is that the weather is so good that the season lasts all year, a prospect even the keenest cricketer might find rather daunting

In all my time there, the Venezuelans never got to understand 'tea'. The players brought sandwiches and cakes but it was left to one of the Venezuelans employed by the Sports Club to make tea. He always had to be told to put the heater on for the water, how many tea bags to put in and so on.

However, some of our normal British habits were different there as well.

One would not normally expect pickle to generate a great deal of excitement. Unfortunately, its non-availability in South America caused the six jars brought into the country in the holiday suitcase to be carefully hoarded in the larder at home, never to be divulged to guests or visitors. The delight on the face of one of the players one Sunday could therefore be imagined as he bit into a cheese and pickle sandwich off the tea table. Similarly one could also imagine the anguish as realisation set in. This was his precious pickle being used to feed the assembled group of flannelled fools when it could have been providing him with many a clandestine snack away from the gaze of any prospective gourmet. Perhaps our ways are just as incomprehensible as those of the Venezuelans.

After the game, incidents were discussed in much the same way as in any English clubhouse. Even in a friendly, feelings could run high. It was way down the legside, could never have been out. Why was the declaration not earlier? If only he had got on with it.

Every year a match was played against the Bogotá Sports Club from Colombia and against Curaçao. These were played on a reciprocal basis and so even our local away matches involved an airline flight!

Bogotá also had a lovely ground. Their pitch was on matting laid over sand treated with oil. The ball used to turn a lot. We always had enjoyable and memorable games with Bogotá, mixing a weekend of cricket with a hectic social life of parties. I can well remember waiting for the arrival of Bogotá one year. It was on our anniversary and they were due at 8.45 p.m. We waited in the Sports Club Bar. Due to a burn-out on take-off of an Avianca 747, they arrived at three in the morning. My wife did not really think playing darts for five hours was her idea of an anniversary treat. The Bogotá team was again generally expatriate but contained a number of naturalised Colombians and the occasional Indian.

Curaçao, a Dutch island off the coast of Venezuela, was basically an oil refinery and oil terminal. It had four languages, Spanish, Dutch, English and Papiamiento, a mixture of all the others. We played on a matting wicket, and there was not a blade of grass on the whole field. As it rarely rained on the island, the outfield was a little dusty and rather quick. If it went past you it was four. Social activities were as important as the cricket and receptions were always generously given. Unfortunately, the decreasing significance of Curaçao as a refinery has led to a decrease in expatriate activity and a consequent falling off in cricket standards.

Undoubtedly, the highlights of the cricketing calendar for the Caracas Sports Club team were our international tours. One year we played Bogotá one weekend, Lima, Peru, the next and in between a visit to Cuzco and Machu Picchu. Another year it was Bogotá and Mexico City, with the Yucatan peninsula in between. The Lima Cricket Club play on grass, a great deal of grass. It never rains in Lima and so every now and again they flood their pitch in order to keep the grass alive. Not the easiest way to keep a fast wicket.

Lima's club is also based on an expatriate community. They have a lovely ground in a delightful setting and are a most hospitable group of enthusiasts. Playing a weekend there and visiting the incredible ruins of the Inca shrine of Machu Picchu has been one of the highlights of my life.

Mexico City Cricket Club are equally enthusiastic. They are the best organised of the Latin American clubs, playing on a grass wicket prepared by Lord's-trained groundsmen. A weekly fixture during the season, printed fixture lists and a club tie of a cricketing Aztec are symbols of the enthusiasm of many members of the Mexico Club.

Entering Mexico perhaps provided me with my most worrying moment as a cricketer. We had played in Bogotá over the weekend and caught a Monday evening flight to Mexico. Now Colombia is the drugs capital of the Americas. Doctors have been known to operate on their children, fill their stomachs with bags of heroin, and take them to the United States in order to make the millions of dollars available to the drug smuggler. So the gleam in the customs official's eye was almost blinding as I put the cricket bag containing two new balls, eight pads, gloves etc. onto his counter. More senior officials appeared from all sorts of doors and I and my bag were isolated from the general throng.

The pads were squeezed, the balls tapped. It looked hopeless. A knife was produced to open the articles to reveal the concealed drugs. How I managed with my broken Spanish to persuade those officials not to dissect my two precious cricket balls I do not know. However, after much arm waving and discussion I was allowed to proceed. I then realised why I had been voted President of the Cricket Section.

A lot of lasting friendships were made on these tours. We stayed as guests in their houses and we played host in our homes when they were visiting Caracas. Club cricket has always recognised that the social side of the game is important. Whether the cricket, the tourist visits, the parties or the friendships were the most important I do not know. What is known is that the total was memorable, exciting, enjoyable and reassuring. Cricket was playing its part in the social fabric of life in Venezuela, Peru, Mexico and the Dutch West Indies just as it does in the United Kingdom.

Mention must be made of the methods by which cricketing gear was brought into Caracas. Obviously it was impossible to buy anything, except a 'box', within Caracas and so every item had to be imported. Devious means therefore had to be resorted to by the committee members to discover who was going back to the UK for annual leave. 'Oh, and while you are there, get a couple of decent bats and half a dozen cricket balls. Yes, I know you will come back with loaded suitcases, but leave a few packets of chocolate digestives out and put in the balls. The bats will be no trouble.'

Several weeks later as the reluctant purchaser queues at customs with an irate wife, screaming kids and jangling nerves, his love of the game is sorely tried. 'I will not let anyone know when my leave is next year.'

One of the joys (for the players) of Caracas cricket is that the season lasts all year. In the rainy season, May to November, some matches may be lost or curtailed, but generally the weather is always warm. I never did see a sweater. Even if it did rain, matches often continued. The wicket was rubber on concrete, so matches were often finished in torrential downpours. Watching the incredulous expressions on some of the Venezuelan spectators' faces was normally worth the soaking.

IAN KEYS

Starkest African Maidens

Box Event

Sierra Leone's far pavilions have yielded a hat trick of anecdotes: a tale of a box and a man and a pair of trousers, a mild case of witchcraft and a terrifying story about the standards of umpiring in Freetown

There was great excitement in Sierra Leone when it came to picking a test team to play against Nigeria for I think the first time (1962?). Your correspondent's father was asked to umpire the test trial, being in the country on holiday and having played a fair bit in the UK. It was a hot sultry day with matting on a concrete strip. Fielding in the deep I blessed the fall of another wicket which took us all one nearer to a glass of ice cold beer. As the batsman walked back a hum floated across the ground from the pavilion area. We all looked up at this unusual sound to see the incoming batsman walking towards us through the haze with a darkish object on his crotch. He approached with a diffident air as if nothing was amiss. As one cricketer to another and in one movement the fielders surrounded him and in a hushed voice my father whispered 'You've strapped your box on outside your trousers!' Confusion reigned, spectators cheered and within a minute or two play restarted with our man properly dressed.

R. W. BUTLER

Sierra Leone v Nigeria

Sierra Leone batted first and scored a reasonable total. However, when Nigeria batted their No. 7 or 8 hit a very high long ball to deep long off. There was no fielder and the ball might have gone for six; however, a spectator ran onto the field and caught it. The bowler appealed and the umpire gave the batsman *out*. Sierra Leone batted again and left Nigeria around 280 to get. They started badly and quickly lost 5 wickets for not many. Came the tea interval and Sierra Leone spectators surrounded the wicket dancing, a full bottle of brandy was poured onto the wicket which was then 'blessed'. Things went wrong, however, as the next two Nigerian batsman knocked off the required runs. One of the Nigerian cricketers remarked, 'A bottle of brandy isn't enough to pay for ju-ju to beat Nigeria.'

The unfortunate batsman was, as I remember, Karen Siepke.

TONY SHARP

Cricket in Sierra Leone during the Second World War

In the course of a game between the RAF and an all-black Sierra Leone Cricket League XI on the Brookfields ground in Freetown I was involved in an incident which I shall never forget. Wing Cdr the Rev. E. T. Killick captained our side (he had played for England v. South Africa just before the war). He was very popular and a real sportsman.

The Sierra Leone umpire, a highly respected and well-known citizen, was a local magistrate with a reputation to maintain. Because of the hard, rather abrasive surface, success with the new ball was all-important to the fielding side. Tom Killick gave me the new ball and set an attacking field. During the course of my first over the opening bat got an edge to an outswinger and was caught by the keeper. Our unanimous appeal was turned down by the coloured home umpire with a polite smile.

Two balls later the same batsman got a thick edge to another late outswinger and was well caught, knee high, by *second* slip. The batsman stood where he was looking 'sheepish' while we waited for him to return to the pavilion. As he made no move I turned to the umpire, who also looked uncomfortable, and quietly said, 'How was that umpire?' His reply was 'I didn't see.' I stood there aghast for a moment and then on my way back to my bowling mark I was joined by Tom Killick from cover point who asked me what the umpire had said. I told him and he stood there quietly for a moment and then said, 'Bad luck – he's a —— cheat.' I never heard him use that word before or since!

F. M. SAUNDERS

Monrovia – Liberia

The following piece emanates from an exotic Bank address. But the subject is in Monrovia, of all places, where it seems cricket is not destined to take root

In 1963 no one had ever played cricket in Liberia. With a small English and West Indian community, we gradually talked ourselves into organising games. There were, of course, no grass pitches so, having had equipment sent into the country through the British Embassy, we duly laid our mat out on the barrack square (to be the scene of many arrests and murders about seventeen years later). Somehow we raised a team and a batting list, and with a little 'jungle drums' type publicity we set off for the middle. The pitch was deadly – the mat being laid on unswept laterite. The opening bowler hurtled to the wicket and stopped. Something was wrong – for there at short square leg was a row of taxis and mammy wagons with enthusiastic spectators agog for the first they'd ever seen of this strange game. Some ten minutes later order was restored to the field of play with their retreat after many arguments, and play recommenced. It was never completed for I believe there were three injuries, the fast bowler tripped over the end of the mat and bowled – your correspondent was felled by a ball to the eye and carted off to hospital in some very gory makeshift whites to the great amusement of the spectators. The British community – such as it was – sustained an irreparable loss, for to my knowledge no one ever dared play cricket in Liberia again and we all decided it was safer (and more fun) to concentrate on the never-ending stream of air hostesses passing through the country!

R. W. BUTLER

In Vino Veritas

*As we have seen, wherever the armed services are
stationed one can be sure that cricket will surface. It is
perhaps surprising, though, to find this hilarious
account of a match in Kenya – where, apart from
anything else, the opposition insisted on including a
witch-doctor in their side – coming from the pen of that
most renowned of all London Frenchmen, the landlord
of the York Minster or the French pub as it is more
commonly known. It is followed by a description of a
game played in Somaliland taken from an account
published in* The Cricketer Spring Annual *in 1968*

It has become quite obvious since that small lovable monster
ET threw back the ball to the boy in the opening scenes of
the smash hit film, that ball games are known and undoubtedly played in the galaxies. It is not, therefore, un-
reasonable to suppose that some sort of cricket is enjoyed.
The following tale has been put together by the writer in an
attempt to make sense of a somewhat garbled story recounted by a group of aging ex-servicemen.

The Annual Reunion had been held year after year,
naturally with diminishing attendance until only five were
left. On this particular evening they seemed quieter and
more subdued than usual and it was after I had served the
coffee that their Chairman called me over to take a glass of
wine and informed me that this would be their last meeting
and if they told me a story would I listen carefully as they had
decided the time had come to 'get it off their chests' and they
felt that I would not laugh them into idiots suffering from
excess alcohol. Very seriously and earnestly they affirmed
that what I was to hear was the sworn truth. I have, however,
taken due note of the passing years and have tried to ignore
the more outrageous accounts which I felt may have become
embellished by time. This is their story.

It all happened in Kenya (that was). The long-drawn-out
war with the Mau-Mau had come to a shaky end, heralding
an equally shaky peace. The bulk of the various military
units had long departed, leaving a somewhat mixed nucleus

of Army and RAF demolition squads destined to clean up generally and deal with all outstanding details. Their zone of operations was an area around Sankuri Post some 200 miles from Nairobi.

As the weeks went by these few stalwarts suffered severely, not from local diseases or fevers, which due to the proximity of the Lorian Swamp were plentiful, but from sheer, utter boredom. The Officers' Mess, a corrugated iron covered shed, held but four officers plus a Kikuyu batman-cum-steward-cum-barman-cum-spy. Of these four officers only two, Lieutenant Campbell-Smythe (Medical) and Flying Officer P. Muggeridge (Admin), could be said to be on active service. The other two were just waiting for their posting home and honourable geriatric retirement. The active ones naturally were called Smiffy and Muggy by some fifteen to twenty other ranks led by Flight Sergeant Drake (Birdie), Sergeant Moldrum (Mouldy) and Corporal Asquith (Corp). In addition were sundry native so-called orderlies performing the duties of washing, cooking and mending etc.; and all keeping a wary eye on the local tribe of ex-enemies, led by Chief N'Kombe and an apparently 200-year-old witch doctor whose unpronounceable name translated into 'He Who Came From The Stars'. He also claimed Masai blood although the tribe were strictly Kikuyu. We will ignore the presence of a few native females, who no doubt did their best to alleviate the appalling boredom reflected in the abject misery of these few remnants of British Imperial might.

Then came a miracle, due perhaps to listening to every word emitted in a kind of wheezing raucousness by the only remaining radio, and the minute study of every month-old newspaper which managed to arrive, together with a scant supply of gin, tonic water and the inevitable Tusker beer, but whatever it was, suddenly everyone spoke of cricket, results of matches, details of bowling and batting, wicket-keeping, catches, nostalgic reminders that rain stops play in other parts of the world. So a cricket match had to take place, but against whom? Chief N'Kombe provided the answer. He and his tribe – among which were several ex-students of the London School of Economics – would form a team, provided that there was no objection to the 200-year-old witch doctor being included.

Nobody could think of any reason to refuse. After all, he could only just about stand, let alone run, so it would be like playing against ten men instead of eleven. Somewhere in the depths of what used to be the NAAFI stores two genuine bats were discovered. A couple of men proved to have once been apprentice carpenters and produced very creditable sets of stumps and bails, and even the pads looked quite professional, made up as they were from green bamboo and leather straps. The ball was the difficulty. Where could a cricket ball be obtained? Nairobi could not help, and field phone links with the few other lonely outposts proved fruitless. It then transpired that 'He Who Came From The Stars' had in his possession a form of clay, and given dimensions as to circumference and weight etc., would be only too pleased to make a ball. After a few days the ball was produced. It looked like a cricket ball, it had the right colour, it felt like a cricket ball, it even had simulated stitches, it handled like a cricket ball and when struck by a bat it produced the most satisfactory sound – the sound of willow striking leather.

I say 'we', because now my companions had almost convinced me I was there.

As expected, Chief N'Kombe's team contained nearly all the ex-LSE students and, of course, the witch doctor. Our team was captained by Smiffy and included Birdie, Mouldy and Corp, as each claimed to be a bowler, wicket-keeper or batsman. Volunteers from the remaining troops made up the team and allowed two reserves. Whether N'Kombe's team practised or not we did not know, but we did and within a comparatively short time developed a team certainly capable of beating a nondescript local native side.

The great day dawned and crowds gathered on the only remaining fairly level piece of the runway. Umpires, one native, one white, prepared for the start of the great cricket match, in which local feeling, propaganda and pride had increased interest out of all proportion to its importance. The toss-up was between Smiffy and He Who Came From The Stars, who to our surprise had been nominated captain of the native team. We lost the toss and were set to bat first. It seemed that everyone except ourselves knew we were going to bat first.

He Who Came From The Stars squatted on the ground at about first slip position, scratched a circle in the dust, made a number of strange marks and despatched his fielders to take up position, while he mumbled a kind of incantation.

The umpires squared up, our opening batsmen Smiffy and Birdie, full of confidence, took up their stances, and the game began. The bare-chested and bare-footed bowler took quite a short run and released the ball which attained an astonishing speed, knocked the bat clean out of Smiffy's hands and then demolished the wicket. 'OUT!' went up the cry and justifiably out went Smiffy. As he passed Mouldy, the next man in, he muttered 'should have worn me sunglasses – didn't even see the . . . ball'. Mouldy importantly took his stance to receive from the bowler a slow bouncer. He smote it mightily, it flew up and up to disappear into the rays of the sun and He Who Came From The Stars, without even moving his body, stuck out his hand and the ball fell into it! 'OUT!' – and so it was. Mouldy stalked over to seize the ball, but it was obviously the same ball. He looked into the eyes of He Who Came From The Stars and discerned nothing but bland amusement.

The next man, a Royal Engineer veteran, planted himself and his bat squarely in front of the wicket, stepped out to hit a slow ball and very nearly collapsed on the spot on hearing the crescendo of noise which said 'OUT!' 'It went right through the bat,' he crooned idiotically, and he was still chanting 'right through the bat' two hours later.

Next man in was a RAF man called Harold. He had an air of competence and faced the bare-footed, bare-chested bowler with a certain air of nonchalance – all to no avail as the ball ricocheted off the edge of the bat to be caught by the wicket-keeper, but not with his hands. It was lodged between his pads! He grabbed it, threw it in the air, caught it and once again up went the cry 'OUT!' This led to a heated argument as to whether a catch between the legs was legal. However, he was the wicket-keeper, the ball had not touched the ground so the 'OUT' was upheld. Runs: Nil. Wickets: 4. Balls: 4.

The crowd, by this time, aided by generous supplies of Tusker beer, were singing and dancing in what can only be described as unholy glee. Harold was followed by Corporal Asquith, who we respected a great deal as he had actually played cricket in his school 1st Eleven. Corp (the noted batsman) took his stance with an air of 'it's time I stopped the rot' to receive from the bowler a slow bouncer. He smote it nobly, as straight as an arrow it headed for the boundary, but suddenly changed course to fall into the ready hands of an outfielder. 'OUT!' went the cry from a thousand Tusker lubricated throats and out went a sorely puzzled Corp while He Who Came From The Stars continued to chant and use his finger to make more mysterious hieroglyphics in his circle.

Our seventh man was a no-nonsense NCO from the AOC. He was built like a wrestler, but in spite of his obvious toughness and size, he appeared ill-at-ease and took his stance a little nervously and hesitantly, almost as if his bat was too heavy for him. However, he faced the savage, half-naked bowler bravely enough. It was a slow ball losing speed as it approached until it was barely moving, then it appeared to stop dead. The big man stared at the offending object as if mesmerised, he did not even move his bat as the ball climbed up it, up his arm, across his shoulder to drop onto the bails. Again the fiendish roar of the crowd – 'OUT!' The big man tottered away muttering to himself 'I'll never touch another drop, never, never.' Thus came the end of the first over, six balls, six wickets all for nil, six batsmen out for the largest duck ever.

The normal over changes took place except He Who Came From The Stars who stayed where he was, but now looked considerably older than his professed 200 years. Our team by now had realised that whatever happened they could not win, but pride, guts and stubbornness forced them to continue.

At his end of the pitch, which so far had seen little or no action, Flight Sergeant Drake's face was moulded in disbelief as eighth man came in. He was our Muggy. Birdie and

Muggy passed a few words between them and it was plain to all that a few runs could now be counted upon. The new bowler was an indescribably ugly little dwarf some four feet tall and dressed in nothing but a loin cloth. He began a long, long run, an easy ball. *Birdie's time had come.* He pugnaciously squared his shoulders, stuck out his chin, hit a spinning ball, yelled at Muggy and they both started to run. The spinning ball hit the ground, reversed direction and hit the off stump before the batsmen were half-way along the pitch. The wicket-keeper, in a single co-ordinated movement, grabbed the ball, hurled it towards the other wicket and spread-eagled both stumps and bails. 'OUT!' and 'OUT!' cried the umpires together with those of the delirious spectators still able to see what was going on. After lengthy discussion nobody could quote any rule to say that two batsmen could not be dismissed from the same ball so 'OUT' and 'OUT' it was.

Nothing could be done but to see the farce through. In came a private called Tom accompanied by tenth man, who was obviously immune to all outside influences. He had started on Mess beer, then on to local Tusker, graduating to the gin and tonic that the officers had lost the heart to defend. He navigated his way to the wicket to face the second ball of the over, which danced its way towards him bouncing to right then to left. It was about waist high when he took a swipe at it, but it stopped just short of his weaving bat then advanced again. Almost demented, he stepped back to take another wild swipe, successfully destroying his own wicket. 'OUT!' – and it was.

Last man in was a civilian technician who had all along protested that he knew nothing about cricket and had only agreed to play to make up the team, never expecting to be called upon to bat. He faced the dwarf holding his bat loosely in front of him, the ball glanced off it into the hand of He Who Came From The Stars which had been held out for it since the bowler had begun his run.

Pandemonium broke out as the crowd, gushing with good humour, congratulated our team on their performance.*

---

*Tom came in for special treatment as the only man *not out*.

Everyone went wild with delight, unconcerned about who won or lost. Even He Who Came From The Stars was grinning in a euphoria of sheer happiness and there seemed no point in calling his side to bat.

Both teams gathered round, someone called for speeches from the captains, someone else called for more beer, then our captain, Lieutenant Campbell-Smythe, asked He Who Came From The Stars if he could have the ball, which was lying innocently on the ground, as a souvenir. Even as he spoke, the ball began rolling, then picked up speed as it went flying through the air higher and higher until it vanished from sight. 'No,' said the ancient one, 'no, it has gone back home.'

GASTON BERLEMONT

Note: Names of individuals have been changed by request.

A Unique Game in Somaliland

In 1945 I was District Commissioner, in the British Military Administration at a place called Las Anod in what was then British Somaliland. I was the only European there and had to make my own interests out of office hours. I decided to teach the local Somalis the game of cricket. I managed to get a couple of old bats, wickets and two and a half pairs of dilapidated pads. I could not get a cricket ball but I got half a dozen hockey balls. We bowled on to a strip of matting taken from an army tent. I had an Indian clerk, who had played cricket at school and he came in as assistant coach.

Our pupils were keen, but slow in making progress, either with bat or ball. But we all got a lot of fun out of the practices. One day I decided that they knew enough about the game to play a match. My clerk and I sat down with a list of the, relatively, more promising players and selected our teams by the one-for-you-and-one-for-me method. Then came a snag. My head *Illalo* informed me that I could not hold a social event like a cricket match without inviting the local Sheik to participate. So out came the name of one of my players and in went that of Sheik Mohammed Mamud.

The great day came. It is a match I shall never forget. The temperature was around 120 in the shade – and we were not in the shade. The Somalis wore their *tobes*, voluminous garments made from twelve yards of white cloth. I could do no better than a lightish pair of khaki trousers. Ahmed Naik sported a pair of white shorts and a violently-coloured red and yellow cap. The whole village was there to watch the game, as indeed they had turned out to watch our practices. By this time, most of them had a pretty good idea of what it was all about. Ahmed won the toss and elected to bat. He opened, with his most promising player. Two shop-keepers from the village, desperately coached over the previous weeks, took up their positions as umpires. What they knew about the laws of the game could be written on the back of a very small postage stamp.

I opened the bowling. Ahmed played a nice game and my first over was a maiden. You had to bowl a pretty good length to hit the strip of matting. My bowler at the other end 'chucked' eight balls in the approximate direction of the batsman, but one was near enough for the latter to take a mighty swipe at it and it landed in the crowd. I reminded the umpire how to signal a four. When they were 53 for 8, with Ahmed still there with 42 of them, I was about to begin my run-up when the Muezzin, from the minaret, called the Faithful to prayer. Every man-jack, players and spectators, spread their robes on the ground, faced Mecca and knelt in prayer. Resuming the game, Ahmed's side were out shortly afterwards for a total of 61, the captain having an undefeated 48.

The Sheik and I opened our innings. My partner was a big, fat fellow and I weighed a couple of pounds short of nine stone. We must have made an odd-looking pair. The Sheik had his ceremonial gilt-handled sword in its gilt scabbard girdled about his ample waist.

I scored six off Ahmed's first over and then the Sheik faced. There was one ball in the over which would have hit the stumps. The batsman stopped it with his massive thigh and then, addressing it as one would a golf ball, gave an almighty swing which connected. It was a certain four, but at that moment the kariff, the gale-force wind which rages almost continuously for some four months of the year, blew up. It got behind the travelling ball and hurtled it along the ground. The crowd gave chase. We got fourteen runs from that classic stroke.

I made 50 and retired when we were 71 for 7. Then one of the tail-enders got his bat in the way of a ball, which trickled only a few yards, called for a run and started off down the pitch. As he ran, he turned his head to see what was happening at the wicket and the two batsmen collided in the middle of the pitch. The 'keeper had broken the wicket and then threw the ball down to the bowler, who broke the other wicket. The batsmen were tangled together on the ground and it was impossible to know whether they had actually crossed or not. The simplest way out was to declare, which I did.

I was transferred shortly after this epic game and my successor was not interested in cricket. So I imagine that was the one and only cricket match ever played in the then British Somaliland.

E. A. CORDELL, *The Cricketer*

Strange Events in Nyeri

Finally, it's back to Kenya for a story which lacks the eccentric witch doctor, but makes up for this with a station-master, a postmaster, a ladies' tailor, a poor bowler and the devil's own luck

During the Emergency in Kenya in the 1950s I was stationed up country in the Kikuyu Reserve in a delightful place, the capital of the province, called Nyeri. The town itself had a large European population swollen by the fact that 70th East Africa's Brigade HQ was situated in the middle of the town, alongside *The White Rhino Hotel*. The town also boasted the even more famous *Outspan Hotel*, gateway to Treetops. Needless to say there was a golf course, also in the middle of the town and a cricket ground which doubled as the fairway for the first hole of the golf course; a fact that seldom deterred keen golfers from teeing up and driving over our heads when we were playing cricket. The ground was saucer shaped and very beautiful. There was no pavilion. We changed in the clubhouse over the road and padded up in a wattle plantation said to have stemmed from the original 'Boma' established by the Kikuyu tribe thousands of years before. In the background the buff and khaki tents of the Brigade HQ gave the ground a slightly festive air – like cricket week at Canterbury.

Every year the Nyeri Europeans would challenge the Nyeri Asians to a cricket match. This was one of the leading events in the social calendar. Because of the Emergency the ranks of the Nyeri cricket team were considerably enhanced by some more than adequate cricketers who were stationed in the town.

This particular year we, the Europeans, taking up the annual challenge had elected to bat first. By mid-afternoon we had amassed a fairly respectable total; I forget exactly how many. The Asians, who had brought with them a colourful band of supporters in two lorries jabbered and cackled among themselves around the boundary, cheering loudly as their opening pair strode out to the matting wicket standing out against the vivid green of the meticulously cut outfield. Very soon the Asians were in trouble. Their opening bat was given out LBW. An outrageous decision by one of the umpires (their own). In fact, the ball hit the poor batsman's bat which was way outside his leg stump. This led to an almost instant collapse of morale and very soon seven wickets had fallen for a total of something like sixty runs. It was obviously time for me to bowl. Fielders were duly dispersed to all corners of the field and I, an indifferent bowler at the best of times, prepared to turn my arm over. I recognised my first opponent. The Nyeri stationmaster, a giant man with sticking-out teeth and a peculiar stance. He eyed me apprehensively as I ran up to deliver the first ball. He was wearing brown trousers and one pad. He thrust his padded leg straight down the wicket, took an almighty swipe and I found the ball flying straight at my face. I caught it. I had taken a wicket. The stationmaster retired crestfallen to the rapturous applause of his saried supporters for he had, the previous over, run three byes. Next there strode to the wicket another man I recognised at once. He was a tall Sikh, the postmaster of the Nyeri post office. It was plain, from his failure to take guard that he was not all that familiar with the game. I waited a moment to give him time to adjust his stance. He stood bolt upright, the bat hanging limply in his hand. I bowled an almighty donkey drop. It sailed through the air, over his head and landed on top of his wicket. He never moved. I had bowled him. Two wickets in two balls. He had to be persuaded to leave the field unable to accept that his dismissal had taken place so quickly. The noisy crowd was hushed.

To the wicket came a seedy youth, chewing. He was, like the previous two victims, instantly recognisable to me. My last opponent was the manager of a shop which rejoiced in the name of Ladies Tailoring. He took guard and held his bat with some degree of professionalism. He had obviously played before. I bowled. An appalling wide. The ball drifted way outside the off-stump, hit one of the iron spikes which was pinning the matting to the ground, broke at a right angle and took his three stumps away. We had won the match. I had done the hat trick. I had dismissed the Stationmaster, the Postmaster and the Manager of Ladies Tailoring in three deliveries. The shadows lengthened as we left the field and the Asians slunk away. I had never done the hat trick before or since. It was a memorable day. I had ruined the game.

L.C.

South Pacific
(Nothing like a game)

Cricket in the Blue

It would be impossible to ignore, in any book on cricket, Sir Arthur Grimble's classic description of the game played in the South Pacific. This extract is taken from that delightful book, A Pattern of Islands

The Old Man was anxious to spread the gospel of the game more widely among the Gilbertese. He told me on Saturday to give the first lesson to twenty-two of the Company's labourers whom the police had inveigled up to the field. At the end of the practice, which had not proved very enthusiastic, I asked them if they would like another trial some time. 'Sir,' replied their spokesman with courtesy, 'we shall be happy to come, if that is your wish.'

I explained that there was no enforcement, but put it to him that the game was a good game: didn't he think so too? 'Sir,' he said again, 'we do not wish to deceive you. It seems to us a very exhausting game. It makes our hearts die inside us.'

I naturally asked why, in that case, he had said they were willing to have another go. He whispered seriously for a while with his companion. 'We will come back,' he answered at last, 'on account of the overtime pay which the Government, being just, will give us for playing on its ground.'

Those early teaching days provided some pretty problems of umpiring. In one case at least, no decision was ever reached. Ari, a little quick man, and Bobo, a vast and sluggish giant, were in together when Ari hit what he judged to be an easy two. He proceeded to run two, paying, as usual, not the slightest heed to his partner's movements. The gigantic Bobo ran only one, with the result that both players were at Ari's original crease when the ball was thrown in.

But it was overthrown; seeing which, Ari hurled himself upon Bobo, started his great mass on a second run, and then himself careered away on his third. Bobo finished his second, but by that time Ari was back at his original crease again, having finished his fourth. He started on his fifth, but collided with Bobo, who was making heavy work of his third, in mid-pitch. Both collapsed there, Ari on top of Bobo, and Ari's original wicket was thrown down. Which of the two was out? In point of fact, it was Bobo whom we sent to the pavilion, but that was not on an umpire's decision. It was because Ari's head had butted with great force into his diaphragm and left him gasping for medical aid.

Another case was much discussed. One Abakuka (Habakkuk) so played a rising ball that it span up his arm and, by some fluke, lodged inside the yellow and purple shirt with which he was honouring our game. Swiftly the wicket-keeper darted forward and grappled with him, intending to seize the ball and so catch him out. After a severe struggle, Abakuka escaped and fled. The whole field gave chase. The fugitive, hampered by pads donned upside down (to protect his insteps from full-pitchers) was overtaken on the boundary. Even handicapped as he was, he would hardly have been caught had he not tried there, by standing on his head, to decant the ball from his shirt-front; and though held feet in air, he resisted the interference with such fury that it took all that eleven masses of brown brawn could do to persuade the leather from his bosom. After so gallant a fight, it would have been sad to judge him out. Fortunately, we were saved the pain, as he was carried from the field on a stretcher.

Ten years later, cricket was popular everywhere, and a better grasp of its finer points was abroad, but odd things still happened now and then to keep us alert. When I became, in my turn, the Old Man on Ocean Island, there was a game between two Police teams in which the umpire of the fielding side, for no obvious reason (since nobody had appealed), suddenly bawled 'Ouchi', which is to say, Out. We were interested to hear what he meant, especially the batsman, but all the answer he gave was 'Sirs, you know not how bad that man is. *O, beere!*' The expletive usually denotes disgust at a nasty smell. We decided that a man's personal odour had little to do with the laws of cricket, and the batsman continued his innings. But, an over or two later, there was a legitimate appeal against him. In attempting a leg hit, he had flicked a strap of his pad and it looked from point's angle as if he had been caught at wicket.

'Ouchi!' yelled the umpire with splendid gusto.

'Ouchi?' queried his victim, 'and for what reason, O eater of unclean things, am I ouchi?'

'Rek piffor wikkut!' The decision was rendered to the sky, resonant with triumphant conviction.

We decided again that the batsman had better continue, but he was so shaken by that time that his stumps were pushed back by the very next ball, a deplorable long-hop.

'Ouchi!' gloated the umpire, 'ouchi-ouchi!' and followed his retreat prancing with glad hoots to the very pavilion.

We learned later that the complex behaviour of a light-hearted village girl was at the bottom of this regrettable business. But the sequel to the story has a nicer flavour for cricketers. Both men gave up playing for a while; a few weeks later, however, they came to the Residency hand in hand, with garlands on their heads, to say they wanted to be taken into practice games again. By that time, I knew the background of their quarrel, and said something severe about umpires who imported private feuds into their cricket. 'Yes, Old Man, of a truth,' the offender answered, 'our sin was to play this game while we were contending over that female person. It is not expedient for men at variance about women to be making *kirikiti* against each other, for behold! it is a game of brothers. But now we are brothers again, for we have turned away from that female.' As a matter of cold, hard fact, it was *she* who had turned away from *them*. But that aspect of the matter was, after all, beyond the cognizance of the MCC whereas his finding that cricket is a game of brothers was sound beyond all argument.

But I like best of all the dictum of an old man of the Sun clan, who once said to me, 'We old men take joy in watching the *kirikiti* of our grandsons, because it is a fighting between factions which makes the fighters love each other.' We had not been talking of cricket up to that moment, but of the savage land-feuds in which he had taken a sanguinary part himself before the hoisting of the British Flag in 1892. The talk had run mainly on the family loyalties which had held his faction together. His remark, dropping out of a reflective silence at the end, meant that cricket stood, in his esteem, for all the fun of fighting, and all the discipline needed for unity in battle, *plus* a broad fellowship in the field more valuable than anything the old faction wars had ever given his people. I doubt if anyone of more sophisticated culture has ever summed up the spiritual value of cricket in more telling words than his. 'Spiritual' may sound over-sentimental to a modern generation, but I stand by it, as everyone else will who has witnessed the moral teaching-force of the game in malarial jungle, or sandy desolation, or the uttermost islands of the sea.

ARTHUR GRIMBLE, *A Pattern of Islands*

Cricket in a Pacific Paradise

Here is another version of the game as played in New Caledonia. In this case the narrator is a well-known commentator whose ability to keep us all enthralled by his cricket broadcasts has done so much to while away the rainy days. This is followed by a specific account of a cricket match in the Fiji Islands together with the score. Another cricket authority describes the further perils to be expected in playing the game in those delightful islands

Just 1,150 miles north-east of Sydney lies an Emerald Isle, 250 miles by 31 – New Caledonia. 'A tropical paradise of blue waters, white sand, lazy, hot days and balmy evenings', says the travel brochure. It also adds that Captain Cook found and named New Caledonia in 1774, that it was a small French colony by 1853, and became a French Overseas Territory in 1946. Amazingly the brochure goes on to reveal that cricket is played on 'this small piece of the South of France with the flavour of Paris'. That is unexpected enough, but it becomes quite remarkable when one learns that only the women play. The reason for this seems obscure. It could be that the men consider it too 'cissy', but seeing the way in which these tough women play that seems extremely unlikely.

What is certain is that cricket was started by English missionaries in the nineteenth century and that there are fourteen teams in the capital, Noumea, and three from the adjoining group of islands, Mare and Lifou. These teams play for a cup awarded annually on 24 September – the anniversary of French occupation. They practise every Saturday 'with ardour'.

Although the laws and conditions of play are somewhat eccentric, to say the least, the game is definitely recognisable as cricket, and bears no relation to the French cricket we all used to play as children. The matches take place on any available land, but usually on a slag pitch because any grass is reserved for baseball and football. The pitch is 62 feet long, the stumps $27\frac{1}{2}$ inches high, and there are no bails. Instead of our bowling and popping creases, there is a $3\frac{1}{4}$-foot square marked out around the stumps, in which the batswoman or 'joueuse' must stand. The bat is long and shaped like a baseball bat, with a maximum length of 39 inches and a minimum of 36. It must be 3 inches wide but can be of any weight. The ball – called 'La Boule' – is made of dried sap and bounces even on a slag pitch. The ladies' bowling actions vary from a blatant chuck to a good old-fashioned lob. They are dressed in loose-fitting, gaily coloured floral smocks and the teams are 15-a-side plus two substitutes. The minimum age for a player is fifteen. They wear no pads, batting gloves, thigh pads or indeed any other sort of protection so far as one can see under the smocks! Perhaps for this reason these smocks are called Mother Hubbards.

Runs count as in our cricket and are called 'pines', but there are no boundaries and the batswomen must run up and down the pitch barefoot until the ball is returned to the wicket-keeper. It is therefore not surprising that the rules allow a 'tired' batswoman to be replaced by the next on the list or to call for a substitute to run for her. Each run is greeted with shrill tin whistles and a hand-clapping version of the Melanesian Pilou-Pilou war song.

The bat must rest on the shoulder and it is forbidden to hold it in the air or to let it touch the ground. If a player drops the bat she must stay in the square until given another one. Incredibly there is only one ball per over, so there is no over-rate problem in New Caledonia!

And now, just in case the whole thing smacks of women's lib, here comes the rub. Both the umpires and the 'off pitch' scorer must be male. They are considered fairer and have authority in a dispute and are capable of breaking up a scrap if the women get excited and fight – as they often do. Here are some of the general rules these umpires must enforce: It is forbidden for players to throw insults (modern Test players please note!), nor must any player enter the field in a state of drunkenness. And here is something that might well be introduced into Test cricket – the umpire has the right to expel a player from the field after a warning. Finally, further proof that the umpires are in complete charge of the game – neither the players nor the public are allowed to look at the score!

There are no time limits and the match goes on until the umpire declares one side the winner. The losers then have to fork out about £5 to give to the winning team. In the matches leading up to the big day on 24 September, points are awarded as follows: win 3 points, draw 2 points, loss 1 point, cancellation or abandonment 0 points.

I hope Rachel Heyhoe reads this article because it would be a great idea if on their next visit to Australia our ladies' touring team could fly up to Noumea and challenge these be-smocked Amazons. But don't forget. No insults or drunkenness please!

BRIAN JOHNSTON, *The Cricketer*

Snow on the Fiji Islands

From the time of the return of the team from Australia, cricket was scarcely played on the island of Taveuni in the province of Cakaudrove for another twenty years. The reason is a rather remarkable one. Just after his Australian tour, Ratu Kadavulevu took the team to Taveuni to play what corresponds closely to a festival match.

In addition to the cricket, in which rivalry would be keen as two old competing states, Bau and Cakaudrove, were opposed to each other, there would be a vast amount of eating. Only those who have seen the enormous quantities of food presented on such ceremonial occasions can accurately visualise the extent of food presented on this event in honour of Ratu Kadavulevu. The chiefly Cakaudrove dish – snakes – was offered and had to be eaten by the Bauan chiefs who would normally never touch them. Great ceremonial accompanied every part of the visit; etiquette was at its highest. The cricket began.

Ratu Lala, Tui Cakau, the highest chief on Taveuni and of great status throughout Fiji (Tui Cakau means King of the Reefs), though not so omnipotent as Ratu Kadavulevu, went in to bat first. This was not due so much to his possessing the greatest ability among his side at the game, which he did not, but to his being of the highest rank. He received a trial ball, as everyone opening an innings does in Fiji whenever Fijians are playing together (and indeed when everyone is playing unless a European is there to point out that the custom died out in the early part of this century). He was out to the next ball, the first one after his trial ball. It is not narrated whether an attempt was made to give him any runs at the beginning. Although of such semi-divine status, which would certainly have accorded him the privilege of some easy runs if he had been playing amongst his own tribe or clansmen, it is unlikely that the Bauan chiefs would have made this gesture on the cricket field. The omission to do so, or at least the fatal error of taking Ratu Lala's wicket, was a diplomatic gaffe on the part of Bau. For Ratu Lala pulled up the shattered stumps and called away his followers from the ground. The match ended abruptly on the first real ball – the earliest abandonment possible in any cricket match. Not only that, but Ratu Lala prohibited the miserable game from being played again in his domains.

This prohibition lasted for very many years, and it cannot be said that even after his death the game has flourished or regal consent been more than lukewarm on Taveuni. If the score could be found it must have a most picturesque appearance. It can be presumed that, if it were kept (probably the scorers had not fidgeted into position by the time of the end of the game), it was torn up by regal command. One can imagine the score to be:

CAKAUDROVE v. BAU at SOMOSOMO, TAVEUNI, 1908
CAKAUDROVE
First Innings

The Tui Cakau, b. Samu	0
Joni Tomasi Kota, not out	0
Extras	0
For one wicket	0

Bowling

	O	M	R	W
Samu	0.1	0	0	1

Match abandoned on account of high dudgeon of High Chief.

PHILIP A. SNOW, *Cricket in the Fiji Islands*

The Rules of the Game

In the early days of Fijian cricket, the tribal chiefs exercised a divine right, one of which was to bat first and to disdain to take any further part in the game. Often, too, the captain of the opposing side would ask the chief's permission to change the bowling against him. The chief's decision usually depended on whether he was comfortable against the existing pair of bowlers. And he was always given a trial first ball.

The practice of trial first balls has, in fact, not died out. Only recently a side promoted from a second league in Suva, the present capital, insisted on starting the game in this way, the stricter rules of the premier division not having been explained to them. In many areas, too, Fijian umpires – who will be members of the batting side – carry with them a bat as an outward sign of their status. Lucky men. With no television in Fiji, all are spared the torments of modern first-class umpires whose every decision is scrutinised at close-up and in slow motion by a multitude of armchair critics.

R. J. HAYTER, *The Cricketer*

The clergy are never far away from the cricket field. The Rev. Elisha Fawcett visits the Admiralty Islands in 1817. This is followed by a piece of Naval history. Although it is not plain which islands in the Pacific Fawcett is referring to, it simply has to be included as does a Scotsman's experience of cricket in Batavia

The Rev. Elisha Fawcett, c. 1817, a Manchester evangelical who devoted his life to teaching the natives of the Admiralty Islands the Commandments of God and the Laws of Cricket. Too poor to purchase a monument to this good man, his parishioners erected his wooden leg upon his grave. In that fertile clime it miraculously took root and for many years provided a beautiful harvest of bats.

REV. MITFORD WARREN, *Carr's. Dictionary of Extra-Ordinary English Cricketers*

A Game of Forfeits

Circa 1860 a British frigate called at some Pacific island and the crew, instead of (or perhaps more truthfully in addition to) indulging in their normal pastimes ashore, played a game of cricket and taught the inhabitants the rudiments of the game. Thereafter the locally embellished game of cricket became a medium for the settlement of differences between one village and another. Each entire village batted and fielded in turn, with the members of each fielding team crowding on to the pitch or retiring to other social pursuits as the mood took them. At the end of the prolonged game the losers were obliged to provide the food for a feast, and also to submit to a number of ignominious forfeits, which included crawling round the perimeter of the pitch on all fours, being inflicted with contumely as offensive dogs, and being obliged to cock a leg (males only?) against every palm tree.

Surely a tradition not to be lost sight of!

H. Sharp

Batavia!

Angus Adair had been invited to take part in a cricket match to be played at the British club in Batavia, which is now Jakarta. He asked to be excused on the grounds that his abilities on the cricket field were non-existent. Pressure, however, was brought to bear and perhaps the matter was clinched by the promise that there would be 'a hell of a good party in the club afterwards'. Not being one to resist such a lure, Angus agreed to play. When in due course the game took place, Angus, batting at the tail-end, astonished everybody by knocking up the highest score of his side. He subsequently added two clean bowled wickets and a remarkable catch in the outfield to his day's performance. When questioned in the bar afterwards about his apparent earlier modesty, Angus insisted that he had no previous experience to speak of as far as the game of cricket was concerned. However, after agreeing to play, he had searched for and found a copy of a book dealing with the sport and had 'read it up during the' plane journey to Batavia'.

Fleming Baird

The Strangest Match in 1980

The setting is somewhere in the South Pacific; but the exact location is in the fertile mind of one of the great Victorian novelists looking far into the future. Well, George Orwell got it a little wrong, too!

Anthony Trollope, the Victorian novelist, is best remembered for his Barsetshire novels set in a cathedral close or for the activities of the Duke of Omnium, Plantagenet Palliser, portrayed on television. One of his strangest books, to which he himself made no reference in his *Autobiography*, was *The Fixed Period* in which larger-than-life characters are set in an environment in which they are apt to appear ridiculous.

To the imaginary island of 'Britannula' off New Zealand sail a community of people pledged to end their lives when they reach the age of 67 and a half. Just before the first of them surrenders to this mass euthanasia, Trollope arranges for a British gun-boat to take over the island. Having done so, the expeditionary force challenges the colonists to a cricket match.

The game took place at Gladstonopolis and was set in the year 1980. The two teams embarked on a month's intensive training so that 'each man should be in the best possible physical condition', though the visiting opening bat, Sir Kennington Oval, also found time to fancy a local girl, the fair Eva. His conduct 'got himself talked about by everyone around'.

When the match itself began, Sir Kennington opened with Sir Lords Longstop. Why these two knights should have been on the expedition we are not told. At any rate, their team is now masquerading as 'England' and England's opening pair are suitably equipped with 'india-rubber guards and a machine upon the head by which brain and features are protected'. But the 1980s-style headgear (anticipated by Trollope over a century earlier) is not against mere fast bowling. Batsmen face a 'steam-bowler ridden to its place by an attendant engineer'. Fifteen minutes are spent setting the machine's sights before Sir Kennington is dismissed first ball, smoke rising from the stumps. A gun is fired to announce the fall of a wicket and Trollope supplies the equivalent of the modern cacophony of noise – 'kettle-drums, trumpets, fifes and clarinets'.

Despite this set-back, England amass over 1,000 runs – surpassing their performance at The Oval in 1938. In their second innings, Sir Kennington makes over 300 and the islanders are set to make 1,500 to win. Jack Neverbend, their captain, scores with such prolific speed that he passes his personal 1,000, dispatching 'every ball into infinite space' in a ground so huge that spectators can see little without field-glasses.

On the last morning, the Britannula islanders still need 560 with three wickets left. Despite all England's efforts, the runs come, and off the last ball of the last over (for the clock has struck six) Neverbend hits a skier – 'perfectly regardless whether it might be caught or not, knowing full well that the one run now needed would be scored before it could come down from the heavens into the hands of any Englishman'. The run was scored and the wicket-keeper made the catch. Either Trollope didn't know the laws or claimed literary licence to ignore them!

Britannula had defeated England in that match set one hundred years or more ahead of his time and placed in this calendar year of 1980. Helmets, noisy crowds, athletic fitness for the contest – Trollope got some of it right in anticipation. He had written his novel when England had begun to play sides 'down under'; he had been to Australia himself; other Victorian novelists – in far more pedestrian ways – wrote about cricket. Even Charles Dickens's Mr Jingle had made 570 in the West Indies.

GERALD HOWAT, The Cricketer

Points East

The Match at Jessore

Dozens of excellent stories from the Sub-continent have had to be 'given out' of this anthology on the grounds that they stem from countries that now enjoy full Test status. The following piece gets past the Umpire since it is set in Bangladesh, a country which is not currently enjoying Test status. And that's to say nothing about the eminence of the author

For several years after independence there was little official support for imported games, and no equipment either. However, the MCC team scheduled for New Year 1977 was the second since independence and Jessore ventured on a more ambitious itinerary. Not for years had the town enjoyed such an opportunity for putting on its own show without guidance from a predominantly Punjabi garrison command.

A little park by a lake known in these parts as tanks was the scene of a civic reception. There were lights and streamers and flags and all the lovely longwindedness that goes with oriental party best. The local band could have been imported from Scotland, virtuosos on fife and drum and, would you believe, bagpipes. And besides the MCC party there was another circus in town, with stalls galore all designed to lift precious taka, the currency of the new state. And in one case literally lift. No stall was more Indian than the mahood and his elephant who provided rides in an area about the size of a small suburban garden. The raj, one thought, used to more spacious times, would revolve in its grave. Was it really so long ago that Ranji took C. B. Fry on all those hunting parties with picnics apparently shipped out from Fortnum and Mason? Still an elephant is an elephant and if a dirty old blanket might not have been Lord Harris's idea of a suitable howdah, nonetheless up the pachyderm's tail climbed the Marylebone Cricket Club. Getting down, and it seemed an unceremoniously long way, was the prelude to the high spot of this apology for a ride. While the mahood stayed aloft indicating that taka should be deposited on the ground, the elephant suddenly revealed himself to be a direct descendant of Colonel Harty from the Jungle Book, developing a hefty snort which blew unacceptable amounts of taka in all directions, forcing the descendants of the cricketing raj to grovel for the precious bits of paper adding to them until his master was satisfied whereupon the elephant's head went up in triumph his trunk curling back so that his boss could pocket the loot. Served me right for not having gold sovereigns about my person for such occasions.

Diversions such as these are all very well on cricket tours, but it is board and lodgings that are the heart of the matter. The Circuit House, again one of many, once housed the Judge and his retinue on their regular peregrinations. If Britain gave India anything, it was reverence for the due majesty of the Law. The Circuit House was therefore the biggest residence in Jessore. At the front was a drive, leading to a porch, and then a hall with ante-rooms which in turn opened into a vast reception room with a high ceiling and huge shuttered windows, now arrayed as a dining area apparently for a cast of thousands, for the two teams in residence were but a fraction of those to be entertained. Beyond the dining room was a terrace and gardens, which if not quite kept to Inns of Court standard, were clearly the object of some attention and affection. At the end of the terrace were the two residential wings and away to one side the kitchens. Architecturally this was single storey Pall Mall clubland.

It is a feature of life on the Sub-continent that order springs out of chaos at one minute to midnight. And sometimes later than that. There were not quite enough beds: nor, it seemed, enough floor space for another. But worry not. In due course cometh the carpenter with board and nails. Two boxes are made to serve as bunks, complete with frame for the mosquito net, a piece of equipment revered since the first Chief Justice established court.

Washing looked a potential problem for there was but one tap for this multitude, a cold one. Once again hospitality triumphed over adversity. Buckets were provided and hot rods to be thrust into them like gas pokers into the fire. These hot rods one noted were made by Siemens, which in ordinary circumstances might have provided reassurance but the technically minded amongst the party noted an absence of earthing and that at shaving time next morning the bath house floor was likely to be wet since the drain seemed to have the same capacity to blow back as the elephant. However no one was electrocuted. Nor were any beards begun that day. An MCC team on tour, one noted with some pride, knows when to take a chance.

Sleep was a chancy business. Apart from normal noises inside the dorm like snoring and men padding off to the pee-hole, there were a series of combats with the mosquitoes which surely could not make such a noise unless they had already penetrated the net. Exhausted by anxiety, worried by the knowledge that one of the party was already very ill, the cricketers dropped off one by one only to be woken at 4 a.m. on the dot, by the sentry's morning prayers. And when he had finished he was followed by the daily dawn recorded announcement from the top of a nearby mosque. At least from 6 to 7 one slept very soundly. At that hour there were shouts of char, and most of a bleary party emerged to drink it in the garden. There the air was still cool and the sun beginning to warm.

Here it should be explained that during the course of the previous day, the leaders of the party had been mightily touched when the hosts asked what they would like to eat at the banquet following the match. The captain, something but not much of an international gastronome, had asked for chicken tandoori, a dish of North India. What prompted this request was not wilful ignorance of the niceties of Indian provincial cooking but the fact that he had seen chickens about the place and did not wish to impose a repeat performance of the first day when relays had to be sent to the cantonment for supplies when the entire visiting team had, after lunch, asked for coffee instead of accepting the proffered tea. Tempers were frayed by the delay in its arrival.

Only when 'coffee just coming, sir' had become an unacceptable answer did it gradually became known that the
coffee had to come ten miles on the back of a motorbike. At
least there were chickens in sight.

Just how visible became unforgettably apparent over the
next morning's early morning cuppa. Four Bengalis, one
older, one younger and two very young and fleet of foot,
appeared in the garden. The two very young ones were
holding sacks, full of mystery and liveliness. Neither was to
last. The younger man reached into the sack and pulled out
a scrawny chicken, holding it in both hands so that the neck
was full extended. Whereupon the older man pulled out his
knife and cut its throat. Off went the very young fellow for
another sack. Now a chicken with its throat cut may look all
right on the marble slab of a Putney poulterer. In a Bengal
garden these poor fowls in their death throes flapped
towards the tea drinkers who were to eat them for dinner.
Some cricketers fled the garden and one at least was said to
have further blocked the aforementioned drain. Others
edged away from the scene. The steadfast, vaguely aware
that some ceremony was being enacted, stood fast. The
farsighted, concerned about their digestive future, sidled
over to the kitchens only to become more alarmed there,
convinced that no judicial stomach would have survived
such an inspection. Meanwhile the score of dead and dying
chickens headed towards the half century. It was going to be
a big banquet.

A few hours later, on the way to the ground one of the very
young from the chicken gang was spotted with his bicycle
chatting up a beautiful young girl of fully six years who was
making fuel for the kitchen by scooping up handfuls of cow
dung and patting them together with bits of straw which
were then left in the sun to dry. The girl offered one of her
little cakes to the players. It was a charming gesture. At that
moment it was all she had to give.

The match, played on a wicket made boringly safe by
generous applications of the same dung, was yet another of
the inevitable series of draws staged on this tour. No one lost
face. Afraid of doing so, I asked the Bangladesh manager
about the ceremony with the chickens in the garden. That,

he told me, was a mark of the highest respect. The guests had to be satisfied that what they were to eat had been alive that morning. That was the healthy way. Less honoured and more likely to suffer were those whose dinners were already dead, of whatever unimaginable cause.

There is a postscript. That summer at Knebworth Park, the home of the family who have now become the Lytton-Cobbolds, an exhibition was created in a disused squash court to celebrate the Delhi Durbar which inaugurated the Viceroyalty of a distinguished ancestor, the very first Viceroy. There on the wall amongst the exhibits was the menu of dinner held in honour of the Governor and Chief Justice of Bengal in the Circuit House at Jessore. The card was longer than a batting order: fish, soup, bird, joints including both beef and pork which suggested one Victorian method of dealing even-handedly with both Moslem and Hindu susceptibilities, dessert and finally Stilton cheese. One wonders how all those throats were cut.

There is also a final irony. It is a fact that there is no documented history of Bengal before the British arrived. In that climate if the damp has not destroyed both the written word and the paper on which it might have been written then either maggots or rats will have done so. However stately homes and squash courts need expensive maintenance if the elements are to be kept at bay. Sadly a hole developed in the roof above that menu and it was dripped on from a height and is now as irretrievably lost as all the other parchments of old Bengal.

ROBIN MARLAR

Mr F. C. De Saram

Sri Lankan tales would likewise be ineligible for a book about non-Test-playing countries. But Ceylon was another matter. Here are two tales from this former Imperial island, one poignant, one a humorous historical footnote

Mr F. C. ('Derek') De Saram, who died in Colombo on 11 April aged 70, was one of Ceylon's outstanding cricketers. He also became politically prominent when, in January 1962, he was sentenced to a long term of imprisonment for conspiring to bring down the government of the day.

Going up to Oxford from Royal College, Colombo, in 1933, he was the first Sinhalese to win a cricket Blue, playing against Cambridge at Lord's in 1934 and 1935. Although he scored 85 in 1935, the crowd of 10,000 rising to him, according to *Wisden*, the innings for which he is best remembered is his 128 for Oxford against the Australians in 1934.

In that year he scored over 1,000 runs for the University at an average of 50, including a hundred in his first first-class match. He was a fine driver and cutter and many years later, when MCC, on their way to Australia, played a match in Colombo, no one stood up more staunchly to the fast bowling of Tyson than De Saram, then 43, which was the score he made.

On MCC's next two visits to Ceylon, en route for Australia, De Saram was behind bars. During the second of them S. C. Griffith, who had played for Cambridge against De Saram at Lord's and was now managing MCC, and Colin Cowdrey went to see him. De Saram had put on his Harlequin tie for the occasion and when his visitors left they were told by the prison governor that when De Saram's time came for release discipline among the inmates would suffer. On and off the field he was a formidable opponent.

The Times obituary column

The first names that occur to me in connection with Colombo cricket are Pauncefoote and B. B. Cooper, both first-class bats. I cannot recall much about the latter, but have a vivid recollection of the former hitting a ball to leg, on the old Galle Face Ground, which travelled into the lake. Vainly the field screamed 'Lost ball!' The ball was in sight, and the batsmen kept on running. Eventually in desperation a native was pushed in to retrieve it, but Pauncefoot had scored 13 runs.

The Ceylon Cricket Annual 1899 (First Year of Publication)

Beware the Wicket Chinaman

Hong Kong Twilight

It is impossible to ignore the game as played in Hong Kong. Anyone who ever had the privilege of playing on that delightful ground in the city centre before the high rise developers got hold of it will relish Tony Lewis's description. And Mrs Thatcher's insensitivity in robbing the Army of one of their best players should not go unrecorded

Throughout the Far East we took the field in colourful and unusual surroundings, but I suppose the conditions for our match against the Hong Kong President's XI were as bizarre as any I have encountered. The ground was so wet that mats were laid each side of the main matting wicket. They certainly aided the running between the wickets and the bowlers' follow-through. It was a very dark, cold and drizzling day. The ground, of course, is famous because it is couched in the city centre of Hong Kong, dwarfed by skyscrapers, probably the most expensive piece of cricket ground in the world. So there we batted, on soaking mats, peering through the gloom, with the trams and the traffic of the city in full view – the ground is open on three sides. The lights went on in the trams towards the end, and this murky ritual was enacted at the feet of the Malayan Bank, the Hong Kong Club, the Supreme Court, the Bank of China and the Hong Kong Hilton Hotel. These giant buildings I am sure nodded their approval. It was everything they must have heard about the cricket game – a spot of English madness! And in case the Supreme Court was having second thoughts, Don Wilson smacked a massive blow right between the upstairs windows, just to prove we meant business.

A. R. LEWIS, *The Cricketer*

On the day of the Sunday League cup final Mrs Thatcher, in Hong Kong on her way home from China, decided to visit the Gurkhas, thereby robbing the Army of at least one player.

'CHINAMAN', *The Cricketer*

Peking Ducks

As recently as 1983 the St George's Club of Hong Kong toured Peking – the first visit of a cricket team to communist China for many years. This account taken from the South China Morning Post *gives some idea of what conditions were like but remains curiously quiet about what the Chinese themselves thought*

The first cricketers to tour Peking since World War II returned to Hong Kong this week with a 100 per cent record and a number of other firsts to their credit.

The St George's Invitational XI won all three of their matches against opponents drawn mainly from the diplomatic community in the Chinese capital. Their victories included a convincing 92-run success in the main match against a full Peking Cricket Club side.

The matches were played at the Peking Gymnasium on a mat laid over the middle of a football pitch. It proved to be a sporty track, and the greater pace of the St George's attack proved to be one big factor in the tourists' favour. Their greater strength in depth and consistency with both bat and ball also proved decisive.

The highlight for the St George's team – apart from the fabulous sightseeing and marvellous hospitality provided by the opposition – was the first century since Peking cricket restarted twelve months ago. Malcolm Grubb earned the title 'Wun Tun' for his maiden three-figure score as he helped St George's recover from a precarious 54 for four with 117 in the main match of the tour on Sunday. Dave Whitefield also earned a new nickname when he gained the tourists' first – and only – Peking duck, also in Sunday's match.

Former St George's player John Ashton, the principal tour organiser, skippered Peking, and after winning the toss, invited St George's to bat first.

Fahmy Jawharsha made his usual bright start with six runs from the first over before giving a catch to mid-on in the second. Tony Turner made 20 and was out giving a return catch to fellow Kiwi Alan Young, who also dismissed tour manager Barry Ellis for nine.

Then came Whitefield's well-received duck, delighting fellow batsman Alan Swift and three others who drew him in 'Peking Duck Stakes'. Swift, who opened the innings and viewed the exit of his first four partners with gathering dismay, continued to bat patiently when joined by Grubb. Swift was eventually dismissed for 24 with his first aggressive stroke in 118 minutes.

Grubb was joined by Graham Sims and began to take full advantage of the very short leg-side boundary and loose attack. He was particularly severe on slow left-armers Ashton and Richard Fletcher-Cooke, hitting three sixes in one over from the latter. Grubb hit a total of eight sixes and seven fours, facing 97 deliveries in 123 minutes. He was out with just one of the scheduled 45 overs left. With Sims he almost doubled the score from 114 for five to 227 for six.

There was one more drama before the St George's innings ended. Bharat Gohel attempted to hook medium pacer Bruce Nicholls and top-edged the ball into his face. Gohel needed a trip to a Chinese hospital for two stitches in a cut near his eyebrow. On his return he bowled three overs for 33 runs, most coming from the bat of the unrepentant Nicholls.

The St George's total of 237 for six was a formidable one – indeed, it was the largest score seen in Peking since Watford beat the Chinese national soccer team 5–1; the largest, in fact, on record.

Peking made a spirited reply. They lost Ashton early, but then David Irvine (28) and Sabhawal (21) prospered until both were bowled by Turner. Jim Middleton also picked up three wickets and Grubb rounded off a successful day with three for 28. Nicholls hit six fours and a six as he top-scored with 36. Will Dennis collected 25 with some good-looking shots, leaving Peking with a respectable reply of 145.

The other two fixtures were with divisions of the Peking Cricket Club, against the Gentlemen of Jehol, a combined Australian and Indian side, and then against Lord Macartney's XI, a combination of British and Pakistanis.

Gohel's five for 13 sent the Jehol Gents reeling to 52 all out, with none of them reaching double figures. Whitefield guided St George's to an eight-wicket win with a breezy 33 not out.

St George's again batted first in their other match and they again topped the 200 mark. Jawharsha led the way with 55, and there were 20s from Gohel and Robert Muirhead. A late 44 from Bill Schaefer pushed the score up to 215.

Macartney's XI lost both openers quickly. Then Dennis took advantage of Eddie Wake's little-used off-spin (or was it leg-spin?) to make the hosts' top score of the tour, 37. With 26 from Sarfaraz they reached 139. Mark Haegele returned the best bowling figures of three for nine.

Generally, the Peking cricketers were short of match practice, but made up for that with enthusiasm. The Peking Cricket Club now has more than 100 members and, if they can survive the next twelve months during which three or four of their key officials will be leaving, they should succeed in setting up a new centre for cricket in Asia.

South China Morning Post

A Long Matrimonial Spell

True or false, England's own 'Typhoon' may have one of the best stories concerning the clash of Western and Eastern cricketing cultures

A certain England fast bowler, not familiar with the customs of foreign parts, was inveigled into taking part in a social tour of the Far East. A number of friendly games were arranged in the Muslim sheikdoms and during one of these matches the team was invited to a reception given by the local ruler.

The sheik entered the room followed by his harem, and

the fast bowler goggled as the procession of women in purdah filing past seemed never-ending. The fast bowler turned to his neighbour and inquired, 'Who are all these women?'

'These are the sheik's wives,' replied the local informant.

'Good God! How many has he got?' was the next question. 'One hundred and ninety-nine,' came the reply.

'Well,' said the fast bowler, 'at least he can look forward to something. Another one and he can take the new ball!'

FRANK TYSON, *The Cricketer who Laughed*

Snow Balls

Polar Cricket

'Students of the game's history,' wrote F. S. Ashley-Cooper, 'are aware that the present universality of cricket can be attributed largely to the efforts of those in the Navy and the Army, for, as Mr Pycroft observed over seventy years ago, "our soldiers and sailors astonish the natives of every clime, both inland and maritime, with a specimen of a British game". This being so, it is only natural to find that occasionally a man-of-war's team has taken part in a match on ice. Such a game was played one night between the ships of the Training Squadrons at Recherche Bay, Spitzbergen (latitude 78° north), and was described as follows in the Graphic *of 28 September 1895, by a correspondent on board HMS Calypso.' The icy tale continues as follows*

The sun was shining brightly, shining with all his might,
And this was odd, because it was the middle of the night.

We started for the shore between 9 and 9.30 p.m., and reached it in safety, after bumping into not more than a dozen or so icebergs, the *Volage*'s men going so far as to land on one and start a slide. The *Active* and *Calypso* took the field – or, rather, the side of the hill – at about 9.30, the *Ruby* and *Volage* having won the toss. The pitch consisted of soft, mossy earth, with lots of stone and mossy hillocks; and the outfielding was, if possible, worse, as it included several dry watercourses. Our fast bowler made a start at the glacier end. The first ball, pitching to leg, altered its course at right angles to the off, and was chased by the batsman, who made one off it. This sort of thing continued till one pitched on the wrong side of a hillock and stopped altogether, allowing the batsman to walk out and have a shot at it sitting. We were lucky in getting this man out with a ball pitching wide to the off taking his leg bail. Then came the stand of the innings, in spite of the efforts of long stop, who was fielding in a valley, and cover point, who was smartly saving boundaries – i.e. the sea. However, we eventually ran one of them out, as a ball, after being hit pretty hard, bounded from a rock towards the wicket, much to the disgust of the batsman. This appeared to demoralise our opponents and we got rid of the rest in various uncouth ways for a total of 57. The in side were indulging in duck shooting close by and bagged one duck. When we went in we made a better show, as we had begun to understand the eccentricities of the wicket, and soon knocked up 58 and won a glorious victory with five wickets in hand. One midshipman made 29 for us by vigorous hitting, and upset the preparations for supper off a full pitch to leg. We then all had some cocoa and something to eat, and returned on board at about 12.30 p.m.

F. S. ASHLEY-Cooper, *Cricket Highways and Byways*

The First South Pole Cricket Match

Ashley-Cooper records other pioneering attempts to bring cricket to the Arctic regions; but it took Sir Ranulph Fiennes and his Transglobe Expedition to achieve the ultimate record – the first cricket game ever to be played at a Pole. We challenge The Guinness Book of Records *to correct us*

As far as we knew, cricket had never been played at the South Pole. Scott's expedition had lacked the time and equipment, and Sir Vivian Fuchs's team of the fifties seemed to have made no attempt on the record. Of course the Americans from their nearby camp had probably got there first with bat and ball, but these would have been of the base kind.

Our Aircraft Engineer, Jerry Nicholson, was determined that our party would make history for cricket and to this end he had ensured that a Gunn & Moore was packed into our survival kit.

I have to confess that the conditions were not ideal. A temperature of minus 27 degrees combined with a 10 knot wind would certainly have caused Umpire Dickie Bird to wonder if play was possible, although the light, as it happened, was intensely bright. Indeed batsmen risked dismissal through snow blindness. Again we faced the constant interruption of Hercules transport aircraft flying into the American base, not to mention a serious shortage of fielders.

Fortunately our Jack Russell dog Bothie, stepped into the breech and I opened the bowling to Nicholson into a very stiff breeze. The wicket keeper and everyone else wore gloves, including the bowler. In many ways the wicket was ideal for bowling; it offered a fair amount of encouragement to my late inswinger and I've no doubt that Freddy Titmus would have been able to produce a prodigious amount of spin, assuming he had been able to move his fingers.

I had two catches dropped off my bowling. One went to ground under a Hercules aircraft with Bothie, another, an absolute dolly, would surely have been pouched by Ran (Sir Ranulph Fiennes) at square leg had he not been busy photographing the occasion.

Future expeditions ought to look carefully at the problem of pitching stumps – metal screws might help. Again I think it would be worth trying to develop a more adhesive ball. Finding sufficient fielders is always going to be a problem; but certainly the next polar expedition is going to need more reliable dogs.

CHARLES BURTON WITH THE TRANSGLOBE EXPEDITION

The Moon's a Cricket Ball

Touring Outer Space

The first black man, the first woman and now the first German – it can't be long before we see the first cricketer in space. Writing some years ago in the Journal of the Cricket Society, *the distinguished astronomer and leg-spinner, Patrick Moore, assessed the prospects of play*

Men have reached the Moon, and will one day go to Mars and even beyond. Naturally they will take cricket with them. I am absolutely confident of this, because only a highly-developed civilisation can hope to colonise other worlds; and it is axiomatic that all highly-civilised people play cricket.

Now, on the Moon there is one-sixth g, and no atmosphere at all. Playing in a space-suit would be somewhat cumbersome. It is all very well for Admiral Alan Shepard to hit a golf-ball, but playing a leg glance would be infinitely more difficult (anyway, he sliced his drive). We must therefore reconcile ourselves to playing in an enclosed dome. The low gravity will provide interesting hazards, because a hefty hit will go for an extremely long way. New rules will, I feel, have to be considered by the MCC. For instance, I envisage that driving the ball beyond the boundary will remain a six, but clunking the top of the dome will merit at least eight.

I rather fear that the Moon will be a batsman's paradise. The luckless bowler will have a very hard time of it. Swinging will be 'out', and the run-up will have to be modified. Personally, I might be in a better position than most, because at all times my run-up is long, leaping and peculiar; one local paper described me as being the bowler with a run like a kangaroo doing the barn-dance, and I would be the last to quarrel. But would my leg-breaks spin on lunar anorthosite? I wonder. Alas, I will never know.

On, then, to Mars, where we have one-third g, but an atmosphere which is about as useful as a sick headache as far as cricket is concerned. What can one do in a tenuous mantle of carbon dioxide? The same problems will certainly have to be faced, and, in addition, the MCC will have to recognise that after Mars has been colonised, and there are people who have lived all their lives there, home teams will be at a disadvantage. A Martian wicket might make even Underwood lose his length.

There seems no point in discussing cricket on Venus (temperature a casual +900 degrees F) or Jupiter (no solid surface on which to lay a wicket; I for one do not fancy playing on cold, gooey ammonia/methane and hydrogen). So let us be bold, and look even further ahead.

Our Sun is a normal star, and it is surrounded by a family of nine planets, including one where civilisation has developed sufficiently for the evolution of cricket. Elsewhere there must surely be other planetary systems, some of them Earthlike and some not. As yet we cannot contact them or reach them; a journey to, say, Alpha Centauri in an Apollo-type rocket would take about half a million years, which is rather lengthy even for an away Test Match. But eventually the time will come. We may manage interstellar flight; we may be visited in our turn; and, of course, there will come the question of fixtures.

On a terrestrial-type world there should be no difficulty at all, but, remember, we cannot guarantee that all intelligent beings are of the same form as Homo Sapiens. I envisage a team made up entirely of beings with, say, four arms and eight legs. This would cause utter chaos in the l.b.w. laws, to begin with, and if an opponent has more than two eyes he will be at an unfair advantage. What I fear is that in the long run this may lead to a serious cosmical crisis. When we contact our brother civilisations, light-years away across the Galaxy, we want everything to be amicable and smooth. At all costs we must avoid a tedious wrangle about how many bats can be used by a ten-armed Sirian, or how many legs must be in front of the wicket before a bowler can justifiably appeal.

I realise that I am looking far into the future but we should remember the Scout motto: Be Prepared. And if visitors in a convoy of flying saucers do happen to arrive, knock at the gates of Lord's and demand to be taken to our President, we should have decided what attitudes we are to adopt.

It may be too early to form a Select Committee to discuss the matter, but at all costs we must not be taken unawares. I hope that this warning is salutary. No doubt there are many interesting episodes ahead of us. And as a parting shot – I wonder just who will go down in History as the first Martian W.G.?

PATRICK MOORE, *The Journal of the Cricket Society*

The Ultimate Tour

Long before men landed on the moon, generations of elderly cricket enthusiasts have sat by winter firesides composing all-time World XIs, presumably with the conquest of space in mind. With his eyes on the furthest pavilion, American writer Marvin Cohen pictures a world where cancer and heart disease have been eliminated and the problems of war, crime, homicide and mortality successfully cracked, and better still where 'as a symbol of these solutions, cricket is abundantly played in every town, city and country of the world'. The stage is thus set for the despatch of that all-time team; but politics raises its head even in this demi-paradise

First, whom to select, and before that, whom to select as selectors? And whom to select the selectors of the selectors?

But let's not get stalled at the start. Let's get on with it. This vast, collective reaching-out . . . a hand not across the sea, but dark aeons of space, to perturb the ancient slumber of the unknown.

After much bickering, a committee of selectors is appointed, with Yorkshire's formidable Lord Hawke as its hard head and chairman. The other selectors are India's celebrated passivist, Mahatma Gandhi; Warwick the King-maker; Neville Chamberlain, the arch appeaser; and De Gaulle, the imperious statesman of the democratic French monarchy.

Lord Hawke was determined to win at all costs against all forms of interplanetary galactic opposition; furthermore, to trounce, thrash, and humiliate them. 'You're a brute!' Gandhi and Chamberlain objected.

Gandhi went on to argue: 'The mission of this tour is by all means foremost a peaceful one. We should not en-deavour to massacre our gracious but remote hosts as the British Raj used to do. We should give them every sporting chance to fairly acquit themselves.

'In short, we must *not* send our greatest team of first-rate immortals. We should send second-rate cricketers who will do us proud as our foremost representatives of ethics, humility, modesty, and morality. These virtues will in-fluence our hosts to match them, in equal graciousness. That will ensure peace over the entire cosmic system.'

De Gaulle stood up, to his full height. In league with the hawkish Lord, he pronounces: 'But *non*! There is but one objective: at any cost, to win!'

'You're ruthless!' Chamberlain disputed.

De Gaulle condescended to counter this: 'To a per-fidious Englishman like your inglorious self, my ears sub-limely are tight shut.'

Lord Hawke, the Chairman, intervened: 'Emperor De Gaulle, I agree with you. But down to practical matters. We'll do our opponents illustrious honour by vying at them with no less than the glorious utmost that earthly humanity has yet achieved. To this end, I propose, then, this true team of my real dreams:

'Opening bat on the World First Eleven is J. B. Hobbs of mighty England. Victor Trumper is number two, followed by his fellow Australian Donald Bradman. At four and five are two of England's – Walter Hammond and W. G. Grace. Then come two all-rounders: Garfield Sobers of the West Indies and K. R. Miller of Australia. Then is Alan Knott, England wicket-keeper. The two spin specialists are Australia's "Demon" Spofforth and England's Jim Laker.

The two fearsome fast bowlers are both Aussies: Ray Lindwall and Denis Lillee.'

'Bravo!' applauded De Gaulle: 'Nothing but the best! Excellent! They should serve fair warning to any alien planet that we mean business!'

'But our purpose,' assertively but passively interrupted that martyr of survival, Gandhi, 'is to promote and propagate peace. . . .'

'Poppycock!' Lord Hawke plainly put forth: 'No dove of India shall drop such rubbish on my hallowed head.'

Warwick the Kingmaker then rose, in deferential address to the selectorial chairman: 'My lord, the World First Eleven you propose is excellent. May I humbly submit my candidates for thirteenth man?'

'Pick several,' Lord Hawke kindly assented: 'We'll spare no expense with our outward bound tourist party, astronomically transported, numbering possibly fifteen.'

Encouraged, Warwick submitted: 'Include, then, Vinoo Mankad of India, Ponsford of Australia, Wilfred Rhodes of England, and Ranji of Sussex and England.'

'Who's captain?' demanded De Gaulle.

'My noble friend, W. G. Grace,' indirectly boasted Lord Hawke.

Chamberlain the appeaser dared next to speak: 'As a compromise between sending our very *best* men or an *inferior misrepresentation* of our cricketing honour, I propose sending our very best "Second XI". I have here a piece of paper with the players.'

'That's no compromise!' objected Gandhi, the premier passivist.

'Objection overruled,' sneered Lord Hawke, the bully. 'Let's hear the reduced magnitude of your secondary choices, Chamberlain.'

The latter obediently obliged: 'Len Hutton of England and Barry Richards of South Africa as the opening pair. Then England's Peter May and Denis Compton, followed by two West Indians: Frank Worrell and Viv Richards. Then Imran Khan of Pakistan, England's Evans for wicketkeeper, Grimmett of Australia, and the two England fast bowlers, Larwood and Trueman.'

Warwick the Kingmaker then applauded Chamberlain's 'compromise' squad, and went on to suggest, as extras in the touring party, Pollock of South Africa, Woolley of England, Gibbs of the West Indies.

'Gentlemen!' angrily piped up Killjoy Gandhi, 'surely this so-called "second best" team is not inferior to our first best as a dangerous threat to the harmony of the Spheres.'

'Defeatist!' angrily denounced Lord Hawke and De Gaulle jointly. 'You lily-white dark man!' Hence racist acrimony.

'Where's our pride?' exasperatedly declared the hawks!

But a theoretical speculativeness spun itself over the committee, since Gandhi withheld approval, in adamant stubborn passive resistance, holding out for a *good will* tour in the interests of secure interspatial peace. 'If you want war, send your belligerent First Eleven, but captained by Jardine, who'll provoke space fury leading to a crisis with the threat of catastrophe's outbreak and the unleashing of maniacal interstellar mayhem.'

Due to Gandhi's insistence and persistence, the others – even Lord Hawke and De Gaulle – backed down bit by bit.

De Gaulle complained: 'Can't we *beat* our rivals, outplay the competition, *win* the matches, without compromising our bid for harmonious peace and security up and down the whole solar system? Wouldn't they construe this as conde-scension?'

Replied Gandhi: 'They wouldn't know we're conde-scending. We'd make them think that our touring party is the most powerful we can muster. We'll conceal our feign-ing meekness, and pretend the pomp of our highest might.'

Lord Hawke, backing down: 'Are you sure that thereby Earth's peace, safety, and security shall benefit by our inferior show on the successive wickets of space?'

Gandhi: 'Precisely. By losing matches we gallantly try to win with inferior players, we display an Earth meekness designed to prove that our planet, though game, is insuf-ficiently belligerent to constitute a threat to the other planets.'

Gandhi won. So the Earth Eleven who went on board the sleek enormity of our space rocket capsule piloted by award-winning astronauts, were as follows: Mike Brearley as opening bat, but not as captain. Co-opener, the Reverend David Sheppard, now Bishop of Liverpool. Then Sir Pelham Warner of Middlesex. Then Jack Fingleton of Australia. Then W. G. Grace's less adept brother, Doctor E. M. Grace. Then D. R. Jardine, but decidedly *not* as captain (and not allowed to talk to the press, either, in any of the officially visited spheres that float on the vast astronomical table). Then the Nawab of Pataudi, India's crown jewel. Then Scotland's Douglas Home, former Prime Minister. Then Lord Harris, Field Marshal Alexander for his early promise at Harrow, then fellow Harrovian, the poet all-rounder Lord Byron, and India's own D. B. Vengsarkar (one of Gandhi's special heroes), Neville Cardus, John Arlott and R. C. Robertson-Glasgow.

So it was that a touring party of veritable doves blasted off for their first fixture in space. No one in the universe was able to accuse the Selectors of having pulled their punches, for the party was redolent with distinguished interplanetary household names. At the same time its combined talents were not such as to endanger the harmony of the spheres. Till the new ball is claimed, let the Earth ever remain the first gentleman of the globes!

MARVIN COHEN

On the following pages are details of Arrow books that will be of interest.

TALES FROM A LONG ROOM

Peter Tinniswood

Those were the golden days: WG and Spofforth were locked in mortal combat at Lord's; MCC rule held sway throughout the Empire; and the world had not yet been darkened by the spectre of aluminium bats, Geoffrey Boycott and underarm bowling.

The brigadier remembers it all. By the flickering firelight of a long room, he takes us back to some surprisingly little-known incidents and characters from cricket's heyday. It's all here – the MCC's ill-fated Test against a Pygmy XI, Scott and Amundsen's historic match at the South Pole, the inspiring story of Mendip-Hughes, Somerset's most distinguished one-legged off-spinner, and, of course, the promising but tragically short career in first-class cricket of the late Queen Victoria.

Tales from a Long Room is the tallest, most hilarious collection of stories in the history of the 'summer game'.

DIARY OF A SOMEBODY
Christopher Matthew

'Quite definitely the funniest book I've had the pleasure of reading.' *Tribune*

At weekend houseparties and the elegant gatherings of the London season, at trendy Workers' Workshops and in the expectant crowds at the new National, Simon Crisp is always noticed. He's the one with the coffee stains on his trousers, the air of punctured dignity and educated worry. Humiliated by hurled apple cores and exploding plastic pants, by practical jokes in the office and in his West London flat, he's a fall-guy for our times.

This is his diary. It curiously resembles that classic of ninety years ago, *The Diary of a Nobody*. Especially in one respect: Simon never sees the joke.

But we do. And deliciously so.

'A genuinely funny book.' *Benny Green, Spectator*

'Spellbinding. I read the diary in one sitting.' *The Times*

GULLIBLE'S TRAVELS

Billy Connolly

He has travelled from the majestic deserts of Doha (twin town of Drumchapel in Scotland) and the teeming markets of Bletchley to the splendour of the Sydney surf and the exotic decadence of the Crawley Leisure Centre.

And here it is — a unique guide to the world, travel, life, death and camel-smells, as seen through the eyes of

'the gangling Glaswegian doyen of bad taste' *Daily Telegraph*

'the man who makes Bette Midler look like Jess Conrad' *The Stage*

'one of the most outrageous Scotsmen ever to have vaulted Hadrian's Wall' *Daily Express*

'the laughing laureate of the loo' *The Times*

the inimitable (thank God) BILLY CONNOLLY

Compiled by Duncan Campbell

Illustrated by Steve Bell

THE TESTAMENT OF ANDROS

James Blish

A disaster-investigator of the future, whose craft is the reading of dead men's minds . . .

A polluted, dying Earth where power is in the hands of the almighty International Brotherhood of Sanitary Engineers . . .

Minute aquatic human colonists, genetically bred to settle an underwater world . . .

A woman space pioneer who unwittingly brings hetero-sexuality to the primeval life of Titan . . .

All this – and more: the best of the best from one of the true giants of modern SF.

THE UNLUCKIEST MAN IN THE WORLD
and similar disasters

Mike Harding

Born in the picturesque spa of Lower Crumpsall, he spent his early years in the brooding shadow of a cream cracker factory. At the age of seventeen he bought a set of Mongolian bagpipes and joined a rock and roll band. Much of his manhood has been spent waiting for a girl wearing red feathers and a hula skirt to come into his life. He is the incorrigible, irrepressible and slightly mad Mike Harding.

The Unluckiest Man in the World takes us into the world of Mike Harding with an inimitable collection of happy, sad, ridiculous, profound and simply hilarious songs, poems and stories.

BESTSELLING NON-FICTION FROM ARROW

All these books are available from your bookshop or news-agent or you can order them direct. Just tick the titles you want and complete the form below.

☐	THE GREAT ESCAPE	Paul Brickhill	£1.75
☐	A RUMOR OF WAR	Philip Caputo	£2.50
☐	A LITTLE ZIT ON THE SIDE	Jasper Carrott	£1.50
☐	THE ART OF COARSE ACTING	Michael Green	£1.50
☐	THE UNLUCKIEST MAN IN THE WORLD	Mike Harding	£1.75
☐	DIARY OF A SOMEBODY	Christopher Matthew	£1.25
☐	TALES FROM A LONG ROOM	Peter Tinniswood	£1.75
☐	LOVE WITHOUT FEAR	Eustace Chesser	£1.95
☐	NO CHANGE	Wendy Cooper	£1.75
☐	MEN IN LOVE	Nancy Friday	£2.50

Postage _____

Total _____

ARROW BOOKS, BOOKSERVICE BY POST, PO BOX 29, DOUGLAS, ISLE OF MAN, BRITISH ISLES

Please enclose a cheque or postal order made out to Arrow Books Ltd for the amount due including 15p per book for postage and packing both for orders within the UK and for overseas orders.

Please print clearly

NAME ....

ADDRESS ....

....

Whilst every effort is made to keep prices down and to keep popular books in print, Arrow Books cannot guarantee that prices will be the same as those advertised here or that the books will be available.